Finding Phoebe

Praise for *Finding Phoebe*

'Understanding the world is often easier from a shifted viewpoint, and this is what Extence does so perfectly. The eponymous Phoebe lives with ASD, and it is her navigation of the strange and often inexplicable world of the "normal" that is so warm and utterly captivating. Neurodiversity has a voice, and it's witty and uplifting and enlightening all at once'
Jasper Fforde

'Totally enchanting, it's warm and funny with such a kind heart, just like Phoebe, who is a wonderfully charming character to spend time with'
Ciara Smyth

'A humdinger of a story packed with infectious humour and heart, *Finding Phoebe* is reading for pleasure at its absolute best'
Jessica Scott-Whyte

'A lovely story with a compelling and unique protagonist. Extence tackles a subject that has almost become taboo these days and deserves to see the light in YA fiction'
Susin Nielsen

Finding Phoebe

Gavin Extence

ANDERSEN PRESS

First published in 2023 by
Andersen Press Limited
20 Vauxhall Bridge Road, London SW1V 2SA, UK
Vijverlaan 48, 3062 HL Rotterdam, Nederland
www.andersenpress.co.uk

2 4 6 8 10 9 7 5 3 1

British Library Cataloguing in Publication Data available.

ISBN 978 1 83913 331 2

Printed and bound in Great Britain by Clays Ltd, Elcograf S.p.A.

For
Amelia

1

The Interesting Clouds
and the Car in the Sea

Dear Mum,

2018 was the year Bethany went off the rails. It was the year many things happened, but Bethany is the main thing I need to talk about here. After all, she was pretty much the catalyst for everything else, from my doomed attempt at self-improvement to my decision to flee the country for an indefinite period. I'm not trying to absolve myself of responsibility. I should make that clear. I made my own decisions, some of which ended up causing a great deal of damage. All I'm saying is that I had to respond to a situation that was often beyond my control, and even further beyond my comfort zone. This continues to be something I struggle with.

I am, however, getting ahead of myself. I need to start at the start, on the evening my routine was broken. It was a turning point because it marked the exact moment my life stopped feeling safe and predictable.

It began with the car in the sea.

I was walking Gladys, our Welsh Border Collie, back from the north beach when the screaming became audible. It was faint at first, barely distinguishable from the shriek of a gull carried on the wind, but as we made our way across the dunes, the sound gradually resolved, becoming more human. It was unfortunate because prior to this, everything had been going well. There were some extremely interesting altocumulus clouds gathering in the northeast, under lit by the setting sun. The rest of the sky was turning a pleasing shade of pink, and the air smelled of salt and sand and wet vegetation. But now I worried that our walk was about to be ruined. Gladys had started yipping in response to the screams, and I was faced with a dilemma.

On the one hand, I already knew what the problem was – or I had a very strong suspicion, based on the time of day and phase of the moon – and it was unlikely that anyone was going to die. If I avoided the causeway and stuck to the dunes, then I'd be home by eight o'clock and could continue my evening as scheduled, with no harm done.

On the other hand, this was probably not the 'right thing to do'.

Unfortunately, I didn't have time to draw up a flowchart of options and potential outcomes. The screaming was ongoing, and it was having a significant impact on my ability to think. I resolved to take a peek at the situation to assess the danger; afterwards, I'd be able to make an informed decision about what action, if any, was required.

When we reached the top of the dune abutting the causeway, the car was approximately twenty metres distant. It was stationary in a couple of feet of swirling seawater. I doubted that any water had got inside the car as cars are designed to be watertight, but the woman in the passenger seat had started to panic nevertheless. She was halfway out of her window, trying

2

to climb onto the roof, while the man in the driver's seat was shouting at her to calm down and stop being so bloody hysterical. In response, she continued to scream hysterically.

I observed the scene for a minute or so, taking in the relevant facts. The car was a BMW, and it looked sporty and impractical: certainly not suitable for driving on a flooded road. As for the people, the woman looked to be approximately twenty-five to thirty years old. She had dark hair and was wearing some kind of flimsy wraparound beach dress and was not very good at climbing. The man was mostly bald, red in the face, and I estimated his age to be fifty years minimum. My first thought was that he was probably the woman's father, except he kept shouting at her and telling her to get back in the car and stop being such a fucking drama queen, and this didn't seem like the sort of thing you'd say to your daughter. So it was also possible that he was her much older husband or boyfriend. I was unable to draw any firm conclusion.

I was loath to go down to them, but Gladys had decided that enough was enough. She darted down the embankment, plunged into the sea and started barking again, with great enthusiasm. This caused both the man and the woman to turn and look in my direction, which was not easy for them because the man had to pivot in his seat and the woman was still clinging to the side of the car. And it was not easy for me because I don't like being looked at, especially not by strangers. This is something else that hasn't changed in the last six years.

'Oh, thank *fuck*,' the man said. 'Listen. We need you to get someone to tow us out of here. Can you do that?'

I told him I could not.

And there was a small pause as the waves continued to lap against the BMW's wheel arches. Then the woman started screaming again. Or that's what I thought at first. After a moment's reconsideration, I decided that she was actually laughing, but her laughter was peculiar – a series of strangled, high-pitched yelps. Since the situation was not humorous, this was a confusing development.

So I explained, carefully, that there was close-to-zero chance that anyone else was going to attempt the causeway with the tide this high and still rising. And anyway, from the angle their car was at – approximately 45° to the straight line of the road – I found it unlikely that it could be freed so easily. My hypothesis was that at least one of the back wheels had come off the tarmac – probably the result of a poorly executed three-point turn – and was stuck in the marshy ground at the bottom of the embankment. The vehicle would be going nowhere until the tide had fallen sufficiently, which would be some time close to midnight.

'*Midnight?*' the man repeated.

'The next low tide is at 3.06 a.m.,' I shouted to him, 'but the road is clear three hours before that. Give or take fifteen minutes. It depends on the wind speed and direction and the atmospheric pressure.'

The man stared at me. I don't know why. It's possible he was awaiting further information. But in the meantime, the woman had finally managed to scrabble out of the window and onto the roof. She started pounding on the metal with her fists, which made Gladys bark again. Gladys was finding the situation extremely exciting.

'This genius said we'd be OK!' the woman shouted. 'He said it would be just like going through a ford!'

'It's not like a ford,' I told her. 'It's the North Sea.'

She ignored this and kept pounding on the roof, and the

4

man kept shouting at her to stop because she was making this ten times worse than it had to be, and I closed my eyes and bit the skin around my fingernails. It's a habit I've been trying very hard to break, but right then, I needed the pain to distract me. The noise, the people, the situation – it was all very distressing.

'He's right,' I told the woman, because she really was making everything worse. But she didn't hear me, so I just kept repeating it – 'he's right, he's right, he's right' – until she did.

'Who's right?' she yelled. 'Who's right?'

This seemed an odd question, given there was only one person I could be referring to. Moreover, it put me in a rather awkward position, not knowing the nature of their relationship. I decided the safest option was to hedge my bets. 'Your father or significantly older partner.'

The woman started screeching again. I decided she was mentally unstable, and looked at my boots for a while.

Then the man said: 'For fuck's sake! Go and get someone else. Go and get a grown-up.'

I phoned Daddy.

'Two tourists have driven their car into the sea,' I told him.

'Oh, Christ,' he said. 'Are they OK? Are *you* OK?'

'I'm OK. I'm on the embankment.'

'Stay on the embankment.'

'Of course I'll stay on the embankment.'

'I know you will. What about the tourists? Are they OK? Have they called the coastguard?'

'They're not in any immediate danger,' I said, 'and the coastguard is not required; they got stuck at the first dip in the road, before they made it out into the channel. But the woman has climbed onto the roof and is intermittently hysterical. The man is still in his seat. And they keep shouting at each other. It's highly unpleasant.'

I was having to shout a little bit too, because the wind was gusting and the phone line was not great. The tourists were both glaring at me.

'OK. Just hold tight, Phoebe,' Daddy said. 'I'll be there as soon as I can. I love you.'

'I know. Please hurry.'

I hung up and told the tourists that my father was on his way.

'Is he bringing a tow cable?' asked the man. 'Please tell me he's bringing a tow cable.'

'He's not bringing a tow cable,' I said, rubbing my temples. 'No sensible person would try to drive on this road.'

I sat on the grass and watched the sky for the thirteen and a half minutes it took Daddy to arrive. Gladys knew that he was approaching before he'd even appeared in the distance. She had been dozing at my side, but I suddenly felt her muscles tense against my leg. Her ears pricked up, and a moment later she was hurtling across the top of the embankment, wagging her tail and barking happily. Daddy appeared a moment later; he bent down so he could pat her head, but without really breaking his stride, since there was a more pressing matter to attend to (i.e. the car in the sea).

'Hello, Phoebe,' Daddy said.

'Hello, Daddy,' I replied.

He put his hand on my shoulder. 'You're OK?'

'It's been stressful, but I'm OK.'

He nodded, then turned his attention to the tourists. The

irate bald man had also climbed onto the roof now, and the sea had risen almost to the top of the wheel arches and was presumably starting to ruin the engine. He tried to place a hand on the woman's back but she shrugged him off angrily. As you know, I sometimes miss the nuances of human body language, but in this instance, there was no nuance. Their feelings were as easy to read as Gladys's.

Daddy addressed the tourists: 'I think it's probably best if you leave the car,' he said.

'Can't someone tow us out?' the man asked. 'There must be someone with . . . I don't know, a tractor or something.'

'I'm sorry. You'll have to wait until the tide falls.'

And even though this was almost exactly what I'd told the man fifteen minutes ago, this time his reaction was very different. He just nodded a couple of times, then looked at the woman, who refused to look back. This is very typical of people. They don't care about the facts or logic of a statement. They care about who's saying it.

'Listen,' Daddy said. 'I can give you the number of a garage on the mainland. They'll recover the vehicle as soon as possible. But in the meantime . . . well . . .' He gestured at the water. 'I'm afraid you're going to have to get a bit wet. There's nothing else for it.'

The woman barely hesitated. She slid herself down the side of the car and immediately gasped as the water rose up past her knees. It was 3rd September, so I'd estimate the sea was approximately thirteen degrees Celsius (based on the daily average, which I've just looked up). The man threw his shoes and socks onto the embankment, rolled up his trousers, and then also slid into the sea and started swearing again. Daddy ignored this. He helped the woman onto the embankment and

7

then took off his coat and wrapped it around her shoulders, which was kind but probably of little practical use since it was her lower half that was cold and wet.

'I parked as close as I could,' Daddy said, 'but it's still a bit of a walk to the car.'

These were troubling words.

'You're not going to bring them to our house?' I enquired tactfully. 'It's just that I have school tomorrow. I'd find it extremely disruptive.'

Daddy held up his hands, the same way he might if trying to calm traffic. 'It's OK, Phoebe. I'm sure they'll be far more comfortable at one of the hotels or B&Bs. There's bound to be room somewhere.'

I nodded, instantly relieved.

The bald man was out of the water and putting his shoes back on. He looked at me, then Daddy. 'You know, your daughter's been pretty rude to us,' he said, quite unfairly.

'Just leave it,' the woman hissed.

'I will not leave it! She could see we were in trouble and . . . well, she was deliberately insulting. Sarcastic. There's no other way to put it.'

Sarcastic? I was baffled. All I'd done was try to help!

Daddy also appeared speechless. That, or he was counting in his head, which was a strategy we'd been taught in a workshop on Managing Difficult Emotions. He looked at the man for a full ten seconds, then said: 'I very much doubt that.'

The man said nothing.

'Phoebe, you can go home now,' Daddy told me. 'Take Gladys. You've done really well.'

I didn't need to be told twice. I went home.

2

The New Boy

It was almost dark by the time I got back, twenty-four minutes later than planned. I put fresh water down for Gladys, set the timer on my phone, and then spent an additional five minutes in the garden, hitting the punch bag beneath the beech tree. I reasoned that this would be time well spent, as my encounter with the strangers had left me with a lot of pent-up frustration.

Yet afterwards, as I removed my boxing gloves and conducted a swift body scan, I noted that my muscles felt just as tense as before, and my mind was still racing; all I'd achieved was an elevated pulse and aching wrists.

I continued with my evening ritual: I showered, brushed my teeth and changed into my pyjamas. When I picked up my phone to check the time again, I found a missed call and a WhatsApp message from Bethany.

I dropped by but no one answered the door. Everything OK?

In other circumstances, I might have told her what had just happened, but I knew I wasn't at my best, and the thought of a protracted conversation, even with Bethany, was daunting. My priority now was to get my evening back on track: wind down, get a full night's sleep, and be adequately refreshed for the first day back at school.

I'm fine, I wrote. *Just got out the shower. Did you want something in particular?*

Bethany replied almost at once. *Just wanted to chat. I'm feeling a bit all over the place TBH.*

I read the message twice; it was frustratingly vague, and possibly self-contradictory. How could you feel *a bit* all over the place? I spent a minute or two contemplating this puzzle, and was just about to ask what she meant when another message came through, saving me the trouble.

It's fine if you're too busy. Don't worry about it.

I am a bit busy, I admitted. *I've been re-watching Game of Thrones and was about to start another episode. I don't want to leave it too late or it will disrupt my sleep!*

I had to wait quite a long time for Bethany's response to come through, considering how short it was.

Fine, forget it. See you tomorrow.

See you tomorrow.

It was a relief that we'd managed to resolve the conversation so amicably, and with minimal further disruption. I resumed my *Game of Thrones* re-watch and was approximately thirty-nine minutes in when Daddy poked his head around the bedroom door. He indicated by gesture that he wanted me to remove my headphones.

'I wanted to check that you're all right,' he said.

There was a long, rather dramatic pause. I waited.

Daddy gave a small sigh. 'Are you all right?' he asked.

'I'm all right,' I told him.

'I was worried that you might be . . . You know, a little wound up.'

I took a moment to consider this. 'I am somewhat wound up. It's no big deal, though. I'm focused on relaxing before bed.'

'Right . . . What are you watching?' he asked.

'Season six, episode nine. Battle of the Bastards.'

He looked at me blankly, so I turned the laptop so he could see the screen. An extra had just had a sword pushed through his throat and there was blood coming out his neck and mouth and eyes. The practical effects were extremely impressive.

'Maybe stop after this one?' Daddy suggested. 'I'm not convinced it's as relaxing as you think it is. And let me know if you need anything.'

'Thank you. I don't need anything.'

'OK. Sleep well.'

But I did not sleep well. Once Daddy had left, I found it difficult to re-immerse myself in *Game of Thrones*, and it was even harder to settle down after I'd shut down my laptop and turned off the light. There were intrusive thoughts of the car in the sea, and how it was probably leaking petrochemicals and damaging the local ecosystem. Then there were intrusive thoughts about how awful it had been trying to converse with the tourists, and how badly it had gone. I attempted a short breathing exercise to calm myself again, but it didn't really help, and I spent the next several hours staring at a dark ceiling.

Consequently, I did not feel like doing my ten-minute trampoline workout when my alarm went off at six-twenty the following morning. This was a worrying sign for the day ahead. Low intensity aerobic exercise is a non-negotiable part of my morning routine, and has been for the last four years. It's vital because, aside from the general health benefits, it also releases endorphins, which lower anxiety, raise energy levels and improve mental performance. But this morning I had to force myself, and afterwards I felt neither energised nor mentally stimulated. It was impossible to calculate my sleep deficit because I didn't know exactly when I'd fallen asleep, but the last time I remembered checking my phone it was 3.13. My usual bedtime is no later than 23.20, so, at best, I was dealing with a loss of three hours and fifty-three minutes, or fifty-five per cent of my normal sleep requirement. I compensated by drinking one cafetiere's worth of coffee, using the extra-strong Sumatran beans from the refrigerator.

When Daddy and I pulled up outside the vicarage not long afterwards, Bethany was not there. She was late. Entirely typical of Bethany, but I'd hoped things might be different today, with it being the first day back after the summer holiday.

Daddy said: 'Well, at least she's consistent.'

This is a 'joke' he makes often when we are waiting in the car for Bethany. It's not funny, obviously, but I do enjoy the repetition, and it's an accurate appraisal of the situation. Bethany is *always* late, which means I am usually able to factor this into my plans. If she were occasionally punctual, it would be far harder to manage.

After a minute of waiting and a couple of beeps on the horn, I told Daddy I was going in. Reverend Collins answered the door when I knocked and waved me into the hallway.

'She told me she'd only be two more minutes,' he said with what I took to be an amused smile. 'Admittedly, that was about three minutes ago. You know what Bethany's like.'

'Yes. I know.'

'I'm almost ready,' Bethany shouted down the stairs. 'Stop ganging up on me!'

Reverend Collins chuckled and raised his eyes heavenward. 'How are you, Phoebe? Looking forward to Year Eleven?'

'I'm tired but otherwise fine,' I told him. 'I've drunk a lot of coffee.'

'Well, the first day back's always the hardest, isn't it?'

'Often, yes. How are you and Mrs Collins?'

'No complaints, Phoebe, no complaints.'

'Excellent.'

There was a small silence; because I hadn't anticipated the need to chat to Reverend Collins, I had run out of small talk. Fortunately, Bethany appeared at that moment at the top of the stairs. It was obvious why she'd taken so long. Her blouse was untucked on one side, but her hair was immaculate. She had tied it in double Dutch plaits, which is where you centre part your hair and arrange it in two symmetrical plaits using a reverse weave to thread in extra strands of hair as you progress from front to back. I know this because I quizzed Bethany later on, and then looked up additional details on WikiHow. It was an impressive artistic accomplishment, I'll admit, but not the sort of thing I'd ever have the dexterity to accomplish myself. My hair was in a ponytail, as always.

'You're four minutes late,' I told her, as we exited the vicarage.

'It's nice to see you too,' Bethany said.

I ignored the *non sequitur*. 'It's probably because of your hair.'

'Thank you,' she replied. 'I'm glad you noticed.'

Bethany is socially adept and reasonably intelligent, so it was surprising that she'd missed the point in this way. I had to consider the possibility that she, too, was suffering from insufficient sleep. But I didn't get a chance to ask, because as soon as we'd climbed into the back of the car, Daddy said: 'All set for the new term, Beth?'

And Bethany replied: 'Yes, thanks, Mr B.' And their conversation continued unbroken for another four minutes and thirty seconds until we reached the stranded BMW.

I had hoped that it would have disappeared in the night,

13

like an unpleasant dream, but it was still stuck at the bottom of the embankment, blocking half the causeway. The falling tide had left an ugly patina of sand, mud and seaweed smeared across the door panels.

'Yikes,' said Bethany. 'Another one?'

I put down my book, *American Gods*, on the seat between us and began a detailed account of the events of the previous evening. Bethany seemed interested, but I hadn't got far when Daddy interrupted.

'Can we do it without the swearing, please?'

'I'm quoting verbatim. *Stop being such a fucking drama queen*. That's what he said.'

'You don't have to quote verbatim,' Daddy said.

I looked at Bethany, who grinned and rolled her eyes. I'm not certain what this was supposed to signify, but I felt a momentary flash of pleasure nonetheless – as if I was being included in a small conspiracy.

'They were definitely a couple,' Bethany told me, once I'd finished my truncated account. 'But you shouldn't have mentioned the age gap. It's no wonder things got awkward.'

This was useful feedback, but clearly ludicrous. If I'd drawn attention to something that was *obvious* – at least to most people – then why get offended? Also, relationships involving age gaps are not a taboo, and are actually rather common across primate communities. Thanks to a documentary on mountain gorillas I'd seen on *National Geographic*, I was able to outline for Bethany the evolutionary pressures that underpin this configuration, whereby females often select older mates based on social status, access to resources and the ability to support numerous offspring. Conversely, males often select younger mates who are more likely to be fertile.

14

'Please tell me you didn't compare them to mountain gorillas. Not to their faces?'

'I did not get the chance.'

'Well, that's something,' Bethany said.

As we exited the causeway and approached the main road, a tow truck passed us coming the other way. It was a very welcome sight.

The early drop-off, owing to the mid-morning tide, meant that Bethany and I were the first people in class, and had almost forty-five minutes of unstructured time to fill before registration. This was far from ideal. The litre of coffee I'd consumed with breakfast had left me agitated – 'tired but wired' – and I sorely needed something to occupy my mind. Fortunately, I'd prepared for this eventuality. I asked Bethany if she'd like to test my vocabulary using a worksheet I'd printed out the previous afternoon – '100 words to sharpen your expression', which would obviously be useful for my fiction writing – but she declined. She said she would prefer to do nothing at all! It was a weird choice, but not the worst outcome as it meant I could spend the time reading without fear of interruption. But before I could initiate this plan, Mrs Holloway walked in with an unfamiliar boy. He was tall and lean, with dark floppy hair, flawless skin and super-white teeth; he looked as if he'd been grown in a lab as part of a project to create the next terrible boy band.

'Hello, girls,' Mrs Holloway said. 'This is William. He's new this term. Can I trust you to make sure he settles in OK?' She was looking at Bethany here, so I assumed the *you* was singular and I was not being included in this request. I was one hundred per cent on-board with this decision. Bethany could handle the situation while I stayed as uninvolved as politely possible.

Mrs Holloway left and William sat at the desk in front of ours; and by sat, I mean slouched. His posture was closer to horizontal than vertical. He'd rotated his chair so that he was half-facing us. He gave a slight nod. 'Hey.'

'Hey yourself,' Bethany replied. Because that's the kind of thing Bethany says sometimes.

I stuck to the safer formula and said: 'Hello, William. It's nice to meet you.'

'It's Will,' William said. 'I prefer Will.'

Bethany shrugged. 'Will it is.'

I decided to adapt this remark with a witty twist, and said: 'As you will, Will.'

Will looked confused. Bethany was fiddling with one of her plaits, looking unusually flushed. Since no one was saying anything, I concluded it was the optimum moment to escape the interaction, and, citing a genuine need to use the lavatory, I exited the classroom. It was a shrewd move, because when I returned, Bethany and Will were happily exchanging banalities, and I was able to slip back behind my desk with minimal fuss.

I managed to read eight pages of *American Gods* before the next problem arose. The problem was Jessica Chapman, who arrived in the classroom and immediately stole Bethany for a lengthy reunion ritual that entailed copious hugging and squealing. Happily, I wasn't asked to participate in this, but it did mean that I was left alone with Will, who took out his phone and started scrolling. This presented a conundrum as the use of mobile devices in the classroom is prohibited at all times. Under normal circumstances, I wouldn't have attempted to police this rule – firstly, because I'm not a fan of it myself, and secondly, because past interventions have not ended well. But this was not a normal circumstance. With it being his first day, it was possible Will had not yet had time to familiarise himself with the school rules, and was thus acting out of ignorance.

My duty was clear. I cleared my throat twice, and, when this failed to elicit a response, clicked my fingers a few inches from his ear. It may have been a small violation of social protocol, but I didn't want to make an unnecessary scene in front of Bethany and Jessica.

Will looked at my fingers. He looked at my face.

'No phones in the classroom,' I explained. 'I'd advise reading the Thorton Park Student Handbook. It's available as a PDF via the school website.'

His response was unexpected: after a few moments of silence, he started to laugh. Obviously, I didn't reciprocate because I didn't see the joke and don't partake in pro-social laughter – i.e. fake laughter used to facilitate in-group bonding. I only laugh when I find something genuinely funny.

Will stopped laughing and gave me a look that I couldn't interpret. 'Oh, shit. You're being serious?'

I confirmed that I was.

'Thanks for the advice,' Will said, 'but I think I'm gonna risk it.'

And he went back to whatever he was doing on his phone. Just like that!

Daddy often tells me that I'm too quick to judge people, but in this instance, I felt justified. I decided that I did not like Will, and I would avoid interacting with him in the future.

3

Biology

I can tell you the exact day I stopped liking school. It was four years and seventeen days ago, following an incident in a Year Seven Biology lesson. Before then, I'd been wavering a bit. I loved learning, but I found the larger ecosystem of secondary school hard to cope with. Moving from a small school to a large one was intimidating, as was having to meet so many new people in such a short space of time. I only felt secure when I was with Bethany, when I could take my social cues from her and achieve a kind of automatic acceptability as her friend. It wasn't that the other pupils were actively unkind, or even unfriendly. It was more that I was growing increasingly aware of my own 'peculiarities' – of all the ways in which I stood out from the crowd.

Nevertheless, I'd always believed that this situation was manageable, that if I worked hard to understand all the hidden codes and rules of the schoolyard, I'd be able to adapt and blend in. I was never going to be conventionally popular like Bethany, nor did I want to be, yet I hoped I'd be able to carve out a niche for myself on the periphery of school life, as unobtrusive as a barnacle clinging to the underside of a whale.

The Biology Incident was the turning point – the thing that shattered this aspiration. You will be the only person I've ever told this story to, Mum, although I think about it often. It was extremely humiliating.

It started out as an ordinary school day, except that I'd been suffering mild stomach cramps all morning, a fact that I'd hitherto attributed to a particularly sharp grapefruit I'd eaten for breakfast. It was only when I went to the toilets at the end of morning break that I noticed I'd bled in my underwear.

I wasn't particularly alarmed at this point. You and Daddy had done a good job preparing me for puberty, from quite a young age, and once I'd comprehended the problem afflicting me that morning, my mind turned immediately to practicalities. This being my first period, I did not have any pads with me. The obvious thing to do would have been to go at once to the school nurse, but I was conscious that this would make me late for class; I'd have to walk in late and I'd have to explain myself in front of everyone, which I wanted to avoid if possible. Bethany had gone ahead and would already be taking her seat, so I could not enlist her help.

Under time pressure, I decided my best option was to use toilet roll as a temporary pad. The bleeding seemed light, and I'd be able to go to the nurse at lunchtime to address the situation properly.

I realised this plan was not the best almost as soon as the lesson began. My hypersensitivity meant that I was acutely aware of the alien sensation of having toilet roll stuffed in my underwear, and I was certain that its position had shifted, either during the walk to the lab or when I sat down. The possibility that I might bleed through my uniform now worried me. I didn't know how likely this was, but once I'd had the idea, there was no shifting it. The scenario just kept circulating in my head like air in an unventilated room, stale and suffocating.

I think I made it through about fifteen minutes of the lesson before I decided I couldn't go on. Mr Jameson, our Biology teacher, was demonstrating how to test for glucose using a dried apricot and a phial of Benedict's solution, but I couldn't concentrate on a word he was saying. I'd tried to ground myself by counting my breaths, but this had only made me aware of how shallow and ragged my breathing had become, and how quick my heartbeat. It seemed to me, at this point, that I could suffer the minor embarrassment of excusing myself from class, or else risk the major embarrassment of *actually* bleeding through my clothes. That was if I didn't suffer a meltdown first, or an all-out panic attack.

That it would be a minor embarrassment, at most, was my genuine belief at the time. After all, people did excuse themselves from class now and then, either on medical grounds or to answer the call of natural bodily functions. I couldn't see why this instance should be any different, and I knew the correct protocol to follow: raise your hand, ask permission to leave, state your reason.

I raised my hand, and Mr Jameson noticed me straightaway.

'Yes, Phoebe. You have a question?'

I nodded. 'May I be excused to visit the school nurse? I'm menstruating.'

The giggles started at once, followed by the whispers, and then more giggles, along with some isolated expressions of disgust. Within a few moments almost everyone was laughing. Everyone except Mr Jameson, who was red, angry, and shouting for calm, and Bethany, who had her head in her hands. She later told me that I had provided too much information. I should have kept things vague and said that I was feeling unwell. In fact, I didn't even need to say this much.

No teacher was going to interrogate a twelve-year-old girl who suddenly needed to see the school nurse. But being vague does not come naturally to me.

Before he turned to teaching, Mr Jameson used to be in the army. He commanded troops in Afghanistan and Iraq and does not, in normal circumstances, struggle to maintain discipline. But on this occasion, he had to pound his fist on the workbench. 'SILENCE!'

The effect was immediate, but, to be honest, it did not make the situation much better. An eerie hush fell across the laboratory.

'Phoebe, you're excused. Would you like Bethany to go with you?'

I looked at Bethany, who no longer had her head down. She gave a small smile, which I took as a sign that she was willing to help me if I wanted her to. But I was too humiliated to talk in that moment – even to Bethany. I needed a moment alone, to process my error and avert a total shutdown.

So I just shook my head, retrieved my bag and left. Each action felt utterly strange. It was almost as if I was watching myself from the outside, in slow motion. I don't know when I started crying, but I suppose it must have been after I'd left the room, otherwise I'm sure Bethany would have been sent with me. I spent some time outside the nurse's office trying to compose myself, but I couldn't have been all that successful, as the nurse tried to give me a hug as soon as I'd explained my situation, and I bumped into a filing cabinet trying to evade her. She made me sit down and got me a cold glass of water, then told me I was exempt from the rest of the Biology class. This was good, as it gave me the time I needed to go to Boarding and change my underwear.

Later that morning, someone threw a tampon at me in the corridor. It struck me on the back of the head, causing me to jump and cry out, then fell to the floor with a muffled slap. I heard giggling from behind the lockers but decided not to investigate further. I didn't want to know who the culprit was, and had no intention of reporting the incident. I just wanted to forget it.

I was still upset at lunchtime, and planned to spend the whole hour in isolation, reading or playing chess against my phone (assuming I could concentrate on either). But my priority was just to stay away from the dining hall, where I was sure I'd face further teasing. I picked up a sandwich from the canteen and sat on the grass on the far side of the playground, partly hidden by a broad sycamore tree. I suppose Bethany must have seen me leaving and followed; she turned up a couple of minutes later and sat down beside me.

'I thought you might want some company,' she said.

'Thank you. As long it's not too embarrassing for you. I know people are still laughing at me.'

I suppose my words could have appeared sarcastic, even though I hadn't intended them that way. Bethany looked slightly wounded for a moment, before giving a firm shrug. 'That's their problem, isn't it?' She put her arm around my shoulder. It felt a bit awkward, but I was grateful nonetheless. I understood that she wasn't just trying to comfort me; she was telling me that she wasn't embarrassed to be with me, in the strongest way she could. 'How are you feeling?' she asked.

'It hasn't been the worst morning of my life,' I told her, 'but it's still pretty bad.'

'I'm sorry I wasn't more help. In class, I mean. It's just . . .'

Whatever Bethany had been going to say, she apparently changed her mind. 'It's just nothing. It wasn't OK for me to stay silent while everyone was laughing.'

'I'm not sure what else you could have done.'

'I could have said something. I *should* have said something.'

I shrugged. 'It's OK. It's hard in those situations. I understand.'

'Is there anything you need now?' Bethany asked. 'What can I do to make it better?'

I thought about this for a few moments. 'I don't want you to tell your mum when she picks us up. I'd rather no one else knew.'

'Are you sure? My mum would want to look after you too. You know she would.'

'I'd rather just forget about it,' I said, fearing this was, in fact, impossible. It was already difficult not to keep replaying the events of the morning again and again in my head. It was like picking at a wound.

Bethany stayed silent for a while and then nodded. 'If you're sure. What about your dad, though? Will you tell him?'

'I don't think he's qualified to deal with something like this. Plus it would make him sad.'

'What would? Knowing that *you're* sad?'

'Yes. I don't want him worrying about me. I'll just tell him to add sanitary towels to the shopping list like it's no big deal.'

Bethany gave a small smile and squeezed my shoulder.

'Could you tell me what I should have said?' I asked her. 'I'd like to know exactly what I got wrong.'

So Bethany talked me through the various ways in which I could have handled the situation differently. I suppose it was useful in a practical sense, but it didn't make me feel much better about myself. If anything, it just left me more aware of my own limitations, of my failure to grasp the basic rules of the classroom – the unwritten rules – or not until it was too late.

When I got home that afternoon, I let Gladys out in the garden, then spent several minutes cuddling her on the lawn. It was consoling, but not enough. So I went to my room and attempted to comfort-read some of the first fantasy books you'd given me as a child, such as *The Hobbit* and the *Chronicles of Narnia*. When I couldn't concentrate on this, I turned to the self-help section of my bookcase and located the first letter you ever wrote to me, when I was five years old. I've read this letter many times over the years, so I know it by heart, but I still like to hold it in my hands every now and then, when I need to feel close to you.

> *Dear Phoebe,*
>
> *This is very important information because it's all about you! Daddy and I hope that you will read it and then keep it safe, so you can read it again, whenever you need to.*
>
> *As you know, everyone is different. Everyone has things that they are good at, as well as things they are not so good at. Not everyone likes the same things as everyone else. Everyone has things that they are scared of, but not everyone is scared of the same things.*
>
> *Phoebe, one of your differences is that you have something called ASD, which means Autistic Spectrum Disorder. You may also hear it called*

just autism, or even Asperger's, or Asperger's Syndrome. They all refer to the same thing really, so we'll just call it ASD. It's a bit like Mummy having ME, but ASD doesn't make you poorly. It changes the way your brain works. I hope that learning a little bit about it will be helpful (and interesting!) for you.

ASD is the reason you find some things harder than other people. It's the reason you don't always like looking at people, especially at their eyes, and it's why you sometimes find it difficult to talk to people and understand what they are saying. Your ASD means that you struggle with your balance sometimes (like when you have to tip your head back to have your hair washed), but it's also the reason you love the feeling of spinning and swinging. And it's why you have some really _amazing_ skills, like reading so well and remembering things brilliantly.

These are not all the things you are good at or all the things you find difficult. It's impossible to write down every single thing about anyone. But I hope it gives you an idea of why you feel the way you do about some things.

The most important thing for you to understand is that having ASD isn't good or bad, or right or wrong. It's just a part of you, and another thing that makes you who you are. Mummy and Daddy think you are the most wonderful daughter in the world. You may not *always like to ask for help, but we love you very much and will always be here for you, whenever you need us. So, please, never be afraid to come to us with any problems or questions, and if there's anything in this letter that you'd like to know more about or don't understand, then please ask us about that too!*

With all my love, now and forever,

Mummy

Reading this had always brought me comfort in the past, but today it did not. Because I'd had a realisation. That I could ask for advice endlessly, from Daddy and Bethany. I could read countless books on social protocols and appropriate behaviour. I could read all the self-help books in existence. And there'd still be things I didn't get. No matter how much I learned, and how many errors I tried to correct, there'd always be something else, some universal expectation that was obvious to most people but alien to me.

I processed these thoughts for a long time, and eventually came to a sort of muted acceptance. Passing as 'normal', blending in, was not a realistic behavioural goal, and it never had been. The logical response was to adjust my ambitions accordingly, and aim lower. A first step would be to restrict myself to the most basic social interactions, the ones that were unavoidable, routine, and carried the least risk of committing a serious mistake. Talking to large groups or in class should obviously be avoided at all costs, as the risk of large-scale humiliation could not be justified by any potential benefit – even the very large benefit of acquiring additional knowledge on an interesting subject. If I needed to discuss the curriculum with my teachers, I could do so before or after lessons.

Having made some practical decisions, I felt a little better. I was still certain that I'd face teasing over the next few days, and possibly weeks, but I hoped that it would peter out eventually. Even if people didn't forget, it seemed unlikely that they would still be throwing sanitary products at me a year from now.

As for the wider implications of my social withdrawal, I told myself that these would be very limited. If I were to be honest, Bethany was my only true friend. I'd always tried to exchange pleasantries with my classmates in the past – so as not to appear aloof or discourteous – but Bethany was the only person my own age with whom I actually felt comfortable. We'd grown up together. We shared a bedroom in the school boarding house five nights out of fourteen, whenever the tide times stopped us from returning home in the evening. The point is, when I ran through these facts in my head, I felt reassured that I had one friendship I was happy with and would never have to worry about. Or so I thought.

4

The Argument

It was the second week back when I spoke to Will for a second time. Or rather, he spoke to me. In keeping with my 'minimal engagement' policy, and in light of the poor impression he'd made first time round, I would not have approached Will for a conversation unless it was a matter of the gravest importance. Possibly not even then. There was a disturbing rumour circulating that he'd been kicked out of his previous school. Kicked out! I don't often listen to gossip, in part because I'm seldom in a position to hear it, but in this case, Bethany was unusually eager to share. She'd heard the story from Emily, who'd heard it from Sienna, who'd heard it from Callum, who'd heard it from 'the horse's mouth'. Yet, when pressed, she admitted that nobody seemed to know what Will's crime had been. I concluded that the rumour might not be one hundred per cent credible, like the time when everyone was whispering that Natasha's father was a hitman who used to work for the Russian secret service but he turned out to be a chartered accountant (though there were some who still maintained this was just his cover story). Nevertheless, I could not dismiss the gossip entirely. I already knew that Will was a rule-breaker, so a prior expulsion from school was not out of the question.

He approached me at lunch break. I was sitting in the portico at the south entrance, using one of the fluted pillars for back support and partial concealment. Will must have spotted my ankles and shoes from the path at the bottom of the steps.

He loomed in front of me for a while, then waved an annoying hand in front of my face. I realised at this point that he probably wasn't going to leave unless I acknowledged him, and with great reluctance, I removed my headphones.

'Aren't those on the list of banned electrical items?' Will asked. He was probably making fun of me, but I decided it was easiest to answer the question at face value.

'They're frowned upon, for unspecified Health and Safety reasons and because most of the teachers find them irritating, but they're not technically prohibited, as long as you don't wear them in class or in the corridors. If you want further information, you can go to the office and ask for the Policy on Electronic Devices. I'm sure they'd be happy to give you a copy.'

I tried to keep my tone neutral, but it's possible that I was glaring at him. Bethany says this is my default expression during most conversations. Nevertheless, Will showed no sign of offence. He also showed no sign of leaving.

'So what are you listening to?' he asked.

'Music,' I told him.

He made a whirling gesture with his hand, which I interpreted as a request for yet more information.

'I *was* listening to Nightwish.'

'Never heard of them.'

This was unsurprising. 'They're a Finnish symphonic metal band. They're relatively niche in the UK but have a significant following across Northern continental Europe.'

'Metal? You're into metal?' For some reason, Will seemed to find this hilarious.

'I'm into Nightwish,' I told him. 'They're *symphonic* metal.'

'What's the difference?'

'In addition to the normal set-up of heavy guitar, bass and drums, they also have synthesised orchestral arrangements, and a classically trained soprano on vocals. And the music is more layered and complex.'

'Jesus,' Will said. 'What do you think of K-Pop?'

This was an odd question. 'I'm not an expert, but based on what I've heard in the corridors, I find it trite and uninteresting.'

'It was a joke . . . Forget it. What else *are* you into? Other than Nightwitch.'

'Nightwish. Do you mean music or in general?'

Will rolled his eyes. 'Music. The thing we're currently talking about.'

This question was much easier to answer. 'Nothing.'

'Nothing?'

I nodded firmly. 'Nothing.'

'You mean . . . like . . . ?'

'Correct. I listen to Nightwish exclusively. I've tried a variety of different artists in the past but always found the experience less rewarding. My conclusion was that I'd rather not waste my time listening to inferior music.'

'Don't you get bored?'

'I do not. They have eight studio albums and several live recordings. That's plenty. And they've had three different lead vocalists in the last twenty-two years, and their music has evolved significantly. It's not like pop where it all sounds identical and follows the same basic template.'

I'd tried my best, but Will still looked baffled. The conversation was clearly going nowhere.

'Was there something you actually wanted?' I asked politely.

Will nodded; I think he was as keen to move on as I was. 'You're good friends with Beth, right?'

'Yes, we're best friends.'

'Cool. So I was wondering, is she, like, you know ... unattached.'

'To what?'

Will rolled his eyes and spoke very slowly. 'Does she have a boyfriend?'

'Oh.' I took a few seconds to think. Not because of the question itself, which required zero thinking time, but because of the possible intent behind the question, which was more problematic. I decided to clarify matters straightaway. 'She does not have a boyfriend. Are you asking because you want to know if she'd be interested in you in this capacity?'

'Yes.'

'Absolutely not.'

No one likes to receive bad news, obviously, but all things considered, I felt Will's scowling at me was unjustified. The phrase 'don't shoot the messenger' sprang to mind.

'OK. Thanks for that, *Phoebes*. Can I ask, why not?'

'Numerous reasons. But the main one is that her father definitely wouldn't want her dating. He's extremely religious.'

'Religious?'

'He's a vicar.'

'A vicar? You're kidding, right? Not a literal vicar?'

'No, he's a literal vicar. In the Parish Church of St Mary the Virgin, Holy Island.'

Will ran his fingers through his hair. 'Beth seems . . . really normal.'

'She is normal.'

Will sniggered at this. 'Yeah. No disrespect, but you may not be the best person to judge that.'

'Touché,' I said; Will gave me a funny look. 'However, I've known Bethany all my life. You've known her a week. I'm obviously in a better position to judge than you are.'

'Yeah, but . . . So she's super-religious, right?'

This was an interesting question. I assumed Bethany's faith was still strong, but I didn't actually know. Following some advice from Daddy, I hadn't spoken to Bethany or her family about religion since the infamous Easter of 2015, when I'd presented Reverend Collins with some of the more unusual arguments I'd found against God's existence – the Problem of Animal Suffering, the Argument from Disappointment, the Impossibility of Omniscience (AKA: How Does God Know He's Not in *The Matrix*?).

'If you want to know about Bethany's beliefs, you should ask Bethany,' I told Will. 'But it's really a moot point. There's zero chance that her father would approve of any romantic relationship at this stage in her life.'

Will snorted at this. 'And does Beth always do what her dad tells her to?'

Another question without a straightforward answer. But the priority, I decided, was not to give Will false hope. 'Maybe not *always*,' I said, 'but she's not going to get into a big argument with her parents over something trivial like this. It would have to be something that actually matters to her.'

He mumbled something unintelligible. I asked for a repetition.

'I said *whatever*,' Will said.

And he left. This was good because I'm not always able to discern when a conversation is over. I estimated that we'd been speaking for at least five minutes, which was the longest I'd spoken to anyone other than Daddy or Bethany in quite some time. On the whole, I thought I'd done pretty well. Having to dispense romantic advice was entirely new territory for me, yet I'd managed to deter Will from what was obviously a pointless endeavour without making it personal – i.e. I'd only mentioned external problems and hadn't had to draw attention to any of his character defects. And I'd saved Bethany from the embarrassment of having to deal with Will's unwanted advances in person. All while evading the most common pitfalls of unplanned social interaction.

I gave myself a virtual pat on the head, and went back to my music.

The next day I had put the conversation out of my mind, since it seemed unlikely that there would be any follow-up. It was the hour between after-school Enrichment and dinner, and I'd returned to our shared room, where there was no sign of Bethany. I was sitting cross-legged on my bed, reading the thesaurus, when she burst in.

'What *exactly* have you been saying to Will?'

I'm not used to being asked for an exact reproduction of discourse, especially not by Bethany; usually, it's the opposite, and she interrupts me to insist on 'the shortest possible summary'. I wasn't certain why this normal protocol was being reversed, but from Bethany's posture and intonation, I diagnosed that she was angry, and I was eager to clear up any misapprehension on her part. Since I'd not said anything rude, unkind or inaccurate about Bethany, I had to assume that Will had presented a misleading picture of our conversation, either directly to Bethany or via some intermediary. This was a common and annoying problem, and provided a strong argument for the superiority of exact words over a vague synopsis.

After a false start, when Bethany told me I should skip the entire Nightwish prelude, I was able to provide a full and uninterrupted run-down of the previous day's conversation. I expected this to quell her anger, but, bizarrely, the opposite happened. She seemed more and more annoyed, until she, metaphorically, exploded.

'For God's sake, Phoebe!'

'Is there a problem?'

'Yes – you! You're the problem!'

I've grown practised at suppressing negative emotions, especially in the school environment, and I think it served me well in this instance. I was feeling extremely confused and anxious, but I managed to keep my voice and demeanour calm. It helped that I still had the thesaurus open, so I could focus on the pages rather than having to maintain eye contact.

'I'm afraid you'll have to be more specific. I don't—'

'You made me sound like a child!'

This was specific, but still unhelpful, as the problem was in no way obvious. By any standard definition, Bethany *was* a child. She was fifteen. She wouldn't be an adult for another two years, seven months and three days. This was an indisputable fact. But I was reluctant to state it outright, for fear of provoking further inexplicable anger.

'I'd appreciate it if you *didn't* talk about me in the future.'

Despite the polite language, Bethany didn't sound any calmer. 'I don't need you interfering in my life, and I especially don't need you embarrassing me again.'

She left the room.

I decided it would be best if I stayed put until dinner time.

5

The Symbolic Hug

It took me the rest of the school week to analyse the problem
with Bethany. This task was, of course, made vastly more difficult
by my decision that I shouldn't ask Bethany herself for further
clarification, which was something I'd always felt comfortable
with in the past, when I'd breached some unfathomable social
code. But now I suspected that any such enquiry would be
counterproductive, and perhaps met with further hostility. This
wasn't just because Bethany was making it obvious that she did
not wish to discuss the subject anymore; I'd also discerned early
on that my inability to understand the nature of the problem
was, itself, part of the problem. This was frustrating in the short
term, but it did mean that if I could figure out what I'd done, I'd
already have made progress towards correcting my behaviour.

Bethany spent the evening after the argument in the main
common room on the boys' floor, while I stayed in our bedroom
and attempted to think. It would have been far better if I'd
been at home, with access to my punch bag and Gladys and
a variety of soothing nature walks, but the week's afternoon
tides meant that I was stuck at school until Saturday, with few
therapeutic options. I didn't even have my trampoline, as
there was no space for it in our shared room, or no space
where it had not been deemed a 'fire hazard'.

Lacking a good alternative, I lay under my weighted blanket with my eyes closed and did a breathing exercise. When this failed to bring clarity, I listened to *Dark Passion Play*, which is Nightwish's sixth studio album, and one of their moodiest. The distraction was welcome, but it was only a temporary fix. At 9.30, I had to hand my phone and laptop over to Kevin, one of the House Parents, so that he could lock them in the store cupboard in line with school's policy on Good Sleep Hygiene. Bethany returned to our room shortly thereafter, but she said very little, and I still had no idea what to say to her.

After Lights Out, I lay motionless for some time – I'd estimate an hour – and then started to compile, by torchlight, a list of the things I could be certain of.

1. Bethany was upset and angry with me.
2. I had embarrassed her. I had made her sound 'like a child', and even though she was a child, this was a big problem.
3. She did not want me to talk about her or 'interfere' in the future.

This last point was especially perplexing, as it implied that I'd already interfered in some non-specified way. But as far as I could see, I'd only provided accurate and relevant information in response to direct questioning. Moreover, my contribution had averted a potential misunderstanding.

I attempted to turn the issue around and look at it from Bethany's perspective. How would I feel in her position? It was hard to come up with a reasonable parallel, but I imagined a scenario in which Bethany had relayed to a third party the correct information that my father was an atheist coffee shop-owner, which, in turn, may have impacted on my own belief system – since I was also an atheist, and drank a lot of coffee.

But *was* Bethany still a Christian? Three years ago, the answer would have been an unequivocal yes, but today matters were not so simple. Bethany had changed in all sorts of ways since we started secondary school – she had changed far more than I had, both in terms of her interests and in how she presented herself to the world. In the old days, she'd made an overt display of her faith. She'd worn a small silver cross around her neck and wristbands bearing the WWJD acronym (What Would Jesus Do?). But I hadn't seen these adornments for a long time, and certainly not at school. She didn't listen to Christian rock anymore, either; she listened to Ariana Grande and Shawn Mendes and, more recently, BTS. Yet was any of this actually significant? Just because Bethany's taste in jewellery and music had changed, it didn't mean that her core beliefs had. And surely she would have told me if there had been some seismic shift in her worldview?

I turned these thoughts over and over in my mind before finally concluding I was getting nowhere. As far as our argument went, the precise nature of Bethany's faith made no difference. I'd said nothing about it to Will beyond telling him to ask Bethany himself. Which was the opposite of interfering!

I tried to start again, going back to the bare facts I could be sure of, but no matter how I examined the puzzle, it refused to yield any useful information. The minutes ticked by, I became increasingly tired and frustrated, and by the time my brain shut down, I was no closer to finding a solution. In truth, I felt further away than ever.

*

Despite my poor night's sleep, I was the second person up in the boarding house, as was standard. I awoke at 6.20, completed my ten-minute callisthenics workout in the bathroom, then dressed and went through to the main lounge. Suzi was preparing breakfast in the kitchenette. You don't know Suzi, obviously, but she is another of the House Parents, responsible for looking after the forty-two full- and part-time boarders at Thorton Park. Suzi is forty-eight years old and has grey hair at her temples which she does not attempt to hide with cosmetics. This is one of the things I respect about her. She has made the positive decision not to wage an unwinnable war against time. She is also comparatively easy to talk to.

'Morning, Phoebe. Did you sleep well? Can I get you a coffee?'

'No and yes, please.'

'Oh dear,' Suzi said, as she put the kettle on. 'Is there anything the matter?'

'Yes. I'd like to discuss the night-time ban on electronic devices.'

'Oh . . . again?'

'I've been doing some additional research since our last conversation, and while I understand the rationale behind the current policy, and don't disagree with it *per se*, I do think it's failing to achieve its intended goal, at least in my case. It might even be exacerbating my insomnia.'

'OK.' Suzi's initial smile had been replaced by a small frown. 'Would you like to talk me through it? What has your research uncovered?'

It took seven minutes to outline my argument, including the time needed to find paper and sketch the bell curve representing the varying sleep requirements of children aged

14–17. I marked the mean with a dotted line at 9.25 hours, then drew a cross significantly to the left of this to indicate my own estimated position on the graph.

'So you're struggling to fall asleep?' Suzi summarised. 'Is that it?'

'Yes. That's exactly it. At home I go to bed between eleven and ten past, and in general I have far less trouble falling asleep.'

'Have you tried reading?'

'Of course. I purchased an LED headlamp for exactly this purpose, so I can read late without disturbing Bethany. Unfortunately, it's still less than ideal. Reading a book in bed is not as comfortable as reading on a phone.'

'But less likely to keep you awake,' Suzi countered.

'I've downloaded a blue-light filter on all my devices to minimise disruption to my circadian rhythms. In addition, I require a phone so I can have the option of listening to relaxing music. In the past, you've suggested that this would be a breach of Health and Safety, because of the headphone issue. But having considered it further, I think your argument is flawed. If the house was on fire, I assume Bethany would alert me to this fact before making her own escape.'

'Yes. I'd hope so too,' Suzi said. 'I'll talk to Kevin, but I honestly don't know if there's much we can do. It's difficult to make exceptions when it comes to phones. I'm sure you understand why.'

'It would be viewed as unfair?'

She nodded.

'What if I got a doctor's note?'

'Saying . . . what? That you have to take your phone to bed with you on medical grounds?'

I could see that Suzi was coming round to my way of thinking. 'Exactly. The phone would be used only to combat insomnia, which is a legitimate medical concern. Poor quality sleep has been linked to all sorts of health issues: high blood pressure, diabetes, stroke, heart attack, death by accident—'

Suzi held up her hands. 'OK, I get it. Many health issues. Listen, Phoebe, I understand that you've done a lot of reading, and you clearly know more on the subject than I do. But maybe there's a simpler reason you're finding it hard to sleep? Is there anything else worrying you?'

This change of direction threw me a little. I do not like lying and I am not good at it, but I was determined not to talk about Bethany, in keeping with her injunction. I sipped my coffee and waited a few seconds to show that I was thinking. 'Nothing whatsoever.'

Suzi looked unconvinced. 'You know, Phoebe, you can always talk to me or Kevin, about anything. Or if you don't feel comfortable with that, there's the school counsellor. You have lots of options.'

I nodded, somewhat disingenuously. There was no way I was going to talk to the school counsellor again. Not only had our past interactions proven ineffectual, but I also had my doubts about her professional credentials; yet when I'd probed this topic in one of our sessions, she'd become rather abrupt and defensive. This did nothing to assuage my doubts.

I told Suzi: 'If you could continue to consider the phone issue, I'd be extremely grateful.'

I added a website reference to the sleep distribution graph, then passed it back to her. I hoped it would be useful for her upcoming discussion with Kevin.

*

The breakthrough came on Friday evening while I was playing chess against my phone. Usually, Friday evening was designated as Film Night: Kevin and Suzi prepared bowls of popcorn and cashew nuts and all forty-two boarders were encouraged, and to some measure expected, to attend. But this week the film was *Beauty and the Beast*, starring Emma Watson, AKA Hermione from *Harry Potter*. A quick internet search revealed that it was a romantic musical fantasy, and not a fantasy in the same sense as *Game of Thrones* – not high fantasy. I was not interested, and managed to persuade Suzi that I needed some 'downtime' after a tiring week.

I was locked in a complex pawn-and-bishop endgame when the moment of inspiration arrived. It was astonishing, really – first, because the idea seemed to come from nowhere, and second, because I had close to zero supporting evidence. All I had was this sudden intuition – a revelation, almost – and the certainty it was correct. This is not the sort of thing I'm used to.

I ambushed Bethany the moment she returned to our room from Film Night. 'I'm sorry,' I told her. 'I didn't realise you liked him.'

After a couple of seconds of apparent confusion, Bethany blushed, very deeply. Hypothesis confirmed. I felt a surge of satisfaction, not only because I'd solved a social puzzle, but also because the awkwardness that followed wasn't *my* awkwardness. It was turning into an evening of novel experiences.

'If you want, I can tell Will that I made an error. Although I'm still not convinced that—'

'No, definitely not!' Bethany sat on her bed, seeming to regain some of her composure. 'I'm sorry. I sound like a complete cow. And I know I said some things that were really unfair. None of this is your fault, it's just . . .'

I was able to fill in the blank. 'You want me to stay uninvolved? Even better. I have zero interest in talking to Will ever again.' In all honesty, I had no idea what Bethany saw in him. He was clearly an idiot, whereas she was smart, popular and, objectively speaking, extremely attractive, with her fine blonde hair, well-proportioned breasts and hips, and a delightful smile – though the latter was currently absent. Bethany was wearing a small frown. 'No offence,' I added. 'Obviously, my opinion should have no bearing on yours. Each to her own, as they say.'

Bethany rolled her eyes. 'Phoebe, it's fine. I know you find this stuff awkward to talk about. We don't have to. I mean, we never really have, have we? It would probably be weird if we started now.'

I considered these statements. Bethany was correct that we didn't, in general, talk about this 'stuff' – by which I assumed she meant boys. Relationships. But it wasn't that I found it awkward, or was unwilling to try. It was more that I felt I had no relevant knowledge or experience to bring to such a discussion.

'I suspect I'm asexual,' I told her.

'Jesus . . .' Bethany had her hands to her mouth, apparently to stifle laughter. 'Where did *that* come from?'

I shrugged. 'I've been considering it for a while. I watched a TED Talk on the subject. It was extremely interesting. I can send you the link, if you like?'

Bethany seemed to find this hilarious as well. I'm not sure why. 'I'm sorry, I'm not laughing at you,' she said, once she'd composed herself. 'It's just the way you come out with these things. I've literally known you my whole life, but every so often, you still find a way to floor me.'

'Oh. Well, I just wanted to clarify my position. I don't feel awkward talking about this stuff. I just don't get what all the fuss is about.'

'You've never had a crush?'

'I don't think so. I was a bit infatuated with Magnus Carlsen for a while, but I decided it was purely intellectual.'

'Who's Magnus Carlsen?'

'He's the world chess champion.'

'Of course he is.'

'But admiring someone's strategic prowess isn't usually a symptom of a crush, is it?'

'Not in my experience, no.'

'To be honest, I don't feel any differently about boys than I did when we were eight. They've got taller, their voices have got a bit deeper, some of them have grown more annoying, but . . . yeah, that's basically it.'

'OK . . . And what about girls?'

'What? Do you mean do I feel differently about *girls*?'

'Yes. Have you considered the possibility?'

I took a moment to consider it now. 'I think it's equally implausible. I mean, I can recognise when girls are pretty, like Zendaya in *Homecoming* or Tarja from Nightwish. The first vocalist,' I clarified. 'The one who dresses kind of like a gothic princess.'

Bethany nodded. 'Right.'

'But noticing that someone is pretty isn't the same as having a crush, is it? And neither is enjoying them as an artist.'

'No. They're three different things. And I'm not sure you

need to overthink this. Crushes aren't generally something you need to diagnose. You're just kind of aware of them.'

'OK. But sometimes I'm not even aware of very basic feelings. Like if I'm hungry, for example. I'll interpret it as a stomach ache. Then I'll realise I haven't eaten for eight hours and put two and two together.'

Bethany laughed again, a warm laugh. 'Honestly, Phoebe, I don't think this is something you need to have all figured out yet. I'm sorry I've been so moody. It was really unfair of me.'

She got up from her bed and spread her arms wide open; it took me a moment to realise that she wanted to hug. Hugging is not a usual feature of our friendship. But since it seemed intended as a formal gesture of reconciliation, I went along with it.

And even though I'm not a fan of close physical contact, it was surprisingly enjoyable.

6

The Careers Debacle

The week after the Symbolic Hug, I deduced that Bethany and Will had ceased their former state of being 'unattached'. Now they were very much attached, to each other, every spare minute of the school day. The best thing I can say about it is that Bethany seemed extremely happy, which was, of course, nice to see. But it didn't mean the new situation was wall-to-wall fun for me.

Will started sitting with us every lunchtime in the dining hall. He and Bethany ate very slowly, seeming far more interested in gazing into each other's eyes, huge grins plastered over their faces. Often, they played with their hair; sometimes, they played with *each other's hair* – which I felt came perilously close to contravening school's very sensible policy against Excessive Public Displays of Affection. Yet it appeared that the lunch staff were either oblivious or willing to turn a blind eye. I coped by trying to adopt the same mindset I had when viewing the mountain gorilla documentary. I imagined David Attenborough's voice in my head, quietly informing me of the grooming rituals of primates, and how they'd evolved to facilitate close pair-bonding. When this failed, I started bringing a book to lunch.

This would have been a good solution, but, eventually,

Bethany regained enough perception to worry that I was being 'left out'. Obviously, I was being left out – and that was definitely not the issue! Yet despite my efforts to reassure Bethany on this front, once she'd become conscious of my continued existence, she was clearly uncomfortable leaving me to read for extended periods of time while she and Will flirted and talked and flirted some more.

I couldn't really engage with their conversations about pop music, which I did not listen to, or *Riverdale*, which I did not watch, but increasingly they seemed willing to drop these subjects and talk to me about the subjects I was familiar with. I also noted that Will was being far less smug and obnoxious than he'd been in our first conversations, and I did appreciate the effort that this must have cost him. He asked me about my interests (other than Nightwish), and listened patiently while I explained the plot of *The Fifth Season*, which was the novel I was trying to finish reading. Furthermore, he did not belittle me when I told him about my own writing ambitions. Will wasn't really 'into' books, but he did like sci-fi films, and we had quite an interesting discussion about *Infinity War* and its ramifications for the final Avengers movie. Meanwhile, Bethany beamed at him, evidently proud that he was trying his best to win me over.

One lunchtime, during a brief lull in the conversation, I decided to ask him if he'd actually been kicked out of his previous school, since I'd heard nothing conclusive either way – just Bethany's assertion that she didn't 'think' it was true.

'Phoebe!' Bethany shrieked. 'You can't ask that!'

'Why not? That's why these rumours persist, isn't it? It's much simpler just to ask and get the matter settled. Anyway, Will's clearly not offended.'

Will was grinning broadly – it was an expression that I thought was almost impossible to misinterpret. 'It's fine,' he said. 'Honestly. I'm familiar with the rumours. And they're just rumours.'

'Of course they are,' Bethany agreed, placing her hand on Will's arm. 'I don't think anyone actually believes them.'

Will kept grinning.

'So, just to be one hundred per cent clear, none of it's true? You weren't kicked out?'

'Phoebe! He's already said it's just a rumour!'

I nodded. 'Exactly. And I want to know if it's a true rumour or a false rumour.'

Will laughed and held up his hands. 'It's *just* a rumour, OK? You know what rumours are like . . .'

This, of course, was terribly frustrating! 'I like to have certainty,' I told Will, hoping this might finally persuade him to give me a straight answer. Which it did not.

'If you want certainty, you should just ignore all rumours,' he said. Then he winked at me.

I looked at Bethany, but she was nodding as if he'd uttered some profound piece of wisdom. I decided that the best option, for the sake of my own sanity, was to give up. Either Will had been kicked out of school and he was ashamed of it (though he didn't seem ashamed!), or he hadn't been kicked out of school but was happy to let the rumours continue (which was just plain baffling!). I supposed it was *possible* that he was trying to maintain a kind of mystique or ambiguity about himself, which Bethany seemed to appreciate, but to me, it was just evasiveness, and rather annoying.

All in all, I still didn't know what to make of Will. Having now had several conversations with him, I was able to acknowledge that he wasn't nearly as awful as I'd first imagined, but neither was he as witty or charming as Bethany clearly thought he was. I could see that he was very self-confident, and seemed to have amassed plenty of friends in the short time he'd been at school. But my strong suspicion was that if it wasn't for Bethany, we would not get along; or, more accurately, we'd have no compelling reason to make the effort.

Yet for as long as he and Bethany were wrapped up in each other, I determined that my personal doubts about Will were largely irrelevant. Moreover, as the days passed, I found a new and more pressing issue had arisen, this time in relation to a careers guidance meeting, mandatory for all Year Elevens.

A few days before the meeting was scheduled to take place, my form teacher, Mrs McManus, drew me to one side to make sure I understood the format: the meeting was to be one-on-one, she told me. It might last up to half an hour, and was outsourced to a specialist careers advisor, who visited school a couple of times a year. I assured her that I did understand this, and attempted to walk away.

'Phoebe, we're not quite done,' Mrs McManus told me. 'I wanted to ask if you need any additional support. Someone can sit in with you, if it would help?'

It took me a moment to realise what she was driving at. The unstated assumption was that I might struggle to communicate effectively with someone I didn't know. This was a justified assumption, since my awkwardness in conversation is, as a rule, inversely proportional to how well I know the person I'm talking to. But in this case, there were mitigating factors. I assumed the conversation with the careers advisor would be highly structured, and without much in the way of sarcasm or subtext. I also had the advantage of having already decided on my future career. I predicted the meeting would be focused and efficient, and told Mrs McManus that no assistance would be required.

The travelling careers advisor was called Mrs Shepherd, which I found both reassuring and somewhat amusing. I'd prepared a small joke prior to going in, about her 'shepherding' us into our future careers, which, sadly, I did not get to use.

Things started well enough. Mrs Shepherd complimented me on my projected grades, noting that I must be the top student in my year. I made appropriate eye contact and confirmed this was the case. My excellent memory for facts and figures, combined with my general enthusiasm for learning and ability to think logically and systematically, meant that I did well in most subjects. I only really struggled with PE and Art, where I was somewhat hampered by my lack of physical coordination, and Computer Science, which I found rather tedious. I'd also found French tricky in lower school, but had fortunately been able to drop it in favour of Spanish, which I much preferred and was of far greater practical use to me.

'Have you decided on A Levels yet?' Mrs Shepherd asked.

'Yes. English Literature, Psychology, Physics.'

'OK. It's an unusual combination, if you don't mind me saying.'

'How so?'

'They don't exactly fit together. You've got a natural science, a social science and an art. It's more usual to specialise at this stage.'

'Oh, I see. Well, I suppose I think of myself more as an aspiring polymath. Reading is my passion, but I'd also like to know a lot more about the human mind and the fundamental laws of nature. These are very interesting subjects as far as I'm concerned. I don't mind if the combination is a bit unusual.'

'It's very unusual. I mean, it's great to follow your interests, obviously. But it's difficult to see the through-line.'

I thought for a while, but must have spent too long. Mrs Shepherd started speaking again.

'Have you thought about your career, what sort of area you might want to go into? It's fine if you haven't. Plenty of people are unsure at your age.'

Not me. This was my time to shine. 'Author. Author of adult fantasy fiction.' Mrs Shepherd's eyes widened, and I realised that I needed to clarify. 'Adult with a small "a". Fantasy for adults, not erotica. I don't think I'd be very good at that.'

Mrs Shepherd did some unnecessary pro-social laughter. 'Phew! You have no ambition to be the next . . . gosh, what's her name? That dreadful woman from a few years back?'

I told Mrs Shepherd that I couldn't help here, as I had no idea whom she was referring to.

'Never mind. Let's back up a little. It's wonderful to have a dream, it really is. But it's a long way outside the remit of what we're trying to achieve in this session. Perhaps we should discuss something a bit more immediate. What are your plans for university?'

This was a little confusing. I explained that I did not have any plans for university, as, clearly, a degree was unnecessary for my chosen career. I planned to write my first novel as soon as I finished my mandatory schooling.

'Yes, there's nothing stopping you from pursuing that, of course. But you've already said that you love learning. Surely university is the next logical step?'

I considered this for a moment. 'I have good research skills and am very self-motivated when it comes to acquiring new knowledge. I think I'd probably do just as well as an independent learner.'

'Yes, but you'd still have plenty of opportunity for independent learning at university. Have you thought about studying English? Or Creative Writing?'

'I've thought about it. My conclusion was that I can read books at home, without the need to travel, and they'll be the books I want to read. As for Creative Writing, I've read many authors who suggest that writing is best learned through just sitting down and doing it. Stephen King, for example. He says the only way to become a better writer is to read a lot and write a lot. And Stephen King has a lifetime's experience. He's sold over three hundred and fifty million books! I think we can agree he knows what he's talking about here.'

'Yes, I wouldn't dispute that. However . . .'

I waited to see where Mrs Shepherd's *however* would lead. I'm not certain she knew, either. She spent a considerable amount of time looking at her notes. 'Phoebe. Maybe we could just explore *all* the options? I mean, with your academic ability you could go anywhere. Literally anywhere. Oxford, Cambridge. It would be such a shame to limit yourself.'

This made no sense. Why would I travel hundreds of miles to read books or learn more about writing when I could do both from the comfort of my own bedroom? I couldn't understand why Mrs Shepherd was being so stubborn about this!

'It's not that I'm trying to deter you,' she continued, 'but it's also sensible to have a Plan B. You can see that, can't you? Being an author is a niche career. There's no certainty that it will work out as you hope it will.'

'I have a Plan B,' I told her. 'I can work in my father's coffee shop. And I can continue to live at home indefinitely. My father is perfectly happy with this arrangement. We have an agreement.'

'Do you think you'd be happy with that?' Mrs Shepherd asked. 'Working in a coffee shop?'

'Is there something wrong with working in a coffee shop?'

'No, of course not. But there are so many things you *could* do.'

I didn't know what to do with this statement. There were lots of jobs I could do – that was obvious. I could be a marine biologist or an antiquarian bookseller. I could be an actuary, like Daddy had been before he decided he hated it and bought a coffee shop. I had no idea what I was supposed to say at this point.

Mrs Shepherd also seemed to be struggling. She looked down at her notes again, at her agenda. 'What about work experience? Have you thought about a placement for next half term? If you have any ideas, you should let your school know in good time so they can help you arrange it. I mean, as long as it's realistic.'

She gave a small smile. I did not smile back. Not only was I distressed at her lack of enthusiasm for my chosen career, but I was also starting to have serious misgivings about the wisdom of continuing this appointment.

I decided not to.

I told her that I'd be sure to let the school know my work experience plans in good time, and I got up and walked out. We'd used approximately seven minutes of our scheduled half-hour.

*

It might have been because she was busy on her phone at the time – probably messaging Will – but I found Bethany was unsympathetic when I told her about the careers debacle.

'Well, what did you expect?' she asked, not looking up from the screen.

'I expected her to advise me on my career. And I don't see what's so wrong with that. It's literally her job title!'

'You should have told her you want to be . . . I don't know, a teacher or journalist or something. Something unproblematic. That's probably all she wanted.'

'I should have *lied*?'

'Well, it's not like she's asking you to sign a legally binding contract. What difference does it make?'

'It makes all the difference. I don't want to be a teacher or a journalist. I want to be an author.'

Bethany sighed and put her phone down on her bed. 'Phoebe, careers advice isn't for that sort of stuff. I thought you knew that?'

'I did not know that! And why isn't it? Author is a perfectly valid career. There are literally hundreds of thousands of books published every year. They didn't write themselves!'

'Yes, but there are some jobs that are just . . . I don't know . . . Irregular.'

'*I'm* irregular! At least in that sense.'

'Yes, I know. And that's fine. But it doesn't mean the careers service is set up to accommodate every conceivable possibility. Plus, it's obvious that they'd encourage you to apply to a top university. It reflects well on the school, doesn't it?'

This was incredibly annoying. First, because it hadn't been

at all obvious to *me;* I guessed it was yet another of those things that everyone else understood so well that it had never needed stating. Second, because it was completely unfair! How my career plans reflected on the school should not have been a consideration. It was *my* career, not school's!

'Is there something inherently ridiculous about my wanting to be an author?' I asked.

'Of course not. You're missing the point.'

'What is the point?'

Bethany sighed again, as if she were exercising an astonishing feat of patience. 'I'm just saying it's not a conventional career path and it's not something that can go down on the form they have to fill in. I doubt "fantasy author" is one of the drop-down options under Post-School Plans.'

'Fine! So what did *you* tell her?' I asked. 'Since you obviously made far better use of the session than I did.'

'We talked about A Levels. We talked about university. The usual stuff. I told her I'd probably do languages or something.'

'Languages or *something*?' Unbelievable! 'What languages? French? Arabic? Ancient Sanskrit?'

'Just languages. Modern foreign languages.'

'And that was sufficient. She was OK with that?'

'Of course. Why wouldn't she be?'

I had run out of words.

Bethany just lay on the bed with her eyes closed.

After a minute or so, I asked: 'Do you actually want to go to university and study modern foreign languages?'

Bethany shrugged again, not bothering to open her eyes.

'You must have some idea.'

Bizarrely, Bethany did not answer this question directly.

Instead, she said: 'You know, Will spent a year living in New York. Manhattan. His dad worked on Wall Street.'

I frowned. 'You want to be an investment banker? I don't think your maths is good enough.'

Bethany threw her pillow at me. 'I'd like to see a bit more of the world, that's all. Like Will has. He's been all over the place. The States, Singapore, Dubai. He hasn't spent his whole life in the same tiny village.'

'Oh.' I hesitated for a moment, choosing my words carefully. 'So, is this about what Will thinks? Because, if it is, I honestly don't—'

'Phoebe, it's about what *I* think! What I'd like to do.'

'Right. And you'd like to . . . see a bit more of the world?'

'Yes!'

'To what end?'

'Seriously? Don't you ever want to . . . just go somewhere new? Experience new things?'

I thought about this. 'No. I mean, I do like to experience *some* new things, but generally I prefer it when I don't have to travel to do it. I think that's one of the reasons I like reading and writing so much. You get to explore all these new ideas and places, but without having to leave your house.'

'What about when you visit your gran in Spain? You always seem to enjoy that.'

'Yes, but that's different. It's more like a home away from home. I know that Gee will look after me. Plus, I've done it so many times that it's a routine. It's not stressful when I know exactly what to expect.'

Bethany looked at me for some time before shaking her head. 'I think it's the exact opposite for me. I don't want things to be predictable all the time. And I definitely don't want to stay on Holy Island for the rest of my life. It's got to be the most boring place on the planet.'

I understood that her final sentence was just an opinion, and perhaps born of frustration, yet I didn't think it should go unchallenged. By most measures, Holy Island is an excellent place to live, with a unique landscape and fascinating heritage. Over the summer, it's home to thousands of migratory birds. It has a sixteenth-century castle! But Bethany was not interested in engaging with these arguments. I couldn't have been talking for more than two minutes when she interrupted and told me that I just didn't 'get it'. Then she picked up her phone, said she was going to go and get a drink, and left the room.

Later, when I thought about our conversation, I didn't know what to make of it. For some reason, it had left me feeling uncertain.

On Saturday, I decided to get a second opinion at breakfast. I did not have long because Daddy was somewhat late getting up and had to be at the shop at 8.45. I gave him a swift but thorough run-down of the careers situation as he ate a piece of toast.

'Did I do something wrong?' I asked him in conclusion.

Daddy scratched his chin. I was aware that he'd probably want to shave and shower before leaving, which lent an extra time pressure to our discussion. Fortunately, conversations with Daddy tend to be efficient as he has a logical mind and knows how to stay on topic.

'You didn't do anything wrong,' he said. 'It's more . . . differing goals.'

'I didn't like Mrs Shepherd,' I told him.

'You might be judging her a little harshly. How long did you talk to her?'

'Seven minutes.'

'OK. And what did she say that particularly bothered you?'

'She said I should think about going to Oxford or Cambridge.'

'She did, did she?' Daddy seemed amused by this. 'Perhaps she was paying you a compliment.'

'Perhaps. That's not the point. She wasn't interested in what I want to do. Not really. Bethany says it's because you can't put "fantasy author" on a careers form.'

'Well, Bethany has a point. But that doesn't mean you have to accept it. Sometimes it's good to push back a little.'

'What do you mean?'

'I mean it's OK to do things your own way, regardless of other people's expectations. You shouldn't worry just because your answer doesn't fit neatly on a form.'

I looked at Daddy for a few moments. 'Do you understand that the form is not a metaphor? It's a literal form the careers advisor has to fill out so it can go in your file.'

'OK. But you get the point. There's no universal template for how you should live your life. And if anyone tries to tell you otherwise, they're just plain wrong.'

Daddy poured more coffee.

I waited a moment, then said: 'OK, I definitely agree with you on principle, but just to clarify: do *you* think I should be applying for university? Is it something you'd want me to consider?'

'I don't think you should rule it out,' Daddy said. 'That's perhaps the one area where I do agree with Mrs Shepherd. You might find it suits you more than you think. But beyond that . . . Honestly, I want you to have the confidence to make your own decisions. As long as you're making them for the right reasons.'

'OK. And what are the right reasons?'

'I'm afraid that's another thing you might have to figure out for yourself.'

'I think it would be simpler if you just told me.'

Daddy thought about this while sipping his coffee. 'OK. Let me put it this way: you shouldn't let fear make your decisions for you. Base your choices on what you want deep down – on the things that are really important to you. Does that help?'

'Perhaps. A little. But I'm not always good at making big choices. It might take me a while.'

Daddy chuckled at this. 'Well, you've got a couple of years to work through it all, haven't you? Longer if you need it. That's one thing I *can* tell you. You shouldn't feel pressured to have your whole life worked out by age eighteen. Sometimes, it's more a case of trial and error. You have to try out different things. See what fits.'

'Am I still allowed to stay here as long as I want?'

'Of course. As long as you want.'

'Bethany says she wants to go and live somewhere exotic. New York or Dubai or Singapore. She wants to travel. Is that about seeing what fits?'

'Yes, probably.'

I decided the conversation was at an end, but before I could leave the table, Daddy asked: 'Are you worried about what Bethany told you? About wanting to live somewhere else?'

My response was automatic. 'No, why would I be worried about that?'

Daddy didn't say anything for a moment, then he nodded. 'No reason. I just wanted to check.'

*

After my talk with Daddy, I did feel that I understood the careers incident better, and I was reassured that I didn't have to pretend I wanted to be a teacher, for example, or spend three years living in Oxford or Cambridge against my will. And yet this was not the full picture. When I considered the events of the past couple of weeks, I was still somewhat agitated – beset by emotions that were worryingly muddled. It was like the discomforting sensation of looking at a photograph that's ever so slightly out of focus.

I had planned to spend most of the morning reading, but in light of my ongoing confusion, I decided it would be prudent to extend Gladys's usual morning walk to its maximum possible length, which was approximately eight and a half miles (i.e. a full circuit of the island). This would give me sufficient time to clear my head, and I doubted Gladys would complain, though she'd probably spend the whole afternoon asleep.

I put on my windproof jacket and walking boots, grabbed a tennis ball and some poo bags, and we set off. It was a bright but chilly morning, and still early enough that we didn't encounter many people. We walked past the vicarage, past St Mary's, past the priory ruins, past the harbour, past the castle, past the seals on the eastern shore. I looked at the sea and the clouds and the birds in the hedgerows, and I allowed my mind to drift.

By the time we'd reached the north shore, a number of ideas had consolidated, and I was now able to organise them. I'd faced three difficult social situations in as many weeks, each of which had caused me significant stress. First had been the car in the sea, the thing that started it all. Not only had it been disruptive and unpleasant in its own right, but it had also set off the chain of events that had sabotaged my first day back at school: too little sleep, too much caffeine, and a reduced ability to deal with the social demands of the classroom, resulting in the worst possible start to the new academic year. Then had come the misunderstanding with Bethany and Will, and the argument that had followed. The careers incident was the latest problem in line, and even though it was provoking less anxiety now, I knew it was yet to be resolved. There would be further careers meetings over the coming months, and I still had to arrange my mandatory work experience; I had to come up with a viable placement that would satisfy school without being a complete waste of my time.

Yet, annoying as this was, I realised it wasn't the thing that was bothering me the most. In truth, there was no single thing. It was the accumulation of difficulty upon difficulty – the fact that a worrying pattern was emerging.

There had been a number of occasions in the past when I'd felt as if the rules of the social game had suddenly changed – they had become more complicated, or extra rules had been added without my knowledge. The most notable was the onset of adolescence, when I'd had to adapt without warning to a whole new set of expectations and hidden codes of behaviour, to new ways of speaking and acting and being. Sarcasm was suddenly rife. Clothing and hairstyles became more intricate. Information was conveyed in silent glances – meaningful to everyone else, and frequently impenetrable to me.

The current situation felt similar. I kept getting things wrong, often without even knowing there was a problem until the damage had been done. At the back of my mind, I could still hear the words Bethany had spoken after I'd embarrassed her with Will: *You're the problem!* True, she'd apologised afterwards, and hadn't been so harsh since, but the recollection

61

still hurt. And when I considered everything else that I'd made a mess of in the last few weeks, it became difficult to view her anger as entirely unjustified.

I didn't want to be a problem, and I certainly didn't want to continue making mistakes that might jeopardise my only friendship. Yet this was the spectre that had arisen since the start of term. I'd managed to avert disaster so far, but it would surely get harder if I kept messing up.

I understood now why Daddy had asked if I was worried with regard to Bethany and the idea of her leaving. Bethany and I had *always* been together, by default if nothing else. We'd been born six months apart, and were the only children born on Holy Island in a three-year span. We'd shared a room as soon as we'd started boarding. I'd spent more waking hours with Bethany than I had with anyone else, Daddy included. Of course, I'd always known, on some level, that this situation could not continue forever, that our lives were bound to diverge at some point. But I hadn't been prepared for it to start so soon. And the more I thought about it, the more convinced I became that this was precisely what was happening. In the midst of our relationship was this ever-widening gap. Because of the things she understood that I did not. Because of the things she found exciting or boring that I did not. Because she wanted to live somewhere far away, and I definitely did not.

I was suddenly aware that I had problems – many more problems than I'd thought – and no obvious solutions.

7

The Birthday Letter

My sixteenth birthday occurred on a Wednesday, and I managed to get through school without anyone apart from Bethany knowing. We weren't boarding, which meant I didn't have to worry about Kevin 'outing' me and getting everyone to sing Happy Birthday while Suzi brought out a tray-bake, as had happened on previous occasions. Bethany was sworn to secrecy, of course, but this year she didn't complain. Or not out loud. She did roll her eyes quite dramatically when I reaffirmed my desire for zero fuss at the beginning of the day.

The reason I don't like having my birthday publicly acknowledged is simple. I do not like being the centre of attention. I realise that other people do, but I do not. It makes me uncomfortable, and I honestly don't know why this is so hard to understand.

With my sixteenth, I think it helped that it was mid-week. There's a general dip in enthusiasm on Wednesdays – and not just among my peers. I've noticed that many of the teachers also appear less alert and less motivated, especially by the afternoon, resulting in a small dip in lesson quality. We have a 'suggestions' box at the school office in which I once left a note detailing my observations and proposing a compulsory aerobics session for all staff and students on Wednesday lunchtimes, to blow away the cobwebs. But, so far, no one in the office had got back to me. It's possible that the box does not get checked all that often.

Regardless, what made for a substandard teaching day also made for a successful low-key birthday. The day passed without incident until we were back in Bethany's mum's car, and almost home. At this point, Bethany told me that I shouldn't freak out, but she had a small surprise. I immediately started to freak out.

'OK, relax,' Bethany said. 'It's nothing bad. It's not a surprise party or anything. It's just a present. I mean, it's your *sixteenth*, Phoebe. I had to get you something.'

I relaxed, but only a little. Bethany did not have a good track record of getting me presents. I was sure we both remembered the *Twilight* incident of 2016.

'Many happy returns, Phoebe,' Bethany's mum said from the driver's seat.

'Thank you,' I croaked.

When we stopped at my house, Bethany got out too and retrieved a gift-wrapped parcel from the boot. It was soft and approximately the size and weight of a small cushion. I hoped it *was* a cushion. This would be a completely inoffensive and appreciated present.

'Is it OK if I open it inside?' I asked. 'It's a bit awkward with my bag. I wouldn't want to drop it.'

'It's fine. I hope you like it. But . . . well, I kept the receipt. Just in case.'

This is why birthdays are such a minefield, even without a formal celebration. Thankfully, I knew from experience that *I kept the receipt* was never to be taken at face value. It was the sort of thing people said, but then, when you contacted them to ask for the receipt, things deteriorated rather quickly.

The present was not a cushion; it turned out to be a black denim jacket. A jacket that I assumed was meant to be decorative, first and foremost, since it would offer almost zero protection from the wind or rain. It had wide, rather showy lapels. I imagined it would look very good on a mannequin, but it was clearly not for me. My wardrobe consists of T-shirts, tracksuit bottoms and warm jumpers. My favourite item of clothing is my grey hoodie, which is baggy, free from design features, and extremely comfortable: the sort of outfit that draws no unwanted attention.

I didn't know what Bethany was thinking, but a thank you message was necessary, and could not be delayed. Except I couldn't *just* write thank you. Given the problems we'd had since school resumed, I was paranoid that she'd read dissatisfaction, or some other hidden meaning, in such a terse response. I stared at my phone for several minutes until inspiration struck in the form of the emoji menu. I don't often use emojis, but in this case, they were the exact tool for the job.

I typed **Thank you!** 😊 and hit send.

And almost at once a reply pinged back: *You're welcome. Glad you like it, wasn't sure you would. Phew! X* 😬.

I didn't try the jacket on. Instead, I put it in my wardrobe, where it hung between my waterproof coat and my navy blue fleece like some weird alien artefact.

I had a Skype call scheduled with Gee at five o'clock, which came through exactly on time. As always, it was very pleasant to talk to her. It was six o'clock in Spain and she was on her laptop in the garden; the sky had a pretty yellow tinge.

'Are there any geckos?' I asked.

Gee took me over to the rockery. There was a lizard, apparently, but it ran away when she tried to get the webcam close enough for me to see.

'I'm too old to be chasing reptiles around the garden,' Gee complained. 'Let me sit down in the shade.' There was a short, wobbly silence as she relocated to the table under the olive tree. 'Did you get anything nice for your birthday?' she asked, after she'd sat down.

'Daddy got me an excellent pen,' I told her. 'It's engraved with my initials and refillable. Bethany got me a jacket.'

'How lovely. Did you remember to thank her?'

'Yes, of course. It's not really me, though – the jacket.'

'Why not?'

'It just isn't. It's more what she would wear.'

'Oh.' Gee thought for a moment. 'Why don't you show me?'

I retrieved the jacket from the wardrobe and held it up to the camera.

'It looks very nice to me,' Gee said. 'Have you tried it on?'

'Not yet. It's honestly not the sort of thing I could imagine wearing.'

'Perhaps that's part of the point,' Gee suggested. 'Just because you can't imagine wearing something, it doesn't mean it won't suit you.'

I couldn't think of an answer to this. It was an interesting theory, but perhaps nothing more. Gee was old and wise, but that didn't mean she was automatically qualified to discern the rationale behind Bethany's present-buying. It seemed just as likely – more likely – that Bethany had picked a gift that *she* would like. Case closed.

'What about your mum?' Gee asked after a moment. 'Have you opened her gift yet?'

This came as a surprise. I didn't know that Gee knew about your gift; it wasn't standard, obviously. 'Did Daddy tell you?' I asked.

'He mentioned she'd planned something extra, since it's your sixteenth.'

I nodded but didn't say anything. After a moment, Gee said: 'You know I still remember your mum's sixteenth like it was yesterday.'

'It was thirty years ago.'

'Time gets a bit funny as you get older. It goes quicker and quicker.'

'That sounds scientifically dubious.'

'Yes. It's still true though – wait and see.'

There was another small silence. I swallowed the lump in my throat and said: 'I haven't opened it yet. Her present. I haven't read the letter, either. It's a lot to cope with on a school day. I wanted to leave it until I had a decent amount of time to reflect.'

Gee nodded gently. 'Would you like to do it while I'm here? For moral support?'

'Thank you. That's kind, but I think it's something I'd like to do on my own. I just have to psych myself up a bit first.'

'Of course. But I'm always here if you need to talk, Phoebe. I'm always here if you need *anything*. You know that, don't you?'

'I know that,' I confirmed.

Your gift and letter were on my desk, where I'd placed them that morning. I had planned to wait for Daddy to get home, as

I'd thought it would be a little easier that way, and because he'd want to read the letter too, as he always did. But having spoken to Gee, I found I'd changed my mind. I didn't want to go on delaying. I sat in my desk chair for a minute or so, counting my breaths, and then, using a butter knife to avoid damage, I carefully prised open the envelope.

Dear Phoebe,

Happy 16th birthday, Precious! I can't quite believe it. In all honestly, these are getting harder to write the further we get into the future. It's difficult for me to imagine how much you might have changed by the time you'll read this. Difficult but rewarding, too. I'll let you in on a little secret: often the hardest things in life are the most worth doing. We value the things we've had to struggle for far more than the things that come easily.

And those might be the only words of wisdom you get out of me today! My hope is that you'll need them a little less now, having already survived three years of being a teenager – the hardest years, in my experience! But the truth is I've always admired your ability to cope. Life's thrown up all sorts of challenges for you, and it will continue to do so (because that's what life does, for everyone), but you've always found a way through. You've found the solutions that work for you. That's something you should feel immensely proud of.

You used to struggle with praise, and in case you still do, I'll leave it at that and move on.

In keeping with tradition, let me give you a quick glimpse into the time capsule. Today (my today) is 1st June 2012. It's a Friday, warm and calm, and has been a good day so far. I woke up with very little pain (yay!) and even managed to go for a short walk after breakfast. I sat in the sunshine by the Lookout Tower and watched the tide go out. That was all, but it was very peaceful and relaxing. I'm looking forward to you getting back from school later. I'm hoping that this better spell lasts and we'll be able to spend the whole weekend together, just me, you and Daddy. It's not much, but I'm thankful for it. I'm thankful for all the time I get to spend with my family.

You'll have seen that I've enclosed a gift this year. 16 feels like a bit of a milestone, and I wanted to mark it. It's another thing that's been devilishly tricky, as tastes tend to change over the course of 6 years (!). So it may be that this gift isn't as appropriate as it once would have been. If that's the case, let's just call it nostalgia – me being hopelessly sentimental.

I hope you have a wonderful rest-of-the-day.
With all my love, now and forever,
Mum xxx

I read your letter, read it again, and then put it safely back in its envelope and picked up your gift. Under the wrapping was a plain black box, and in the box was a ring, and a thin golden chain. It was a replica of the One Ring from *The Lord of the Rings*, complete with engraved Elvish runes. It was perfect. I tried it on my left index finger and it fitted, and I wondered if you'd used your own finger as a template and that meant our fingers were the same size. It felt a little strange as I'd never worn jewellery before, but strange in a good way. I spent some time tracing the runes on its surface with the tip of my finger, then I left the house and walked to the Lookout Tower, where you'd sat on 1st June 2012, which was six years, four months and two days ago. It would have been almost exactly six months before you died.

I tried to picture that day and the weekend that had followed. Obviously, I couldn't remember any of it specifically, but I did have a very strong impression of what that summer had been like. It had been very calm, especially compared to the previous one, when Daddy had been working all the time, despite taking on extra help in the coffee shop, and you'd both been tired and stressed. I remembered 2011 as the summer I'd spent a lot of time with Bethany and her parents, and with Gee, who'd looked after me around the time of your cancer diagnosis. But 2012 was the summer when we had spent a lot of time together as a family – me, you and Daddy. We'd spent a lot of time outside in the garden, or at the beach during the quieter times, when the tide was in. It comforted me to think that there was a good chance you'd got the wish you mentioned in your letter – that we'd had the whole weekend together.

I cried for a bit, but they weren't bad tears. I actually felt very close to you, and I was grateful for the advice you'd given me in your letter, which had come at just the right time. Your words had shifted my perspective, pulled me out of the mental rut I'd dropped into during the last few weeks. Because you were right: I'd adapted to challenges in the past and I could do so again in the present. I realised now that I did not have to continue the school year as I'd started it – lurching from one social fiasco to the next. With a little bit of effort and forethought, I could surely make my life so much easier.

When I checked my phone it was 5.39, and the sun was low in the west. Daddy would be heading home imminently, bearing the dairy-free cake that Moira from the shop had made especially for me, even though it was her day off. He'd light the sixteen candles and ask me if I wanted him to sing the birthday song, and I'd assure him that this was absolutely one hundred per cent unnecessary, as I did every year. It would be a happy, stress-free evening.

Then, tomorrow, I was going to make some changes.

8

Self-Improvement

I slept deeply for approximately six hours and forty-five minutes and woke up early, energised and full of ideas. These were clarified further during my trampoline workout, and by six o'clock I'd showered, made coffee and was sitting on my bed with my laptop open.

Change is always a scary prospect, but in this case, the first step was not only straightforward, but also comforting, since it involved making a list. I identified the three areas of my life that required immediate attention.

1. **Social Interaction**. I needed to refamiliarise myself with the main rules of engagement, and possibly learn some new rules as well. The end goal was to be able to make non-weird, non-awkward conversation with a range of neurotypical human beings, as this seemed the surest path to averting future misunderstandings, of the sort that had plagued my life for the past month. In support of this, I also needed to expand my social circle. In theory, there was plenty of scope here, since my existing circle was small. In fact, if you excluded all the people who didn't really count – Daddy, Gee,

Suzi, Kevin, my teachers, Moira, Gladys and Will – my social circle consisted of only one other person. The minimum possible increase was one hundred per cent, and this was an encouraging thought.

2. **Personal Appearance and Presentation**. It may have felt incredibly pointless, but Bethany's gift, the jacket, had reminded me that most people cared about this sort of thing. A lot. The sad truth was that without some visible outer transformation, my other efforts might go unnoticed.

3. **Work Experience**. I had to sort out my placement. To a large extent, this was a side-project, but I added it to the list because it was urgent and causing me distress; and, on reflection, I realised that it would overlap with the two other areas of my self-improvement in some significant ways, since I'd have to speak, act and present myself in a manner appropriate to the work environment. Obviously, I'd had some experience of this in the coffee shop, but that was a familiar and safe environment, where I had Daddy and/or Moira to support me. In the wider world, there was a far greater potential for mishaps, and planning and preparation would be essential.

Having made the list, I felt satisfied that I had taken the first small step. And the second followed immediately. I closed my laptop and dressed for the day.

The denim jacket fitted me well enough, but it still felt odd and constrictive over my school blazer, and I was certain that it looked peculiar when I inspected myself in the mirror. Upon further thought, I decided the correct set-up might be to wear it *in place* of my blazer, which I could carry with my bag and change into before lessons. I made the alteration and it was a definite improvement, though I still felt a little weirded out, viewing this unfamiliar version of myself.

Nevertheless, I kept the jacket on and went through to the kitchen, where Daddy made no comment. This is one of the many excellent things about Daddy. He saw no reason to make a big deal over a change of garment. It's possible he did not even notice.

Bethany was a different matter, of course. 'Oh, you wore it!' she said, as she got into the back seat of the car, three and a half minutes after pick-up time. I didn't know how I was supposed to respond to such a self-evident statement, but I nodded redundantly. 'It looks good!' Bethany insisted.

And even though I felt this to be untrue, even though compliments make me uncomfortable, I reined in my instinctive response and forced a smile.

Bethany was grinning like the Cheshire Cat. She was so obviously happy – at such a small thing! Self-consciously, I touched the small hard lump against my breastbone, the spot where the One Ring hung concealed on its chain. And as the car started moving, and my initial embarrassment began to subside, the strangest feeling overtook me. I felt a flush of warm, genuine pleasure. The most trivial of changes, and already I was reaping the rewards.

For the last three years, my main social strategy had been one of avoidance. It wasn't that I *never* spoke to my classmates or to the other boarders, as this had proven impossible, but I was not in the habit of initiating conversations, and on the rare occasions I did, they tended to be brief and functional. I was aware that it would appear odd, and possibly unsettling, if I now attempted to strike up an unprovoked conversation with one of my peers – and that was assuming I could even think of something suitable to say. As a rule, I find small talk excruciating, and it seems that most people have a similarly adverse reaction to discussing any serious topic in depth. Bethany tells me I should try to 'feel' my way into the conversation, rather than diving straight in with a disquisition on global deforestation, for example. But this sort of advice is too vague to be useful.

What I needed, now, was a concrete plan – ideally, one that involved graded exposure (i.e. starting small and simple and building my way to more complex and demanding interactions). My goal was to find some sort of safe environment in which to practise and gain confidence.

The solution came to me one evening while I was collecting my laundry. Chess Club! It was one of the after-school Enrichment options, and it took place on Mondays at four o'clock. I'd discounted it in the past because, despite my enthusiasm for the game, I could not see the appeal in playing against another human being; I'd always been perfectly happy playing against my phone. But in my current predicament, the advantages of Chess Club were many. I'd be forced to engage with people I didn't usually engage with, but only on a limited basis, between games. Most conversations were likely to be one-on-one, which was immeasurably easier than trying to interact within a group, and we'd already have common ground – a shared interest – to provide a suitable topic. In addition, I probably wouldn't have to worry so much about all the secondary stresses that come with everyday conversation, like appropriate eye contact or what to do with my hands.

There was only one problem that I could foresee. We were supposed to sign up for Enrichment activities at the start of each new term. I was signed up for Jigsaw Club, and we were not allowed to 'chop and change' once the term was underway. However, this was counterbalanced by the fact that I was the only member of Jigsaw Club, so it wasn't as if I was going to be missed. Furthermore, I was always being encouraged to participate in group activities and sports. I decided to informally transfer myself, and attended Chess Club the following Monday. I made sure I was a few minutes late so I didn't have to queue up beforehand, and would not be asked any awkward questions.

Chess Club was run by Mr Finch, my Maths teacher. When I entered his classroom, I saw that there were six other members of the club and they were all boys. I knew four of them: Steven Penrose, who was in my year, and Ishmael, Hu and Johnny, who were all international students and boarders. (Ishmael was from Saudi Arabia, Hu was from China, and Johnny was from Hong Kong.) I did not mind that they were all boys as I generally find boys and girls equally difficult to get along with.

Mr Finch came over to greet me. 'Hello, Phoebe. Can I help you?'

'I'm here to join Chess Club,' I said.

'Oh. That's wonderful; the more the merrier. But don't you have somewhere else you're supposed to be right now?'

I explained the Jigsaw Club situation, and Mr Finch agreed that it was unlikely to be a problem.

'You've played chess before?' he asked.

'Yes. My father taught me when I was ten, and I play against an app on my phone. I also enjoy watching it on YouTube.'

'OK.' Mr Finch scratched his small grey beard. 'Well, we accept all abilities, but I should warn you that you'll probably struggle against the others. They all play for the school team.'

'I don't mind if I win or lose,' I said. 'I'm not naturally competitive. I'm just here to socialise.'

Mr Finch chuckled. 'Well, that's good. It's a nice attitude to have. You can just enjoy a few games.' He glanced at the other six members of Chess Club, who were already paired across three boards. 'I could give you a game now, if you like?' He laughed again. 'Don't worry. I promise I'll go easy on you.'

'Do we have to use a clock?' I asked. I had noted that the other players were using chess clocks in their matches. 'I haven't played under any sort of time constraint before. It doesn't really make sense against a computer.'

'No, I suppose it doesn't. It's fine – we'll just have a casual game to begin with. Would you like to be White?'

I didn't think I should try anything too flashy, so I started with E4, then transposed into the Ruy Lopez. Mr Finch responded with the Berlin Defence. After a dozen moves, we were out of Opening Theory and battling for control of the centre. When I glanced up from the board, Mr Finch was frowning. He'd played his opening quickly, but now he was pausing between moves. It was an odd experience, playing with a physical board and pieces, and I doubt my moves were as accurate as they could have been, but I was still able to hold my own for the next half an hour. At this point, Chess Club was due to end and Mr Finch said we'd better call it a draw. It was a fair suggestion, since neither of us had a winning position, though I assessed I had a slight edge. I looked up and extended my hand for the customary handshake that signified the end of the contest.

'That didn't go exactly as I was expecting,' Mr Finch said. He was still frowning, but I didn't know why. I wondered if I'd made some error with the handshake. 'How often do you play?' he asked.

'Every day.'

'Against your phone?'

'Yes.'

'Do you want to join the school team?'

It was a surprising development, and not part of the plan. I replied instinctively: 'No, thank you. As I said, I'm not really interested in competition.'

'Phoebe, I'd like you to reconsider. The team could use you. Unfortunately, we lost two of our strongest players last year. Sixth formers – they left. The point is, we're not operating at full strength. We could do with some fresh blood.'

'What would it entail?'

'We play against five other schools in the county league, but we've already had one match this year. Which we lost, by the way. But let's leave that to one side for now. It's only four more matches across the academic year, and we don't play during exam periods. It's honestly a very small time commitment.'

I thought for a few moments. 'No, thank you.'

I interpreted Mr Finch's expression as somewhat disappointed, but he didn't press the matter of joining the chess team any further. For now. 'Will you at least come back next week? I'd like to see how you do against some of the boys. Probably Hu, first.'

'OK, then.' I nodded. 'I shall return next week. Thank you for our game. I enjoyed it.'

As I exited the classroom, I couldn't decide if my first venture into Chess Club had been a success or not. I had failed to socialise with anyone who wasn't Mr Finch, and I had landed myself in the potentially awkward position of being asked to compete. Of course, it was gratifying to have my chess competence recognised, but at this point, I wanted to keep my self-improvement plan as simple as possible. However, I was going back next week, I'd have the opportunity to interact with Hu, and I hadn't been reported for my truancy from Jigsaw Club. My conclusion was that even though things hadn't gone perfectly, I should be pleased that I'd tried something different, with few negative consequences.

I hadn't told Bethany about my plan to attend Chess Club in case it came to nothing, but when I got back to our room, having reflected on the experience, I felt sufficiently buoyed to want to share the news with her. Unfortunately, I had to wait. She was engrossed in her phone. I sat on my bed and watched her, trying to be patient. That she was texting Will wasn't even a question in my mind; Bethany had a new smile – a distant, secretive sort of smile – that I'd mentally named the Will Smile, since it seemed to me that she wore it only when texting Will/daydreaming about Will. It was a smile I'd grown very used to over the past few weeks.

Eventually, she put her phone down and noticed me. 'What?' she said, looking confused.

'How's Will?' I asked. 'The same as an hour ago, I trust? You know, the last time you saw him.'

Bethany grinned at me. 'That almost sounded like sarcasm.'

'Don't you run out of things to say to each other?'

'Of course we don't! I could talk to him forever.'

'Right, and you seem determined to do so.'

'Wow. You've got your claws out this afternoon. What's going on?'

'Many things. How was Zumba?'

'It was . . . fine?' Bethany gave me a puzzled look. I waited. 'How was Jigsaw Club?'

'I didn't go to Jigsaw Club. I went to Chess Club instead.'

'Oh . . . I thought we weren't supposed to change mid-term?'

'We're not. I decided to do it anyway.'

Bethany took a long time to process this. 'So you . . . broke a rule?'

'Yes, I did. I decided the rule didn't matter so much in this instance. I also thought it was unlikely to be enforced. Correctly, as it turned out. Mr Finch asked me to come back next week.'

Bethany looked dumbfounded. 'Phoebe, I'm not sure what to say . . . Good on you?'

'Thank you. I found the experience interesting.'

Abruptly, Bethany started laughing. Then she broke one of *her* rules; she blasphemed. 'Jesus Christ, Phoebe! You've illegally joined the Chess Club! I wonder where this will end?'

I smiled. I had no idea where this would end, but I knew what was coming next. I was ready to start working on the next item on my agenda.

9

A Series of Obstacles

Having made immediate progress with items one and two on my self-improvement plan, I was perhaps over-confident when it came to item three (work experience), but by the end of the week, I'd realised this was going to be a tougher nut to crack. Initially, I determined that the best option – or the least bad option – was to follow Bethany's advice and feign an interest in journalism. It was still writing, after all, and it would certainly be preferable to spending a week working in a bank or retail outlet.

There were four local newspapers that I identified as possibilities: the *Berwick Advertiser*, the *Northumberland Chronicle,* the *South Edinburgh Echo*, and the *Scotsman*. I found their contact details online and began drafting a letter of enquiry – and that's where I ran out of steam. In hindsight, the problem was simple: I just didn't want to do it. If I'm interested in a subject or task, then motivation is never a problem for me; I can maintain a laser-like focus for literally hours, often neglecting basic needs such as eating or going to the toilet. But when I'm not interested . . . well, this task was a case in point. Instead of pressing on with the letter, I spent at least an hour re-reading my favourite passages from some of my favourite novels. Then I did a page of creative writing, describing a magical bridge I'd invented linking Earth to a parallel version of itself which appears only on nights with a full moon. Then I drew the bridge. Considering my lack of artistic ability, I was quite pleased with how the drawing turned out, but I had no desire to finish my letter. Beyond the first, horribly insincere sentence – *I'm interested in a career in journalism* – I couldn't think of anything to say.

I knew that I could get help from the careers service if I needed to. In fact, I could probably delegate most of the process; I could nominate my profession and let school do the rest. Yet I found that I did not want to do even this.

The truth was, I felt irritated when I thought about how quick the careers service would be to help me find a *normal* work experience placement. I was still angry when I thought about my meeting with Mrs Shepherd and her talk about realistic options. It's possible that this was an irrational and unreasonable response to what she'd said, but knowing this didn't seem to make any difference. I was reluctant to compromise.

On Friday, I decided that I'd exhausted my capacity to think constructively about the problem. I did need further help, and since I wasn't ready to capitulate to the careers service, I'd have to ask Bethany again. She understood the system far better than I did, and, more importantly, she understood me. Hopefully, she'd have additional ideas for jobs to investigate.

I had to choose a moment when she'd be receptive to this kind of discussion, so I waited until 9.29 that evening, and then volunteered to take our phones to Kevin so he could lock them away for the night.

Bethany eyed me suspiciously. 'Why so eager? I thought you were a rule-breaker now.'

'I don't intend to make a habit of it.' I held out my hand. 'Say goodnight to Will, if you haven't already. It's not fair to leave Kevin twiddling his thumbs.'

'OK, what's this about?' Bethany asked when I'd returned from the common room. 'You obviously want to talk about something.'

'Correct. I need some advice regarding work experience. It could take a while and I thought it would go more smoothly if your phone's not beeping every two minutes. You're easily distracted at the moment.'

'Phoebe!' She sounded shocked, but she was smiling, and she didn't even try to dispute my assertion. Instead, she giggled. 'OK, fine. So the distractions have been removed. I'm all yours.'

Bethany listened patiently for several minutes, not saying a word, while I explained my lack of progress with the newspapers and the considerable stress and anxiety it was causing.

'Do you have any plans for tomorrow?' she asked when I'd finished.

'Just the usual Saturday plans,' I told her. 'Read, write, walk Gladys. Why?'

'Come over for lunch. We'll talk about it then. My mum and dad can help too – they're already helping me sort mine, so I'm sure they won't mind.'

'OK. Sounds good. Shall I email you the research I've done so far? It's not very much – just some contact details and a list of concerns I have regarding various—'

'Phoebe, forget all that. You're over-thinking things. Just come over tomorrow and we'll start again with a fresh perspective. It's not going to be as hard as you think it is, I promise.'

I'm generally sceptical about Bethany's no-need-to-plan attitude, but in this case, I decided to trust her. I arrived at her house at exactly twelve o'clock the following day and brought no notes to our lunch meeting. This was probably for the best, anyway, as there was no room on the dining table for paperwork. Mrs Collins had made a tomato and basil pasta salad, hummus, flatbreads, falafel, spiced fruit punch and a platter of vegan cookies. I was extremely grateful, of course – Mrs Collins always goes out of her way to ensure that I'm well-fed, and I think she sees my dietary requirements as a challenge rather than an obstacle – but at the same time, I worried that Bethany had over-emphasised the lunch component of our get-together and understated the need for focused discussion. Certainly, no one else seemed in a hurry to get past the small talk. After Reverend Collins had said grace, Mrs Collins asked me a series of questions about Chess Club, since Bethany had told her that I'd joined. Then Reverend Collins started talking about Mr Tibbet from the village, who'd just been released from hospital following major heart surgery; Reverend Collins had been providing pastoral support to the family. I didn't know much about Mr and Mrs Tibbet, only where they lived and that their daughter had worked in the coffee shop briefly when I was eight, during the summer when you'd been very ill and Daddy had had to take on extra help to cope during the tourist season. I stayed solemn and silent while Reverend Collins spoke about their recent troubles. It didn't seem like the best moment to segue into a discussion of my work experience woes.

The chance came while Reverend Collins was pouring the coffee. There was a short silence, and I seized the opportunity to remind everyone of the main purpose of our gathering.

'Oh, yes,' Mrs Collins said. 'Bethany did mention you were

having some difficulties. You need some ideas for a suitable placement – is that right?'

Since Bethany had clearly laid little of the necessary groundwork, I spent the next six minutes providing the relevant background to my problem, starting with the disastrous encounter with Mrs Shepherd and ending with my realisation that I definitely did not want to work for a newspaper, even for a week.

'Journalism was just an example,' Bethany said. 'I thought it would be more up your street, but if you hate the idea, you obviously shouldn't do it.'

'I think my street is extremely narrow. That's the problem. I want to be a novelist and every other job pales in comparison.'

'What about a publisher?' Mrs Collins suggested. 'Or a bookshop, or library? Something that's at least in the right sector.'

I thought about this for a while. 'It's not that I hate any of these ideas,' I told Mrs Collins. 'They're all good suggestions, but they still feel like a compromise. It just seems a little bit silly to spend a week doing a job I don't actually want to do. Especially when I know the job I do want to do.'

'Hear hear,' said Reverend Collins. Bethany and her mother both shot him identical surprised looks. 'What? It's wonderful to be passionate about your job. Too many people in the world aren't.'

'Exactly!' I said; I was pleased that Reverend Collins was on my side, but in retrospect, it made sense that he was: he and I both knew what it meant to have a calling. Bethany, meanwhile, rolled her eyes at him.

'Dad, we're not talking about a long-term career. We're talking about one week's work experience. Phoebe needs practical advice. It's not like she can take herself off and be an author for a week.'

'Lots of people are self-employed,' I pointed out. 'It should be as valid an option as any other.'

'Yeah, in your world maybe. But I'm guessing school would disagree.'

'Well, perhaps you should ask,' Reverend Collins said. 'You never know, do you?'

'I think they'd probably require something a little more structured,' Mrs Collins objected. 'I don't suppose there's any chance of actually working with an author, is there?'

'*With* an author?' Bethany repeated. 'Doing what? Watching them write?'

'I was thinking more along the lines of . . . I don't know. Having a mentor, learning the craft. I'm just throwing out some ideas.'

'You could ask Mrs Frost,' Reverend Collins said, then immediately frowned. 'Actually, don't ask Mrs Frost. That's a terrible idea.'

'Mrs Frost? The poet?' I didn't know why this thought hadn't crossed my mind previously. 'Brilliant! I mean, it would be better to work with a novelist, obviously, but I'm sure it would still be fascinating. And I wouldn't even have to leave the island!'

I found that I had leapt out of my chair, as if I were intending to run to Mrs Frost's house directly to present the proposal. To clarify, I wasn't. I was just excited – that was how I knew that we'd hit upon the correct idea, even though Bethany's parents were now trying to talk me out of it.

'I really doubt that she'll be amenable to it,' Mrs Collins said. 'You do know what Mrs Frost is like, don't you, Phoebe?'

'What's she like?' Bethany asked. 'I'm not sure I've ever even seen her.'

'Well, she is a bit of a recluse,' Reverend Collins said.

'She's extremely odd,' Mrs Collins added. 'And quite . . . prickly, too. To be honest, I don't know of anyone in the village who's on good terms with her. I think she really does prefer to be left to her own devices.'

None of this put me off. In fact, I could relate. I also preferred to be left to my own devices much of the time, and I suspected that the majority of my classmates viewed me as 'extremely odd'.

'Am I right in thinking that she lives in the last house on Crooked Lonnen?' I asked. 'The one with the overgrown hedges and the cracked paintwork.' I was confident that I knew who lived in every house on Holy Island, but I thought it wise to make sure.

'Phoebe, I'm not sure you should just turn up at her house,' Mrs Collins said. 'That's not what you're planning, is it?'

'That's exactly what she's planning,' Bethany said.

'You should probably talk to your dad about it first,' Reverend Collins chimed in. 'Not to mention school.'

'Yes, of course,' I said. 'I'll make sure I talk to them.' What I didn't say was that I'd talk to them *first*; this struck me as redundant at this point. It would be far easier to get my plan approved if I already had Mrs Frost's support in place; moreover, I didn't want to go back to the careers service if there was any chance they'd complain that my scheme was unrealistic.

'Thank you for this talk,' I said, addressing the Collins family at large. 'It's been very helpful.'

*

My impulse was to visit Mrs Frost that very weekend, but it was an impulse I needed to resist. I thought it likely, based on what Bethany's parents had said, that I'd only get one chance to put my proposal to Mrs Frost, and I didn't want to rush into it unprepared. I had to treat our impending encounter as an interview and try to make the best possible impression.

I decided, therefore, to schedule our meeting for the following Sunday – i.e. eight days from now – to allow myself adequate time to do some research and to write and memorise my pitch.

In the meantime, I could also continue to work on my personal presentation. Having successfully incorporated the denim jacket into my weekday outfit, I decided to make a further tweak, and set the goal of expanding my repertoire of hairstyles, which currently ran to only two configurations, ponytail and loose.

I decided I would attempt a simple plait. I knew I'd never be able to manage anything intricate, like Bethany's double Dutch, but I thought that with sufficient practice I might be able to 'mix things up' every once in a while, on a limited basis. Furthermore, I regarded a plait as a reasonable compromise between decoration and practicality. Katniss Everdeen had worn a plait (or 'braid') in *The Hunger Games* and it had not detracted from her proficiency in armed combat; in fact, you could make the case that it had saved her life, because when her hair caught fire, the damage was very localised. If she'd been wearing it loose, it's possible she would have been killed or incapacitated.

I watched two tutorials on YouTube and practised in front of the bathroom mirror. It was tedious and abominably difficult, even though the girls in the videos made it look the simplest thing in the world. I didn't know how they were able to intertwine their hair by touch alone – and while talking to a camera! After half an hour, I grew frustrated and a little despondent. I tried setting up dual mirrors by relocating Daddy's shaving mirror to the top of the towel rail, but I became paranoid that it would fall off and smash. And, anyway, it was not a good solution as I had to stay in the exact same position so that I could see the reflection of the back of my head, and this restricted my mobility to the point where even separating my hair into the initial three sections became impossible.

I gave up, but I vowed that this was not the end. I would keep practising every day, for as long as it took.

On Monday, Mr Finch greeted me at the beginning of Chess Club to prepare me for the game with Hu. He told me that we'd each have twenty minutes on the clock, which was as long as could be managed within the confines of Enrichment, which ended at 4.45. It seemed that Hu had already been briefed, as he was sitting on one side of a set-up board, with the chair opposite empty. I took my seat at once and extended my hand.

The contest did not last the full forty minutes. Hu had the White pieces and opened with the Queen's Gambit. I countered with the Semi-Slav, created a passed pawn, and on move 38, Hu resigned.

'I didn't know you played,' he said after our second handshake, which was decidedly limp on his part. He did not look or sound very happy. This was one of the obvious advantages of playing against a machine. My phone did not become sullen when I beat it.

'I don't usually play in the flesh,' I told him.

'You play online?'

'Offline. Against an app on my phone.'

There was a silence.

'Who's your favourite chess player?' I asked. 'Classic or contemporary. I've always been a big fan of José Raúl Capablanca.'

Hu gave me a strange look, even though this was a perfectly sensible choice. Capablanca was widely regarded as the greatest player of the early twentieth century. But Hu didn't get a chance to nominate his preference, because at this point Mr Finch, who'd been keeping an eye on the game, intervened.

'Well done, Phoebe. Excellent endgame! Commiserations, Hu. I perhaps should have warned you that Phoebe's quite a strong player, but I wanted to see how things panned out. Phoebe, may I have a quick word in private?'

Mr Finch ushered me away. I was concerned that he was going to ask me to join the school team again, and I was correct to be concerned.

'Have you thought any more about joining the chess team?' he asked.

'I don't want to join the chess team,' I told him. 'I'm very flattered, but I don't think it's right for me.'

Mr Finch shook his head. He looked agitated. 'I'm not sure what you're basing that on. Perhaps you'd feel differently if you gave it a try?'

'Perhaps. But I think, on balance, I'd rather just . . . not.'

Mr Finch ignored this and changed tack. 'Phoebe, do you know who the best player in the school is at the moment?'

I told him I did not. Since I'd only joined Chess Club last week, it would have been strange if I did know.

'It's Hu,' Mr Finch said. 'Discounting myself, as I'm also

regarded as a fairly strong player. But among the current students . . . Well, it's Hu.'

I did not know what to do with this information. I could feel my face reddening.

'I'm sorry, Phoebe. I wasn't trying to trick you or anything like that. I just wanted to see how you measured up against him. And I have my answer.'

'I'm not competitive.'

'Yes, so you say. And I can assure you that I have no problem at all with that. Whatever works for you!'

I stayed silent. I was feeling a little overwhelmed.

'Phoebe, I just don't want you to sell yourself short because of any . . . preconceptions you may have about what you can or can't do. I honestly don't know why you've never come to Chess Club before, and if you're adamant that you don't want to join the team then . . . well, I shall respect that. Of course I will. But my strong opinion is that you should give it a try. It would be a crime against chess if you didn't!'

I had never seen Mr Finch so animated before.

'May I have a Time Out?' I asked. 'I won't be long. I just need a moment to reflect on matters.'

Mr Finch indicated this was acceptable, and I stepped out into the corridor. I briefly considered running, before realising it would be futile. I'd be seeing Mr Finch on Wednesday for Maths, and I didn't want to make this any more awkward than it already was. The prospect of being part of a team event filled me with dread, but if I backed away from it, I didn't know where that would leave me with regard to Chess Club. Would I still be permitted to attend? Would Mr Finch and the rest of the team think less of me for shirking my responsibility?

The one thing that was clear to me was that I couldn't

spend the rest of Enrichment in the corridor, however much I wanted to. I re-entered the classroom and told Mr Finch that I was willing to try one match, on the understanding that I couldn't commit to anything more at this time.

Mr Finch was over the moon.

10

Propositions

'Hey, Phoebe! Wait up!'

It was Will, and his timing was irritating. I had been on my way out for Second Break, with the intention to spend it all reading; I was at a particularly exciting point in *The Stone Sky*, the third book in the Broken Earth trilogy, and was desperate to get back to it. But now I saw little choice but to stop in my tracks. If I pretended not to have heard him, Will would probably chase me the full length of the corridor, shouting all the time.

'What do you want, Will?' I asked, once he'd caught up with me.

'Wow, OK. Straight to the point today.'

I nodded patiently, ignoring the trademark grin he flashed at me. I wasn't going to be rude, but I had no wish to prolong this encounter any more than necessary.

'I wanted to ask you a favour,' he said. 'Or Beth wanted to ask you, actually. But she felt a bit weird about it.'

This was already confusing. 'What's the favour?'

'Nothing massive. It's just we were going to hang out, at the weekend, or maybe at half term, except apparently she can't, not without permission. So she – well, *we* – kind of wondered if you'd mind covering for her.'

'You need to be specific,' I told him. 'I still don't know what you're asking me to do.'

Will rolled his eyes, as if I were the one muddying the waters here. 'It's not a big deal, really. She said she'd probably be allowed to go to Edinburgh if she was going with you. So . . .'

'You want me to provide a plausible alibi. Correct? She'd say she was going to Edinburgh with me but she'd actually be "hanging out" with you.'

'Yeah, exactly.'

'What would we be doing in Edinburgh, supposedly?'

'I dunno. Shopping or something. It doesn't really matter. It's just got to be believable.'

'Shopping would not be believable. Not for me.'

'How about book-shopping?'

'I tend to research and buy my books online. I'd obviously go in the bookshops if I was there already, but it wouldn't make sense for it to be the *whole* purpose of the trip.'

Will rolled his eyes again. 'Phoebe, you can use whatever works! You decide what makes sense and go with that."

'But I wouldn't actually have to go to Edinburgh, would I?'

'No, I don't see why you would. You can do whatever you want that day – just make sure it's low-key, OK? If you're meant to be in Edinburgh with Bethany, you can't be seen anywhere else.'

'I haven't agreed to anything yet,' I pointed out. I could already see several flaws in Will's proposal. At the very least, I was sure that the deception would prove far more stressful and complicated than he was trying to make out.

'Listen,' Will said. 'I'm not really asking for me. I'm asking for Beth. She's your friend, right? And you know she'd do the same for you.'

The hypothetical inversion was absurd, as it would obviously never happen, but this aside, Will had identified the only factor that was worth considering. I did not want to risk damage to my friendship with Bethany, not when things were pretty much back to normal between us. And she had helped me with the work experience problem; I did want to reciprocate in any way I could.

'Let me talk to Bethany,' I said. 'And in return, you can promise not to shout at me in the corridors in the future. I find it alarming."

'What if I need to get your attention?' Will asked, grinning inanely. 'Or am I supposed to make an appointment first?'

I ignored the second part. In an ideal world, it would indeed have been my preference, but I assumed he was being sarcastic. Possibly, he was teasing me. 'You can just approach me in the normal manner,' I said. 'And speak at a normal volume. I don't see why it's complicated.'

'Phoebe, if you're walking away from me then I won't really be *approaching* you, will I? I'll be stuck stalking you until you decide to stop. You walk pretty quickly, you know.'

I shrugged. 'I happen to have a book I'm eager to get back to.'

'Surprise surprise!' Will said. I scowled at him. 'I'm joking,' he added quickly. 'Seriously, Phoebe, you need to chill out a bit.'

'Reading is what I do to chill out,' I told him. 'The thing you're currently preventing.'

'Fine, I won't hold you up any longer. And I won't shout at you in the corridors. And in return, you'll talk to Bethany about Edinburgh. Deal?'

'Deal.'

And I turned and left.

*

When I talked to Bethany later, it seemed that Will was correct and she did feel 'weird' about the situation.

'I told him not to ask,' she said.

'Well, he asked,' I replied. 'And it's fine. I can help. I mean, it's no big deal.'

'Really?' Bethany frowned. 'I kind of thought it *would* be a big deal for you. That's one of the reasons I didn't say anything.'

This illustrates how complicated it is operating and maintaining even a single friendship. Because Bethany had predicted correctly. Getting involved in any kind of deception was a big deal for me; I knew that I would find it difficult, both practically and morally. But the fact that Bethany also knew this about me, and had tried to spare me the dilemma, made me more determined to help her. Put differently, I felt she had done her bit, by *not* asking me, and now I had to do my bit by pretending that I was happy to help.

'It's fine,' I repeated. 'Just give me some advance warning, so that we can plan it properly.'

My hope was that I'd be minimally involved. It would just be a case of Bethany telling her parents that we were going to Edinburgh together, and me being in place to confirm this as necessary. In the best-case scenario, I wouldn't even have to lie. I could just stay silent.

Sunday morning was cold, so I wore my grey hoodie underneath my windproof jacket, along with plain black tracksuit bottoms, thick socks and trainers. It was a practical outfit, obviously, but it demonstrated a further advantage of applying for work experience with a writer rather than a newspaper. At a newspaper, I guessed I'd have to wear a blouse and skirt and my thin navy cardigan; a freelance writer could wear whatever the hell she wanted.

As I walked east out of the village, I reflected on what I now knew about Mrs Frost, which was still relatively little. An internet search had revealed that her full name was Miranda Jane Frost, born 1953. She had published thirteen volumes of poetry, was well respected within the field, and had won several prizes across her forty-year career. She didn't have a website, but some of her poems were available online, including one called 'Lizards', which was about the end of the world (and also lizards). I enjoyed it very much. The most recent newspaper article I'd found about her had confirmed that she lived alone and was widely considered 'reclusive and eccentric'.

I had to ring the doorbell six times before she answered. I had my opening speech prepared and ready to launch as soon as she said hello. But she did not say hello. Instead, she said: 'You know, usually when someone doesn't answer the door after the first minute it means they don't want to answer the door.'

'Oh. My apologies. I thought you might be on the toilet or something.'

'No. I was ignoring you. *Trying* to ignore you.'

'Right. Well, sorry for disturbing you, but I only need a minute of your time. I'm—'

Mrs Frost cut me off. 'I can save you the trouble. I'm not interested in buying anything. I'm not interested in sponsoring you. I'm not interested in making any charitable donations. Is that clear enough?'

'Yes, it's extremely clear, thank you, but also irrelevant to why I'm here.'

Mrs Frost snorted. 'Well, why are you here? You're not well dressed enough to be a Jehovah's Witness.'

'No, I'm an atheist,' I said. 'I regard all religions as equally improbable.'

'Well, that's something, at least.' Mrs Frost sighed, drumming her fingers against the door post. 'OK, let's hear it, then. You can have thirty more seconds – won through your persistence and lack of religious affiliation. After that, we're done. I'm shutting the door.'

It was a good job I had my pitch prepared, as I did not think Mrs Frost was joking; she had rolled up her left sleeve and was looking at her wristwatch.

'My name is Phoebe Buchanan,' I told her. 'I'm the daughter of Stuart Buchanan, who owns Island Coffee, and Karen Buchanan, deceased. I am an aspiring writer and I wish to spend some time with you as part of my work experience programme. I will accept as much or as little as you are willing to offer. All I really want is to spend some time talking about writing with a professional, although I'd also be happy to carry out any administrative tasks for you. I am also a trained barista and could bring you hot drinks while—'

Mrs Frost tapped her watch, cutting me off. 'Excellent. I'm sure that barista training will come in handy in the future. Tell me, are you interested in poetry?'

'Not especially, no,' I admitted. 'I want to write fantasy novels, so my preference would be to do work experience with George R R Martin, for example. But he lives in Santa Fe, New Mexico. It's too far to commute.'

Mrs Frost laughed theatrically. 'Miss Buchanan. This conversation has been more entertaining than anticipated. I'll grant you that. But it doesn't mean I have any desire to repeat the experience. I don't think there's anything for us to talk about. And as for "administrative tasks", well, there may be some cat shit that needs removing from the lawn, but that's about it.'

'That's fine,' I said. 'I have a Welsh Border Collie and am an experienced remover of ... shit. I expect it will be less unpleasant than having to work in an office for a week.'

Mrs Frost laughed again. 'You're quite amusing, aren't you? Points for that. And points for trying to bribe me with coffee and menial labour rather than resorting to flattery. I do appreciate an honest bribe.'

I stayed silent because neither of the things she mentioned was intended as a bribe, but if she regarded this as a point in my favour, I was not going to correct her.

'Listen, Miss Buchanan – Phoebe? Thanks so much for dropping by, but you must see that there's nothing meaningful I can do for you?'

I shrugged. 'As I said, I'll accept whatever's offered. If it's just one conversation in return for some chores, that's fine by me.'

Mrs Frost pinched the bridge of her nose for some time, before saying: 'When is this work experience to take place?'

'The third week in November. Monday the nineteenth to Friday the twenty-third.'

'And you'll accept a single conversation as payment for some tedious chores?'

'Yes.'

'Very well. Monday the nineteenth, ten o'clock. But you shouldn't expect the conversation to be even remotely useful to you. And I reserve the right to kick you out at any time for any reason.'

'That seems fair. Shall I drop round some of my work-in-progress beforehand? I've written one hundred and ninety-four pages. It's mostly lore and world-building at this point, but—'

99

'Absolutely not! I have as little interest in your fantasy novel as you have in my poetry. You may provide me with one paragraph on a different subject of your choice. That will be sufficient for me to tell you if you have any aptitude as a writer. No more than half a page. If you go over, I'll read none of it. And you can pop it through the letterbox – no need to ring my doorbell again.'

Mrs Frost ended the conversation by not saying goodbye. She just shut the door.

Although I counted my meeting with Mrs Frost an unqualified success, Daddy was not convinced.

'I wish you'd told me first,' he said.

'Why? I wasn't certain anything would come of it.'

'Yes, but Miranda Frost is odd. She's . . .'

Daddy was clearly struggling to find the appropriate word, so I supplied it, quoting from one of the online articles I'd read about her. 'She's a sociopath.'

'Yes, put bluntly. But don't tell her that, for God's sake.'

'I found her fairly easy to talk to. Our conversation was very efficient. Or it was once I'd convinced her I wasn't selling anything.'

'You sold her your labour,' Daddy said. 'At least that's how it sounds. And I can't pretend I'm happy with it. It sounds like she's exploiting you.'

I shrugged. 'It's work experience. The whole idea is that you perform labour in return for new knowledge and skills, without being paid for it. I'm probably getting as good a deal as any of my peers.'

Daddy looked at me for a while, then said: 'Phoebe, the fact is your school's not going to go for it. They're not going to let you do half a day of domestic chores, have one conversation and count it as a week's work experience. I mean, what do you plan to do for the rest of the time? Have you thought about that?'

'I plan to write. I shall treat it as a full-time job and make up the hours I'm not with Mrs Frost.'

'They're not going to go for it,' Daddy repeated. 'Work experience is supposed to be *in* a workplace.'

This was ridiculous. Plenty of people worked from home, and were obviously able to do so without falling into some unstructured abyss. The real problem was easy to infer. It was the *form* again, both metaphorical and literal. My choice was unconventional; it did not fit the mould, and would be rejected purely on these grounds.

'You said it was good to push back a little,' I told Daddy. 'You said I didn't have to do things the way everyone else did.'

Daddy frowned. I knew from experience that he was probably trying and failing to recollect the details of our earlier conversation. It's an annoying problem he suffers from, shared by most other people.

'The conversation took place on Saturday September the twenty-second,' I told him, 'after breakfast. It was a sunny day, but unseasonably cold. We discussed the problematic meeting I had with the careers advisor.'

Daddy thought for a few more moments, then shook his head and sighed. 'Are you determined to do this? It's what you want?'

'One hundred per cent.'

'OK. Then here's what you need to do. By all means, present your proposal to school. If they go along with it, great. But it's more likely they won't. At this point, you can offer them an alternative. The time you're not with Mrs Frost you can spend at the shop with me. You can learn how to run a small business. They can't possibly object to that.'

'I already know how to run the coffee shop,' I pointed out. 'It's not complicated.'

'You can help me do my tax returns. It's an important life skill, sadly. I estimate it will take a few hours at most. The rest of the time . . . well, you know what the shop's like in November. You can spend the rest of your time writing in the corner. Does that sound acceptable to you?'

It sounded more than acceptable. The next day I liaised with Mrs McManus, and the conversation went precisely as Daddy had said it would. She raised objections, I presented the solution, and by the end of the week, the relevant forms had all been completed. My work experience was approved.

11

Edinburgh

Half term came, and with it, the day of the Edinburgh deception. Unfortunately, it had become obvious early on that I *would* have to go to Edinburgh as well. Or I had to go as far as Berwick train station, where Bethany's mum was dropping us off. And since I had no intention of spending the entire day laying low in Berwick, I was going to Edinburgh.

The cover story was pretty much the itinerary I'd planned for myself: cinema in the morning, followed by something healthy for lunch. In the afternoon, I was going to open a bank account and pay in the cheque that Gee had given me for my birthday, along with the cash I'd saved from working over the summer. If I had sufficient time afterwards, there was a museum I wanted to visit, in the hope that it might inspire some new ideas for a race of parallel humans I was developing for my parallel Earth.

Bethany smiled shamelessly as she recounted *our* plan for the day, as if every word were the gospel truth. All I had to do was fill in a few details. For example, she'd clearly forgotten the name of the museum, which was the Anatomical Museum at the University of Edinburgh, home to Scotland's largest collection of preserved remains and medical curiosities. Luckily, this was exactly the kind of detail Bethany *would* forget, and I was able to patch over her lapse without arousing any suspicion.

When we got to Berwick, Mrs Collins gave Bethany thirty pounds to cover our lunch and film costs, which Bethany graciously accepted. On the train, she offered to split the money with me, and I told her I would not be party to financial fraud – which is what this was. If she wanted my advice, she should probably donate it to the Red Cross or something.

It led to a frosty five minutes, but that aside, the train ride was quite pleasant. I watched the coast and countryside of the borderlands roll by, and in truth, found myself uncharacteristically excited by the prospect of a full day out in unfamiliar surroundings. By the time we arrived at Edinburgh, I'd managed to seal away my misgivings about our duplicity. I didn't know it then, but this would turn out to be an extremely useful ability over the coming months.

Will met us at the train station. He was sitting on one of the metal seats outside WHSmith.

'Thanks again for doing this, Phoebe,' he said. 'You're a star.'

I shrugged and told him it was no big deal. It was a good opportunity to practise my lying face, in case I needed it again later on.

I wouldn't say that Bethany leapt at Will, exactly; it was more of an excited skip that ended, somehow, with her sitting in his lap. It was to be expected, I suppose, since they hadn't seen each other for *five whole days*. They kissed. On the mouth.

'Well, I'm going to head off,' I said.

Although I'd been to Edinburgh before, I'd never visited on

my own, and I had been a little worried that I'd find the experience overwhelming. I'd imagined being lost in this dark, turbulent sea of strangers, noise and grimy city smells. So, in preparation, I'd memorised all the routes and street names I'd need, and this, along with my carefully planned itinerary, meant that I was able to traverse the city centre as if I'd been doing this all my life. It was a tremendous boost to my confidence, and within a few minutes of leaving the station and locating my first landmarks, I found that I was enjoying myself very much.

At the cinema, I saw a film called *The Hate U Give*, which I'd read positive reviews of the previous weekend. It was about a black American teenager who witnesses her best friend being shot by a white police officer after they are pulled over in his car. It was emotive and thought-provoking. Afterwards, I went to a quiet independent coffee shop and had an enjoyable chat with the barista about which coffee beans they used and where they sourced them. I had a double espresso and a grilled vegetable sandwich with Moroccan hummus. I set up my new bank account, paid in my cheque, and passed a pleasant two hours in the Anatomical Museum, which was a beautiful building containing many fascinating exhibits.

The outing was brought to a successful conclusion when Bethany arrived back at the train station *on time*; the two polite reminders I'd texted to her had clearly paid off. She appeared at the bench outside WHSmith, *sans* Will, twenty minutes before our train was due to depart, and weirdly she initiated a hug, which I managed to reciprocate with zero difficulty.

'Did you have a good day?' she asked.

'Yes, extremely! I'll debrief you on the train. But, in short, it was highly enjoyable. If you want to do this again sometime, it's fine by me.' There was a small silence, during which I realised that I should also respond in kind. 'What about you? Did you enjoy hanging out?'

'Of course.'

She sounded certain enough, but I'd expected more. Bethany wasn't usually reluctant to talk about anything Will-related.

'What did you do?' I asked. 'Where did you go?'

Bethany shrugged. 'We went to Will's.'

'Right. Is his house close by? Did you walk there?'

'Phoebe, what's with all the questions? How much coffee have you had?'

'Just one double espresso. Sorry, I think I'm a bit over-stimulated from seeing so many new things!'

Bethany smiled patiently. 'It's fine. It's nice to see you so full of energy. But can you take it down a notch? I feel like I just need a few minutes to sit and chill.'

'OK, then. But we should head down to the platform soon, in case the train is early or there's a problem with the ticket barrier. I've bought you a Diet Coke for the journey. It was two for two pounds.'

'Thanks. That's kind of you.'

It was kind, I suppose, but it was also because I wanted to make sure Bethany was alert and attentive on the way back to Berwick, so that we could run through the details of what *we'd* done today. It proved to be a shrewd move as, even with caffeine, Bethany was clearly distracted. It was hard to pin down her mood. She seemed alternately happy and somewhat agitated. I decided that her head was still full of Will; unfathomably, a whole day in his company had not been enough to cure her of this affliction. I wondered if she was *in love*, and briefly considered asking, before deciding it could only lead to the sort of conversation that I was in no way qualified to deal with.

Instead, I took advantage of the fact that she wasn't saying much and began the debrief as soon as the ticket inspector had passed through our carriage.

'The cinema was moderately busy,' I told her. 'We watched a film called *The Hate U Give*, which was a coming-of-age story that dealt with institutional racism in the American police force. The main character was called Starr, with two Rs, and she was a black teenager from a poor neighbourhood who goes to a posh high school where most of the other students are white and wealthy . . .'

After I'd finished, approximately ten minutes later, Bethany nodded and grinned but said nothing. I wasn't entirely convinced that she'd been listening. I decided that if Bethany's mum wanted to know about our day, it might be better if I narrated the story. All I had to do was watch my pronouns.

Reviewing my progress at the end of half term, I was very happy with how my self-improvement was coming along. I had tried a number of new things, such as the denim jacket and Chess Club, and had won praise for my efforts. It was also possible that by changing certain habits I had opened a gateway to enjoying experiences that previously would have provoked stress and anxiety, the Edinburgh trip being a case in point. I had landed a work experience placement that I expected to be stimulating and career relevant, and my friendship with Bethany seemed secure, with the challenges of the last few weeks laid to rest. There was only one area in

107

which I had made limited headway, namely that I had failed to expand my social circle. But I had taken the first small steps, and I felt hopeful that I could build on this in the immediate future.

On the first day back at school, I wore my hair in a passable plait, having finally mastered it over the weekend. It was enough of a change that even Daddy noticed it, and commented that it 'looked nice.' Bethany was more vociferous in her appreciation.

'I didn't realise you even knew how to do a plait,' she said.

'I learned,' I told her, with a cool shrug. I resisted the urge to elaborate and tell her that it had taken approximately three weeks and at least seven hours to perfect, as I knew this would diminish my achievement rather than highlighting it.

'It's so neat,' Bethany said. 'Did you use hairspray?'

'I did not. I found a tip online which suggested washing it less frequently would help to make it more manageable. It's also a healthier option according to several medical practitioners. Over-washing strips the hair of important natural oils and is one of the main causes of a dry, flaky scalp.'

Bethany laughed. 'OK. Just don't get too healthy.'

'I'm not planning to wear a plait every day,' I told her.

12

Several Demotions

I thought I was well prepared for my first, and possibly last, outing with the chess team. I had spent the weekend prior revising my opening theory and playing intensively against my phone. My goal was straightforward: I was determined not to let the team down.

We were playing an away match, against a team from Alnwick, and Mr Finch was driving us there in the minibus. I'd chosen to sit in the front with him, since I wasn't sure what welcome I'd receive in the back, with everyone else. Despite my efforts over the past month, I had been unable to sustain any non-awkward conversations with my team-mates. In theory, it should have been so much easier than in other circumstances, with our shared interest to build upon. Yet this had not proven to be the case. The chess team was an unexpectedly tough clique to break into. This was one of the reasons I was so determined to do well in my first competitive match. I reasoned that they'd appreciate me more if I was defeating an opponent from an enemy school, rather than them.

On the motorway, Mr Finch gave me a briefing on the format of the competition. There would be five boards and we would each play one game. Each player got forty-five minutes on the clock, with another fifteen added after the first forty moves – an hour in total.

'You'll be on board one,' Mr Finch told me, 'as you've probably guessed.'

I had not guessed. Not only this, but I did not understand the significance of the board numbers, since I'd only watched one-on-one chess contests online, and had zero knowledge of chess as a team sport. In hindsight, perhaps I should have done more preparatory research. I asked Mr Finch for a clarification.

'Board one is for the strongest player on each team,' he said. 'Then it works down sequentially, with the weakest player on board five. Excluding the reserve players, of course.'

'Oh.'

There was a short silence, then Mr Finch said, in a lowered voice, 'Listen, Phoebe, I've had a word with the rest of the team, and I'm confident that it shouldn't be a problem. We're all very glad to have you.' He paused for a moment, and then lowered his voice even further; I had to strain to hear him. 'But if there *are* any problems, let me know at once and I'll nip them in the bud. I won't have any petty resentment undermining the team spirit. We're all in this together.'

Resentment? I glanced back at my team-mates, noted their frosty expressions. I could suddenly see the full picture, and I felt like an idiot.

I'd joined the chess team part-way into the competition and had been inadvertently judged the school's strongest player. This meant I was to be assigned to board one, and everyone else was being reassigned, one step downwards. The logic was clear and merciless: Hu would move from board one to board two, Johnny from two to three, Ishmael from three to

110

four, and so on and so forth right down to Alistair, the reserve, who was now, presumably, the *second* reserve.

I had caused every other player on the team to be simultaneously demoted. It was no wonder they all hated me!

I felt like I was going to vomit, which was unlikely to boost my popularity on board the minibus. Mr Finch had his eyes on the road, and I assumed he was unaware of my misery. After several steadying breaths, I managed to find my voice and asked him if it would be OK if I put my headphones on for the rest of the journey.

'Of course. Be my guest.' Mr Finch chuckled. 'Listen to something motivational.'

I listened to 'Planet Hell', turning the volume up loud to block out all evidence of the outside world. I zoned out, zoned back in, and by the time we reached Alnwick, I'd concocted an emergency plan. It wasn't sure to work, and it certainly wasn't honourable, but my new goal was to lose – as catastrophically as possible. My theory was that this would force Mr Finch to re-evaluate my competence and remove me from board one. If I played an *embarrassingly* bad game, he might even remove me from the team. At that moment, it seemed like the best possible outcome.

I had enjoyed previous trips to Alnwick to visit the castle and the poison garden and the second-hand bookshop, but this time round I couldn't wait to leave. The school was large and confusing, with echoey corridors and an unfamiliar smell. A member of staff guided us through to a classroom where strip lights hummed and made the white walls look vaguely jaundiced. There was a table with a water heater, instant coffee, tea bags, disposable cups and digestive biscuits, none of which I touched. I had brought a bottle of mineral water with me, which I had frozen overnight but was now thawed and a sensible drinking temperature.

Infuriatingly, the match did not begin at once. There was a pointless fifteen minutes allocated so that we could settle ourselves and use the facilities if required. I put my headphones on again and stood alone in a corner. The enemy team were all boys, too. Mr Finch talked to the other teacher but no one else fraternised.

Once everyone began to take their seats, I moved over to board one, placed my water adjacent to the board, put my blazer on the back of the plastic chair, and sat down, all without looking at my opponent. My plan was to ignore him throughout, but this was immediately scuppered.

'Do you have a rating?' he asked.

'Excuse me?'

'Do – you – have – a – rating?' The exact same question, but asked at half speed.

'You mean an Elo rating, correct?'

He nodded, also at half speed. He was poised with his pen hovering over a notepad. Mr Finch had warned me that most players liked to record the moves, so that they could review the game later on. I wasn't going to do this because I would easily remember which moves were played, and I doubted that I'd want to relive any part of this game. Regardless of what my opponent played, I planned to respond with the Bongcloud Attack, universally acknowledged as the worst opening in chess.

'I have an Elo rating against my phone,' I told him. 'Is that acceptable? This is my first competitive match.'

'This is your *first* match?'

'Correct. I only started Chess Club a few weeks ago. I have not previously competed.'

The boy sniggered. 'Well, try your best, won't you? That's what matters.'

I didn't have to be good at subtleties in this instance. Previously, I'd been willing to give him the benefit of the doubt and had assumed he'd been trying to enunciate for maximum clarity. Now I understood that he was mocking me, implying that I was some kind of imbecile! I felt a little bubble of anger rise in my chest, tightening my muscles.

He played E4 and pressed the button to start the chess clock. Four and a half minutes later I had not replied, and he started tutting and coughing theatrically.

I glared at him and hissed. 'I'm thinking!'

This was true, but I wasn't thinking about my move. I was thinking about how unfair this whole situation was. I hadn't wanted to join the chess team – I'd practically been forced. And I'd had no knowledge before today about how their stupid chess hierarchy worked, let alone the desire to usurp anyone's position within it. All I'd wanted was to socialise in a safe space, and now I was stuck in this ridiculous situation where I had to spend the next several minutes in an unpleasant classroom, losing to an unpleasant boy just to assuage the guilt I felt about wounding some other boys' pride.

After another five minutes, my opponent got up and went over to talk to his teacher. Shortly thereafter, Mr Finch appeared at my side and asked if everything was OK.

'Yes. It's fine,' I told him.

'Are you going to move?'

'Yes. I'm ready to play my move now.'

My opponent sat down again and I played C5, the Sicilian

Defence. It's called a defence, but it's one of the most aggressive openings Black can play. I'd decided I was not going to lose quietly; by move nine, I'd decided I was not going to lose full stop. We castled on opposite sides of the board. He attacked on the wing, I broke through in the centre, and a bloodbath ensued. On move twenty-one I played an exchange sacrifice on C3 to open up his king, and ten moves later, I checkmated him. We did not shake hands; he stomped off and started talking to his teacher again, gesticulating angrily in my direction. It was not the result I'd been looking for when I sat down, but I can't deny it was extremely satisfying.

I returned to my corner and put my headphones back on.

I revised the plan a second time. My *new* new plan was simply to resign from the team later on. I would wait for an opportune moment and then explain to Mr Finch that the experience of playing competitive chess had confirmed my suspicion that it was not for me. I would be polite and apologetic, but would remain steadfast.

But when everyone else had finished playing, the mood among my team-mates was surprisingly buoyant. Back on the minibus, Mr Finch told me that we'd won the match by four points to one, with three victories and two draws. It was an exact reversal of the first match of the season, which the team had lost by the same margin.

'Of course, it helped that everyone had a slightly easier game this time round,' Mr Finch said with a wink. 'Thanks to our new board one.'

I felt myself blushing as I glanced in the rear-view mirror. Everyone was still smiling, despite this unfortunate reminder of the position I'd usurped. It was difficult to get my bearings with the emotional landscape changing so rapidly; the only thing I felt certain of, now, was that my impending resignation was going to be awkward.

Mr Finch's face turned serious, and he said, 'Phoebe, this isn't a criticism, so please don't take it that way. But your approach today was unconventional, to say the least. You're probably aware, but your opposite number wasn't too happy.' Mr Finch coughed delicately. 'He accused you of gamesmanship.'

'Gamesmanship?' This came as a tremendous shock. 'You mean *cheating*?'

'No, not cheating. But you did take over ten minutes to make your first move. There's no rule against that, obviously, but given the way the game went, your opponent felt it was . . . unsportsmanlike. Psychological warfare, if you will. Of course, I smoothed it out with his teacher. I told him that it was probably just nerves or something. I'm sure you won't make a habit of it, will you?'

In hindsight, this would have been the perfect point at which to tell Mr Finch that I would *not* be making a habit of it because I wished to end my chess career. But at the time I was too stunned to think about my best interests. I explained to Mr Finch that my delayed opening was nothing to do with nerves; I had been incapacitated by anger.

'He *sniggered* at me,' I said. 'I needed the ten minutes to calm down.'

For some reason, Mr Finch seemed to find this hilarious. 'Sniggered, did he? Well, well. I suppose that explains a thing or two. From what I saw, you played a brutal game. It wasn't elegant, but you certainly got the job done!'

He chuckled to himself.

I spent the rest of the journey in silence, working out what

I needed to say. But then, when the moment came, I faltered. Mr Finch had parked the minibus in the school car park and given us permission to leave; half the team were getting picked up by their parents and the rest of us had to head over to Boarding. I hung back a moment and started to approach Mr Finch and, as I did, I felt a tap on my shoulder. It was Hu, whose position at the head of the chess team I'd stolen.

'Are you coming, Phoebe?' he asked.

That was all, but it stopped me in my tracks.

I stood with my mouth open for an embarrassingly long time, and then managed to nod.

We walked back to Boarding.

13

The Mystery Woman

A week before work experience, I posted my half-page paragraph through Mrs Frost's letterbox. I'd put it in a plain envelope without a covering note, as I did not want to test her threat that she would refuse to read it if I violated our agreed word count. Daddy said I was probably being too literal in my interpretation of her terms, but this was one instance where I trusted my judgement over his. Miranda Frost used precise language and had precise thoughts. If she said she wanted a single paragraph, then that was what I'd give her. I hadn't even written her name on the envelope.

After much deliberation, I had chosen to write my paragraph on the car in the sea. It ended up taking me an entire weekend, but I reasoned this was OK because Mrs Frost had set no limit on how long I could spend on it, and I wanted to get it right. I wanted her to say that I had aptitude as a writer.

Monday November the nineteenth was murky and wet. Fortunately, I did not have to ring the doorbell six times; I rang it once, at exactly ten a.m., and Mrs Frost answered within five seconds.

'Shoes off, Miss Buchanan,' she said. 'If you track mud in, you'll be the one cleaning it up.'

She didn't wait for me to hop out of my boots. She went through to a room that turned out to be the kitchen, and, once I'd joined her, showed me to how to operate a steam mop.

'You can go over all the hard floors. It shouldn't take you more than half an hour. After that, you'll find glass cleaner and cloths in the cupboard under the sink. You may do all the windows excluding those in my study, which is where I shall be. The coffee beans are in the fridge and the cafetiere is on the draining board. I take mine black without sugar. You can bring me a cup at eleven o'clock and we shall talk. Before then, I do not expect to be disturbed.'

Mrs Frost's house was uncluttered, minimally decorated and extremely quiet, and I found mopping the floors and cleaning the windows to be a relaxing experience. There was a grey cat dozing on the sofa in the living room and I let it sniff the back of my hand so that it could familiarise itself with my scent. But other than that, I stuck strictly to my assigned jobs. If it wasn't for Mrs Frost's admonition that she did not wish to be disturbed, I might have hummed. I was very happy to be working here, rather than feigning an interest in journalism at the *Berwick Advertiser* or the *South Edinburgh Echo*. Briefly, I found myself wondering if Bethany was enjoying her work experience as much as I was enjoying mine. She was in Edinburgh for the week, working at a specialist travel agency. Ostensibly, this was to further her life goal of a career incorporating *languages or something*, but in reality, I suspected it was to further her more immediate goal of spending as much time as close to Will as possible. He, I'd gathered, was working just round the corner from her at an investment firm, learning how to grow wealth or something similarly absurd. I had no idea if this was a field he was interested in, but it seemed plausible.

'OK, Phoebe. Let's get this over with. The good news is that you're able to string a few sentences together, which is a rare ability these days. The bad news is that your vocation is highly competitive and, in general, poorly paid. I was not joking when I said your barista training will serve you well in the future. If you have any fantasies about becoming rich from your writing you might as well forget them right now. Statistically speaking, you have chosen the fast track to penury.'

My heart soared at Mrs Frost's praise. 'I have zero interest in being rich,' I told her. 'I just want to write.'

'Good. Very good. That's the only reason one should write. But please don't interrupt again.'

I kept my lips pressed tightly together. I hadn't realised that I had interrupted; I'd thought it was my turn to speak. But I made a mental note to allow for a few extra seconds of silence going forward, in case Mrs Frost was executing a dramatic pause.

'Your word choice is interesting and you have a sound understanding of rhythm and cadence. You don't over-embellish or fall into a pit of mindless verbiage, which is the number one crime of inexperienced writers. In short, your writing is simple and effective. How long did you spend on it?'

'Quite a long time,' I confessed.

'How long? Be specific.'

'Thirteen hours and fifty minutes.'

'You found the exercise difficult?'

'Yes.'

Surprisingly, this answer pleased Mrs Frost. She took a sip of her coffee, placed the cup back on her saucer, then nodded. 'Good. You're familiar with Thomas Mann?' She didn't wait for me to shake my head. 'Of course you're not. It's not your fault; it's your school's. Thomas Mann was a German novelist and Nobel laureate. He said that a writer is someone for whom writing is more difficult than it is for other people. You understand why?'

I had to think about this for a while, but Mrs Frost did not seem to mind. She continued to sip her coffee and waited patiently.

'I suspect he meant that normal people, i.e. non-writers, don't struggle so much with their writing, because they're not so concerned with getting it *right*. They're happy to say what they want any which way. Whereas writers want to find the best way of saying something, and that takes time and effort.'

'Exactly! If half a page of writing takes thirteen hours, then that's how long it takes. If your writing starts to feel easy then you're most likely doing it wrong. I'll give you another quote. "The first draft of anything is shit." Hemingway, whom you may even have heard of. If not, you should read him. He seldom wastes a word.' Mrs Frost took another sip from her cup. 'This coffee is excellent. What's your secret?'

'It's not a secret. The main thing is you have to let the kettle sit for a couple of minutes after it's boiled. Coffee infuses best at about ninety-three degrees Celsius. Any hotter and it develops a bitter aftertaste. Too much colder and the water won't extract all the flavour from the beans. Most decent coffee machines are calibrated with this in mind, but it's something you have to bear in mind if you're using a cafetiere.'

Mrs Frost looked at me for some time. 'You're a strange girl, aren't you?'

I shrugged. 'People say you're strange.'

'Yes. And fortunately I stopped caring what people think of me a long time ago.'

'Is that why you wanted to be a writer? So that you could do whatever you wanted, without having to deal with other people?'

'No, that's just one of the perks. Let me ask you the same question: why do *you* want to write? Enjoying your own company is all very well – I'd say it's probably a prerequisite – but if you're planning to write novels, I suspect you're going to need more than that to keep you motivated.'

I thought for a few moments. 'Do you want me to give you the main reason or all six?'

Mrs Frost snorted. 'OK, so you've obviously thought about this before. That's good. Give me all six but try not to ramble. Keep it short and sweet.'

I nodded. 'One: I like to figure ideas out in depth. Writing lets you do that. Two: I like to challenge myself. Three: it allows me to try new things but sort of in safe mode – without having to worry that I might crash my whole system. It's a computer metaphor,' I added.

'Thank you,' Mrs Frost said. 'I'd never have realised.'

'Four: I *do* enjoy my own company. It's when I'm most relaxed. Five: I like being able to go into other worlds. Six: I enjoy working things out according to a set of established rules. It's a bit like chess: you set up your pieces, make one logical move after another, and keep going until matters are resolved. It's far less messy than real life.'

Mrs Frost looked either impressed or amused. I couldn't

decide which. It was a good job she tended to say exactly what was on her mind, as I found her facial expressions quite subtle and difficult to read. She stayed silent and sipped her coffee again.

'Do you mind if I ask a question that might be impolite?' I asked.

'You can ask whatever you want until the moment I throw you out. That was the deal, wasn't it?'

'Yes, more or less. Do you make money from your writing? It's just that you don't seem to be impoverished.'

'There's no money in poetry, Phoebe. If I relied on that I'd have long ago starved. Fortunately, I married well. Or rather I divorced well. That's what paid the mortgage. So there's some advice for you, I suppose. My number one tip for the aspiring writer: marry well, divorce better.'

'I think I'd rather work in the coffee shop,' I said. 'I can't see myself getting married. I believe I'm asexual.'

'Ha! Wonderful! That's how you *identify*, is it?'

'It's just the category that best seems to fit. I watched a TED Talk about it.'

'Of course you did. At the risk of sounding ancient, things were far simpler in my day. You were straight or you were queer, and that was the end of it. All these fine distinctions are a modern invention.'

I frowned. 'Mrs Frost, I don't think you can say they're an invention. They've probably always existed. It's just that they're recognised and acknowledged now. Also, I think it's helpful to be specific in some circumstances. I wouldn't necessarily describe myself as queer, for example. I'm not sure it's the term that makes the most sense for me.'

Mrs Frost scoffed at this. 'Nonsense, Phoebe! Queer

encompasses anything and everything that deviates from unwavering heterosexuality. That's the whole point of the term. You do not identify as straight, therefore you're queer. It's that simple.'

'Yes, but—'

'Don't tell me the term makes you uncomfortable? I don't believe it.'

'No, it's not that. It's more . . . Well, like I said, it's more that it's not the most precise term for how I feel. For who I think I am.'

Mrs Frost actually chuckled at this point – though her chuckle sounded rather like a bark. 'I'd say it's the perfect term for you. I assume you do understand the original meaning of the word queer? You have read some literature written before the nineteen eighties, I hope?'

I nodded. 'Of course. It means something that's not the way it should be. Something odd or strange or different. I guess that's why it used to be considered a slur.'

'Yes, precisely! Society has always been quick to condemn the people who deviate too far from the expected path, from the behaviour that's deemed normal and acceptable. People rather like you and me, wouldn't you say? Rather like anyone who's ever had an original thought. Tell me, how many of your classmates are drinking coffee with a celebrated poet right now? How many are being challenged to think for themselves?'

'Zero are drinking coffee with a celebrated poet. I don't know how many are having to think for themselves.'

Mrs Frost sniffed. 'Also zero. Do you know what most of your peers will end up doing in the future?' She did not wait for me to answer. 'They'll be prostitutes, Phoebe. The vast majority will end up as prostitutes.'

I frowned again. 'I would have thought office jobs or something.'

'Very droll. But we're not talking in superficialities; we're getting to the heart of the matter. They will spend forty years walking the streets of capitalism, selling their bodies and brains to the highest bidder. Their purchasing power will grow and their souls will shrink. That is what it means to follow the expected path.'

I stayed quiet. I didn't know what I could possibly say to this. Fortunately, Mrs Frost was very accomplished at filling silences.

'Phoebe, I have two more pieces of advice for you. The first is that you need to embrace your queerness – in every sense of the term. It's what makes you interesting. The second is that when you find an idea that challenges you, *that's* an idea worth writing about. Write about the things that are difficult or complicated. Write about what makes you uncomfortable. Trust me, it's the only way you'll grow. It's the only way you'll ever discover anything new.'

I sat perfectly still while Mrs Frost took another sip of her coffee. I had a lot to process.

When I got back to the coffee shop, Daddy said I was unusually animated.

'It was an extremely stimulating morning,' I told him. 'Mrs Frost likes my writing and my coffee and we had a deep, philosophical discussion.'

'Good. I'm glad it went well. Did she give you any useful tips?'

'Yes. She said I should write about what makes me uncomfortable. And she thinks I need to embrace my queerness.'

'Right.' Daddy stayed silent for a moment. 'Did she happen to explain what she meant by that?'

'She had multiple meanings,' I clarified. 'She was using the term queer both in its original sense of strange and as an umbrella term for non-straight.'

'Right. Of course. So . . . are you non-straight? Because I have to say, this is a hell of a way to learn about it.'

I shrugged. 'I think I'm probably asexual. But Mrs Frost thinks it's included in the queer category. As is anything that deviates from unwavering heterosexuality.'

'OK . . . Well, that's . . . Well, it's fine, obviously. But I'd like to know why you were talking about this with Mrs Frost in the first place. It's quite a personal subject to be discussing. Actually, it might be better if you just talk me through the whole conversation.'

I was happy to do this. Daddy looked slightly reassured when I explained that it was me who'd brought up the topic of sexuality, and slightly less reassured when I got to the part about my classmates being prostitutes.

'I'm not sure she knows it's better to use the term sex workers,' I told him. 'She is quite old. Also, I think she was being metaphorical. She doesn't think most of my classmates will end up as literal sex workers.'

Daddy shook his head. 'I'd still question why she needs to express everything in such a . . . provocative way. To be honest, I'm just happy that you're not going back there.'

'I'm going back on Wednesday to do the gardening.'

Daddy frowned at this news. 'Listen, Phoebe. Miranda Frost can get away with saying whatever the hell she wants because . . . well, she's old. Like you said. She's old and eccentric, and she's a poet so people give her the benefit of the doubt and assume she has some higher purpose when she says these things. But that doesn't mean she's a good role model. I hope you'll take the advice she gives you with a pinch of salt.'

I understood what Daddy meant. He was worried that Mrs Frost might be a bad influence on me, and I did not disagree with him. Spending time with her probably wasn't going to help improve my social skills. Yet I also knew that I much preferred talking with Mrs Frost than I did with most other people. Because you didn't have to guess what was on her mind, and she asked direct questions and told me when it was my turn to contribute. And everything she said had a *point*.

It was not easy to articulate all of this to Daddy, but I was worried that if I didn't try, he might stop me from going back. I said: 'I think Mrs Frost wants me to make up my own mind about things. She says challenging things so that I'll have to think about them for myself.'

Daddy didn't reply for a while. Then he sighed. 'I don't know, Precious. Maybe you're right. But I can't pretend I'm completely OK with the situation. I don't know the woman well – nobody does – but she strikes me as being very self-centred. I won't have her taking advantage of you.'

'I think she likes me.'

'Christ, Phoebe. I don't know. Maybe she does. In that case, you're in the island's most exclusive club. Just promise me you'll be sensible.'

'Of course. I'm always sensible.'

Daddy waited for a moment. 'Do you want to talk any more about you being . . . probably queer?'

'No, thank you. I'm just going to keep thinking about it for now.'

*

The following morning, Moira came into the shop early with two cakes and a vegetable tart. She then took over behind the counter while Daddy and I sat at a corner table and did his tax return, which he promised would be every bit as stimulating as a morning with Mrs Frost. But he was making a joke, and it was not.

I was back at her house at nine a.m. on the Wednesday, wearing my boots, fleece, gardening gloves and waterproof trousers. It took approximately one hundred and ten minutes to complete all the chores she'd assigned to me. I raked and bagged up the dead leaves. I pruned the shrubs and pulled up weeds and gathered fallen, rotten apples and threw them on the compost heap. As I worked, I imagined what it would be like to have Mrs Frost's life. To spend the morning writing in her study. To have a small house and garden to tend, and a pet cat to keep me company. To not worry about what other people thought of me because I'd long ago stopped caring about such trivia. I have to say, I could see the appeal.

By the time I took the coffee through to her study at eleven o'clock, my head was buzzing with questions, and I started asking them as soon as I was seated. It was another thing that felt especially gratifying about talking to Mrs Frost: she seemed as disinterested in preamble as I was.

When I'd exhausted all my questions about writing and her daily routine, I asked her how long she'd lived in this house.

'Twenty-six years,' she told me. 'Before that, I lived in London.'

'Did you like living there?'

This was the first question that Mrs Frost actually had to think about. She held her coffee cup to her lips without drinking, then said: 'I did when I was twenty. I hated it by the time I was forty. London's a city for the young.'

'My parents used to live in London. But they moved here just before I was born. Sixteen and a half years ago.'

Mrs Frost nodded. 'I remember. Don't look so surprised. Outsiders buy a property and it's the talk of the village for the next year. You can't avoid the gossip even if you want to. Your mother was ill, wasn't she? Chronic Fatigue Syndrome?'

'ME. She hated the term Chronic Fatigue. She said fatigue was something that happened to women in Victorian novels. What she had was exhaustion, and continual pain. When it was at its worst, she couldn't get out of bed. I used to sit and read to her when she was too poorly to do anything else. Or she'd read to me if she was well enough. It was the thing we both loved best, so it was a good way to be together.'

Mrs Frost nodded but didn't say anything.

'She was diagnosed with bowel cancer when I was nine. It killed her a year later.'

It was a fact I'd had almost six years to get used to, but I was still surprised at how calmly I was able to say those words then. Of course, Mrs Frost would have known about your cancer already, just as she'd known about your ME, because *this* was the sort of news that travelled through the village very quickly. It was the same as with Mr Tibbet's heart surgery, or a few years ago when Mr Kingsley had to be airlifted off the island following a stroke. In a community of 160, everyone knows about these occurrences almost as soon as they've happened. Yet, in my experience, most people still don't feel comfortable talking about illness and death directly, or not with the people involved. But since Mrs Frost had been the one to bring the subject up, I suspected she'd prove herself to be abnormal in this sense too. I was largely correct.

After a moment, she nodded again and said: 'Well, it's a shitty hand to get dealt, no question. But such is life. It's seldom fair.' She made an expression I couldn't interpret, scrunching her lips slightly, then sighed. 'I'm sorry, Phoebe. I'm not good at condolences.'

'That's OK,' I told her. 'Neither am I. It's difficult to find the words in real-time. It's another reason I prefer writing.'

The silence stretched for a few moments.

'Shall I come back on Friday?' I asked.

The next afternoon I was alone in the shop. Daddy had gone to take Gladys for a short walk and had left me 'in charge', though we both understood this was mostly a figure of speech. I was in charge of myself and an empty shop, at least for the first ten minutes. I had my notepad open on the counter and was jotting down the key developments in a colonial war I was devising for my parallel Earth. Then the Mystery Woman walked in. I performed my professional smile and closed my notebook.

She looked at me for a moment, removed her sunglasses, and glanced around the shop uncertainly, as if surprised to find herself here. I estimated her age at thirty. She had unnaturally glossy black hair and carried an impractical-looking handbag, adorned with beads and sequins. She was quite pretty, and glamorous by the standards of Holy Island, with wide dark eyes and skin that was more tanned than you might expect for Northumberland in November. My immediate diagnosis was that she was a lost tourist, seeking directions. Except there was something strangely familiar about her. I thought this even before she spoke.

'I was looking for Stuart,' she said.

'He's popped out,' I told her. 'He shouldn't be long. Maybe ten minutes at the most. Would you like to wait?'

She shrugged. 'I guess I will.'

'Can I get you anything?'

'No. Thank you.'

I waited for her to take a seat, then said: 'How do you know my father?'

I thought it was a reasonable question to ask – nothing more than a polite enquiry, really – but her reaction said otherwise. She looked taken aback, as if I'd said something entirely unexpected; I wondered if my expression had slipped into its 'neutral glare' without my realising. I was about to explain that I hadn't intended any insult, but she didn't give me a chance.

'I don't think I'll wait after all,' she said. 'I'll come back some other time.'

'OK, then,' I said.

By the time I'd thought to ask if she'd like to leave her name, she'd already gone.

When Daddy returned, I told him about the Mystery Woman and he listened with a small frown, saying nothing.

'Did I say something wrong?' I asked.

'No, I don't think so. She didn't say what she wanted?'

'No. She just asked for you. That was all.'

'Very odd,' Daddy said. 'But I'm sure it's nothing to worry about.'

'Do you know who she is?' I asked.

Daddy shrugged. 'I guess we'll find out when she comes back.'

But she didn't come back. There were three more

customers that afternoon, but they were all locals. None was the Mystery Woman.

'She didn't actually say *when* she'd be coming back,' I told Daddy, as we were closing up that evening. 'She said "some other time".'

Daddy nodded, then said: 'I expect she'll be back if it was something important. Maybe it wasn't.'

I nodded too. But I couldn't shake the feeling that it *was* important, and that I was missing something – some significant detail. Yet even after replaying our interaction in my head, multiple times, I couldn't identify anything obvious. All I had was this vague sense that I was not seeing the full picture. And that was as far as my intuition could carry me.

Walking to Mrs Frost's house the following morning, for the final time, I was struck by a new insight: what bothered me about the Mystery Woman wasn't just that she was out of place or an unknown quantity; it was that she was a paradox. I knew she wasn't a local because I knew all of Holy Island's 160 permanent inhabitants. Yet she couldn't be a casual visitor either because she knew Daddy well enough to ask for him by name, even if he didn't know her – though this last point was far from certain. He seemingly hadn't recognised her from my description, and he'd implied that he had no idea who she could be, but I realised now that he hadn't stated this outright. When I'd asked if he knew who she was, he'd said *I guess we'll find out*. The implication was clear enough, but in hindsight, I felt anxious that he'd not given me a straight no.

I didn't know if I was over-analysing the situation, so I decided to ask for a second opinion. Mrs Frost had an extremely logical mind, and I felt confident that she'd tell me exactly what she thought, in clear and precise words.

After I'd cleaned the oven and taken her coffee through, I initiated the conversation, outlining the encounter and explaining, as best I could, why it had left me feeling so bemused.

Unfortunately, Mrs Frost's initial response was less helpful than anticipated. 'If you really want to know, you should ask your father.'

I was a little confused by this statement. Not because it wasn't clear, but because I didn't usually have to repeat myself with Mrs Frost.

'I did ask him,' I said. 'He didn't give me a proper answer.'

'So ask him again. I have no wish to get embroiled in your family drama.'

I felt myself blushing a little. Mrs Frost stared at me for a few moments, then sighed, shaking her head. 'If I had to guess, I'd say she was a love interest. It would explain why she was awkward with you and why she didn't want to say why she was there. It would also explain your father's evasiveness – if that's what it was.'

This wasn't helpful either. It was a theory I could instantly discount. I explained to Mrs Frost that Daddy was fifty-one years old. The Mystery Woman was thirty, at a push. She was clearly too young. Furthermore, there had been no one else since you died. Having had the perfect marriage, it seemed unlikely that Daddy would want to replace it with an inferior relationship.

Mrs Frost snorted at this. 'I doubt you know everything about your father's life.'

'I know the important things,' I said. 'We don't have any secrets.'

'Good. Then we don't need to have this conversation, do we?'

I didn't have a response to this. I stayed silent until Mrs Frost shrugged and said: 'Listen, Phoebe. If you want to know, you'll have to ask your father. But if you actually want my opinion, you would do better to forget it. Accept his right to some privacy. Either way, it's the last I'll say on the matter.'

I didn't know how to reply to this, either. The silence dragged for a few seconds.

'Well,' Mrs Frost said eventually, 'it's been a diverting week, but it appears we're done here. If there are no further questions – *writing* questions – you may show yourself out.'

'Oh. OK.' I got up and almost left the study. But I made a half-turn when I reached the door. 'Shall I come back . . . some time?'

Mrs Frost gave me a level look. 'Phoebe. I'm quite content with my life just as it is. I don't think your coming back would be beneficial to either one of us. Good luck with your writing.'

She turned back to her desk, and I left.

Needless to say, it was not the end to the week that I'd envisioned.

14

A Minor Meltdown

I felt flat in the aftermath of my week with Mrs Frost. What was worse, I knew that it was wrong of me to feel like this. Our arrangement had been for the opportunity to talk to her about writing in exchange for the 'administrative' chores I had carried out. Our arrangement had been for a single day, and I'd got three, and there had never been any suggestion that the visits would outlast the week. So why did I feel disappointed with how things had transpired?

My big plan for the weekend had been to continue writing the backstory to my fantasy world, as it had seemed the ideal way to conclude my week of work experience. Yet when I sat down with my notepad, I found that inspiration had fled. It was ridiculous! On Thursday I'd been bubbling over with new ideas: I'd had a full decade-long war brewing in my head! But now there was nothing. All I could think of was how I'd managed to mess things up – how my lack of social awareness had, apparently, let me down. Again. I gave up trying to write and relocated to the garden, where I spent a lot of time hitting the punch bag under the beech tree. Afterwards I spent even more time in my room, sitting very quietly. I then repeated the process. I punched, I sat, I thought.

Mrs Frost had never pretended that she wanted to be my

mentor, or my *anything*, yet I'd thought she enjoyed my company, to some extent. It was possible she'd simply become bored of me, and had decided that she wanted her solitude back. But I had the feeling – a familiar feeling – that I'd got something wrong, without knowing what that something actually was. Perhaps I'd irritated her by treating her as a confidant and telling her about my confusing encounter with the Mystery Woman? It seemed to me that everything had been going fine to that point; she'd only terminated the visit when I brought up what she'd called my 'family drama'.

I didn't know if this was a mistake, but in hindsight, I could see that it had been a complete waste of time. Mrs Frost's theory about the Mystery Woman was absurd, and the more I thought about it, the more I saw that I had been fretting over nothing. The woman hadn't come back to the shop, and Daddy had given me zero reason to think that anything strange was going on. Just because I couldn't think of a good explanation for who the woman was and what she wanted, it didn't mean there *wasn't* an explanation. The sensible thing, and the thing I most wanted to do, was to forget about everything that had happened after Thursday lunchtime. Forget about it and move on.

Unfortunately, this was easier said than done. The problem with intrusive thoughts is they can't be switched off, and it didn't matter how I tried to distract myself. Reading, writing, chess – I could focus on none of these for more than a couple of minutes before the Mystery Woman's face would flash again in my mind, or else Mrs Frost's exasperated expression as I tried to explain my concerns. Eventually, I gave up on doing anything that required effort. I sat in front of the TV and binge-watched *Planet Earth II* on BBC iPlayer.

On Monday morning, I woke at six twenty, completed my trampoline workout and plaited my hair. I checked off the rest of the school preparation tasks one by one, like items on a shopping list, but I found the return to my normal routine neither satisfying nor soothing. It was nice to see Bethany again, of course, but she wanted to know all about work experience, and because of her superior social skills, she picked up on my reticence rather quickly.

'What went wrong?' she asked once Daddy had dropped us off at school.

'Nothing went wrong,' I told her.

'Something went wrong. You were stupidly excited beforehand. It was all you talked about.'

I was annoyed that Bethany assumed that something had gone wrong, and even more annoyed that she was probably correct.

'It was fine,' I told her. 'Uneventful. We talked about writing. I did some odd jobs. Nothing else to report.'

Bethany shrugged, but didn't press the issue further. There was a short, slightly uncomfortable silence as we passed the junior school and continued across the yard towards the main entrance, where a cluster of students was sitting on the steps.

'What about you?' I asked. 'Did you gain any valuable insights into the world of bespoke travel agencies? From what you've said, it sounds like it was a positive experience.'

Bethany gave me a weird smile. 'It was *fine*.'

I didn't know what to make of this statement. She was echoing my words back at me, obviously, but to what end? Was she just making it clear that she still didn't believe me? Or was she implying that her work experience was also *not* fine, but she wasn't going to tell me about it while I refused to do the same? It was so ridiculously complicated! I felt as if I'd been drawn into the kind of guessing game that I detest – and I'd probably brought it on myself by refusing to speak honestly in the first place.

The thing that was holding me back, still, was the rawness of my feelings when it came to the end of last week. I didn't want to talk about the Mystery Woman because she made me feel queasy in a way that I couldn't understand and did not want to confront. Moreover, I did not want to confess to Bethany that I'd messed up yet another social situation – my placement with Mrs Frost – but had no idea what had gone wrong. It was embarrassing. I was supposed to be getting better at these things, and instead I seemed to be getting even worse.

I decided the safest thing would be to shift the conversation to territory that Bethany would inevitably want to discuss: I asked if she'd seen Will in the week, not expecting any reticence here.

'We had lunch together every day,' she said. 'I saw him a couple of times after work, too . . .'

'Well, that's good then.'

Bethany shrugged again, as if it wasn't particularly important.

'It is good, right? It's what you wanted.'

'Phoebe, you make it sound like I picked a placement just so I could be near Will. That wasn't the main reason, you know.'

'Wasn't it? I thought—'

'Of course it wasn't! I am capable of making decisions independently of Will!'

'Yes, of course. I just thought . . .' I trailed off, momentarily confused. Why was Bethany being so prickly about this subject? 'Is there a problem with you and Will?' I asked. It was possibly a bit of a leap, but there was something in Bethany's tone, in her general demeanour, that made me suspicious.

'No, not exactly. It's just . . .' Bethany paused until we'd passed the students on the steps and were inside. 'It's just very intense,' she continued in a lower voice. 'It feels like it's moving a bit . . . quickly. Do you get what I mean?'

I considered her words for as long as I could without derailing the conversation. 'No, not really. I mean, I sort of assumed it was quite intense from the amount of time you spend with him, or messaging him, or – I don't know – just thinking about him, if I'm being honest. But that's only how it appears to me,' I added, noting that her lips were pursed in a small frown. 'I'm sorry. I'm not very good at this stuff, as you know. It's all alien territory to me, but I'm more than—'

This sentence was stopped in its tracks as Mrs Harris, our English teacher, appeared from around the corner, giving a cheery wave as she passed us in the opposite direction. 'Morning, girls.'

We said our good mornings, and I tried to resume what I'd been saying to Bethany, raising my voice to compensate for the background chatter as we reached the busy corridor leading to our form room. But this time Bethany cut me off, speaking in a much lower voice. 'Phoebe, it's fine. I don't think we really have time to discuss it now. It's probably better to leave it.'

I checked the time on my phone. 'Are you sure? We've got another eleven minutes until registration.'

'Honestly, Phoebe. Just drop it for now. Please?'

Her voice had a slight edge to it, but it was hard to diagnose what this signified. Was she embarrassed? Angry? Or frustrated that I didn't automatically 'get' what she was insinuating? If the latter, it was equally frustrating for me. Bethany knew very well that I wasn't a mind-reader! I made a last attempt to offer my support, but she cut me off almost before I had begun.

'Phoebe, forget it! I shouldn't have said anything. It's between me and Will. You don't need to be involved.'

I nodded, glumly. But Bethany either didn't notice that she'd upset me or she didn't care.

I suppose in other circumstances I might have been pleased that I didn't have to deal with whatever turmoil was occurring in her and Will's relationship, which could be annoying at the best of times. But as it was, I just felt useless and rejected. It was yet another example of my failure to be a competent human being.

As is often the case, I didn't realise that I was heading for a meltdown until it was far too late to stop it. It was lunchtime and Bethany was off with Will again, presumably sorting through the issue she had alluded to earlier in the day – the one that I had no hope of understanding because she wouldn't explain it properly.

I was sitting alone in the dining hall, eating an avocado and spiced bean wrap. I needed time by myself to counteract the sense of pressure that had been building all morning and had yet to dissipate. It was extremely strange – a physical heaviness that seemed to be holding me down in my chair, making even basic movements harder than they should have been. The dining hall was not busy and I had several feet of open space all around me, and yet I still felt hemmed in. My clothes felt too tight, even though they were the same clothes from a fortnight ago and it seemed improbable that I'd had a significant growth spurt since then. There were smells of fried vegetables from the kitchen and the hum of a refrigerator and the overlap of half a dozen impenetrable conversations. I would have put my headphones on, but headphones were not permitted in the dining hall *under any circumstances*. Once more, this was due to frustratingly non-specific 'Health and Safety requirements', designed by someone with no grasp of the perils of sensory overload.

I finished my wrap, closed my eyes, and put my hands over my ears. This strategy helped for approximately six minutes, until one of the dining staff came over to check if I was OK. I'm sure it was well intentioned, but when she put her hand on my shoulder it caused me to yelp and jerk violently, hitting both knees on the underside of the table. It was very noisy and dramatic, and everyone in the dining hall immediately looked over. I didn't have any words to answer the dinner lady's question – was I OK – so I got up and left. Which I suppose did answer the question.

Outside, I retrieved my headphones from my bag and put on *End of an Era*, which is a recording of Nightwish's final concert with Tarja on vocals, before she was unceremoniously fired backstage. I also put on my sunglasses, even though it wasn't sunny and people would think I was being peculiar. I didn't care very much at that point.

I walked to the Frowned-Upon Forest, which is the wooded area to the far south of the grounds. As the name suggests, there was nothing in the school rules which explicitly forbade students from accessing this area, but it was common knowledge that we shouldn't go there. I suppose it was because the trees were thick enough to conceal any number of illicit activities, from vaping to inappropriate affection. No one else called it the Frowned-Upon Forest. It was a private joke, existing only in my own head.

Fortunately, no illicit activity was occurring today; I was alone. I sat on the ground with my back pressed against the trunk of a tall oak tree which had lost its leaves. I closed my eyes behind my sunglasses and I drew my knees up toward my chin and hugged my legs and rocked for a while, trying to regain my mental equilibrium. I don't know how long this lasted, but eventually I calmed down enough to have a coherent thought, which was this: school was hard work. It had always been hard work, and it always would be hard work, until the day I left.

I had, of course, been aware of this previously, but having spent a week in a different environment, where I didn't have to put in the same level of effort, the bald fact of it stood out all the more. Trying to blend in was exhausting. Freaking out in the dining hall was exhausting. Talking to people was exhausting and avoiding people or being ignored was a different type of exhausting. And I still had two years and seven months of school ahead of me, approximately five hundred school days. Experience told me that not every one of those days would be as terrible as today. But they would all be difficult.

When I opened my eyes, I noticed that my fingers were bleeding. This was because I had been biting them. There were bright red streaks across my knuckles and darker stains around some of my nails. Nightwish's cover of 'Phantom of the Opera' was playing in my headphones, so I deduced that approximately twenty-one minutes had passed since I left the school building. This meant that lunch hour was almost over. I walked back to class via the toilets, where I washed my hands and rubbed the back of my skirt with a wet paper towel to remove some mud. But it didn't really work. It just spread the mud around and made it look worse.

With no clear alternative, I struggled back into my normal life.

I avoided sitting alone in the dining hall, reasoning that when I *had* to be in a public space, I should take every pain not to withdraw and dwell upon my ongoing anxieties. It wasn't that I felt like being around people. I just needed something external to focus on – something to distract me and reduce the chance of future meltdowns. When Bethany wasn't available, I sat with whichever small group I could join and hovered on the edge of their conversation, trying to look simultaneously involved and unobtrusive. When Bethany was available, I sat with her and Will, and felt only fractionally more at ease.

Observing the two of them together, the logical conclusion should have been that whatever issue had afflicted their relationship, it was now resolved. After all, on the face of it, their behaviour was very much unchanged. There were the same laughs and smiles, the same grooming rituals, the same minutes lost in mutual adoration. And yet, for some hard-to-define reason, I found it impossible to shake the impression Bethany had given me on the morning of the meltdown, that there was more going on than met the eye.

As a result, I started watching Bethany more closely when it was just the two of us together, and, by increments, my suspicions grew. She may have seemed happy enough when she was with Will – she may have seemed as if she was once again fully committed to the 'intensity' of their relationship – but when they were apart, her moods were far harder to categorise. Sometimes, she'd be tapping away at her phone and I'd catch a glimpse of the same uncertainty she'd revealed, briefly, after work experience. At other times, her expression would change so rapidly it was hard to keep up with. She'd go from exuberant to anxious and back again – all in the space of a single minute! It was possible, of course, that these mood swings were just hormonal. Yet my intuition still told me that there was more to it. In better circumstances, I'd have been able to ask her, but I felt that the wall she had put up previously, when she told me not to get involved, was still very much in place. I felt shut out, and consequently, my fears from earlier in the term, that we were drifting apart, started to resurface.

In response, I directed my attention again to my self-improvement plan, which I felt was losing some of its early momentum. Part of the problem was that it was difficult to keep up the same level of enthusiasm for the project over the long term, and part of the problem was that I'd suffered major setbacks – i.e. the social failures that had accumulated since the beginning of November. Thus it was a major boost to my morale when I achieved another small but significant success with the Chess Club.

I was still playing every week, and I took part in a second match with the school team – a home game, which was far less stressful than the previous away game. I won a decisive victory in sixteen minutes and thirty-one seconds, and then sat at the far end of the library reading my book. Hu was second to finish and came and sat beside me.

'Hey, Phoebe.'

'Hello, Hu,' I said in the lowest possible voice, since there were still games being played. 'Did you win? It looked as if you were winning.'

Hu smiled. 'Yes, I won. I won't ask if you did because you always do, don't you?'

I returned his smile – quite cautiously, as I wasn't a hundred per cent certain if I was being praised or criticised.

'What are you reading?' he asked.

'*Red Rising*,' I told him. 'It's basically *The Hunger Games* in space, but a bit more A than YA.'

'Right . . . Any good?'

'Yes. It's not the most original concept, obviously, but it's very well done so far. Do you like fantasy?'

Hu gave a small shrug. 'Yes, what I've read. I'm not an expert. I liked *His Dark Materials* and *The Lord of the Rings*.'

I nodded; this was an interesting development. I had not observed Hu reading in the common room, but this wasn't surprising as most people did not – they used it for conversation or multiplayer computer games. I was the only person who habitually had a book on the go.

I was conscious that we'd fallen silent, and it was probably my turn to speak. So I said the first thing that came into my mind, which was: 'I read *The Lord of the Rings* when I was nine, and *The Silmarillion* when I was ten.' Then, conscious that this might sound like a boast, I added: 'My mum was an avid fantasy reader. She got me into the genre when I was very young.'

Whispered as this was, it felt somewhat like a confession; it was very rare that I'd talk about you at school. I think that many of my peers knew that I only had Daddy now, and I'm sure Hu did, being a fellow boarder and only one year below me. But, excluding Bethany, I wasn't close enough to anyone to share intimate details about my family, either before or after your death. I felt a momentary surge of panic at having now brought you up, in what should have been a light and casual interaction. I felt certain that I'd violated the most basic rule of small talk – that it should be kept small! – and now there was nowhere else the conversation could go. Yet, to my surprise, Hu did not look mortified. I interpreted the brief smile he gave me as sympathetic. 'My mum's a big reader, too,' he said. 'She's always got a book on the go. I used to be the same when I was younger, but I kind of got out of the habit.'

I blinked for a couple of seconds, trying to regain my composure.

'You can borrow this after I've finished, if you like,' I said, holding *Red Rising* aloft. 'We can compare notes afterwards. I mean, no pressure, obviously. But if you do want to get back into the habit . . .'

'Um . . . yeah, thanks. If you don't mind?'

I shrugged, as if lending a book to a fellow pupil was no big deal for me – the sort of thing I did all the time.

And I realise it would be a stretch to say that I'd succeeded in making another friend, but after two months of getting nowhere, this was not the point. I had just sustained a three-minute conversation with a schoolmate that not only wasn't too awkward, but also – astonishingly – felt rather meaningful.

Yet, as is so often the case, a success in one area of my life did not translate to the rest of it becoming any easier. It was more as if there was a cosmic balancing act, so that as one aspect improved, another had to deteriorate.

November became December, and Bethany said that she'd like to plan another Edinburgh trip, assuming I was up for it. This should have been fine, but it led to a ridiculous argument over which film we were supposedly going to see. I suggested *Spider-Man: Into the Spider-Verse*; Bethany said it was too childish.

'You enjoyed *Homecoming*,' I pointed out.

'*Homecoming* wasn't a cartoon,' Bethany said.

'*Spider-Man: Into the Spider-Verse* isn't a cartoon, either,' I told her. 'It's an animated feature film, and it was *Variety*'s "Critic's Choice". The *Guardian* called it dazzling and witty. It has eighty-seven per cent on *Metacritic*.'

'I just don't think my parents will buy it,' Bethany said. 'It has to be something we'd both want to see.'

'But I'm the only one seeing it! You'll be with Will.'

'For Christ's sake, Phoebe! I'm not saying you shouldn't watch it. Watch whatever you want. But let's agree on an alibi that makes sense for both of us. Something my mum and dad aren't going to question.'

I stayed silent. It was not like Bethany to blaspheme.

'C'mon. Why's it such a big deal? It's just to make the story more convincing. You know I'd do the same for you.'

'You won't even *pretend* to watch a film that I want to see! Plus, the more you make me lie, the more I'll struggle. Deception does not come naturally to me.'

'Are you saying it does come naturally to *me*?'

'No. If I'd wanted to say that, I'd have said it.'

Bethany exhaled noisily. 'Fine! We're going to see *Spider-Man in the Spider-Verse*! Just don't expect me to memorise the plot.'

'It's *into* the Spider-Verse,' I told her. 'If you're worried about being convincing, you should at least get the title right.'

Bethany didn't reply to this. Instead, she rolled her eyes, got up from her bed, and left our room.

Afterwards, I wondered why such a trivial matter had escalated in this way. Leaving aside the incident at the beginning of term, Bethany and I did not often argue, but it struck me, again, that her moods had been highly unpredictable recently; and on this occasion, I felt convinced that she was more in the wrong than I was. She was being unreasonable – not to mention paranoid. I didn't doubt that her parents would disapprove of Will, but they didn't even know he existed. Nor had they shown any sign of suspicion before or after the last Edinburgh trip. So why was Bethany so worried about a non-existent flaw in her cover story?

My conclusion was that something else *had* to be going on here. Based on the evidence of my eyes, and the fact that she was still taking pains to keep their illicit relationship going, I was no longer wedded to the idea that it was necessarily a problem between her and Will – or the same problem that I'd failed to comprehend weeks ago. It could equally be some issue I'd never even considered, something between Bethany and her parents, for example.

Knowing it would not be the first time I'd missed a crucial detail, I vowed that I would pay even more attention to Bethany's behaviour over the coming weeks. With our friendship under strain, I didn't think it would be wise to ask her outright; but if there *was* something else underpinning her recent agitation, I was determined to discover what it was.

15

Paradigm Shift

Despite the friction that preceded it, the second Edinburgh trip went off without a hitch, following the same pattern as the first. After *Spider-Man: Into the Spider-Verse*, which was excellent, I went to the same independent coffee shop, where I had a double espresso and a sesame stir-fry wrap. I browsed the fantasy section in Waterstones for half an hour and bought a book called *The Poppy War* by R F Kuang. The remainder of the afternoon was spent in the Scottish National Gallery, which was not as interesting as the Anatomical Museum but still enjoyable.

Unsurprisingly, Bethany was again distracted and disengaged on the train ride home – so much so that I decided there was no point even attempting a full debriefing on what we'd supposedly done that day. I gave her only the broadest outline and left it at that. This proved a sensible choice, as Bethany's mum asked zero questions about the film or where we'd eaten, *et cetera*. She asked if we'd had a nice time and Bethany and I both confirmed that we had. She asked if the city was busy, and we confirmed that it was, which was to be expected ten days before Christmas.

That seemed like it was going to be the full extent of the conversation. An excellent outcome – no need for further deception, and half an hour of silence to rest and unwind on the drive home. But as we were leaving Berwick, Mrs Collins started talking again: she asked me if I'd be joining Bethany for carols the following weekend. Usually, I would have been able to reply without thought. I still sing carols at St Mary's every Christmas, and I continue to enjoy it very much, despite the general lunacy of the nativity story. But on this occasion, being tired and unprepared, it took me a few seconds to process the question. In the intervening time, Bethany muttered something. I heard her the first time, as we were sitting in the back of the car together, but Mrs Collins did not.

'What was that, darling?' she asked.

Bethany raised her voice. 'I don't remember you asking *me* if I wanted to sing.'

There was a short silence. I decided that this meant it was my turn to talk. 'Yes, I'd like to join you for carols. I don't mind if Bethany is there or not.'

Mrs Collins addressed Bethany. 'You always sing, darling. Why wouldn't you?'

'I didn't say I wouldn't. I said it would have been nice to have been *asked*.'

'Do you have other plans?'

Bethany snorted. 'On December the twenty-third, on Holy Island? Obviously not.'

'So, what's the problem?'

I was also wondering this.

Bethany said: 'I just think you should have asked me rather than assuming.'

Mrs Collins considered this for several seconds before responding. 'Maybe we could discuss this when we get home. I'm sure Phoebe doesn't want to hear it.'

This was correct. I would have preferred silence after a busy and over-stimulating day. But I thought it was more important to be polite. 'I don't mind at all,' I said. 'If you want to continue your discussion, you can.'

'Forget it,' Bethany said.

Mrs Collins said nothing.

After a few more minutes had passed, I felt it was safe to assume that the discussion wasn't going to continue, and I went back to gazing out the window.

It was only the next morning, after a long and refreshing sleep, that I started to reconsider the conversation in the car. I suspect my brain had been processing the scene overnight, as it would explain why I woke up with Bethany immediately in my mind, and why it took me very little time to decide that I needed to text her to find out what was going on. Why had she been so stroppy with her mother, and over such a trivial matter? Obviously, I'd phrase the question more diplomatically than that, and I'd wait a few hours to send it, as it was 6.15 in the morning, and I knew from past experience that if I tried to instigate a conversation with Bethany now, she'd be stroppy with me too. Or she'd just ignore me. If I wanted a sensible answer, patience was the key.

I got up and bounced for ten minutes. I fed Gladys, breakfasted with Daddy, and then read *The Poppy War* for two hours. At 9.30, I composed and sent my message to Bethany, figuring she'd be up and showered by then, ready for her father's ten o'clock Sunday service.

Hi. Just thought I'd better check in after last night. Is everything OK? You seemed a bit stressed.

Despite my best efforts, it seemed that I must have

mistimed the text, as it took her a surprisingly long time to reply: two and a half hours.

I'm OK now. Just a bit tired.

It wasn't much. I decided to press for more.

Have you made up with your mum?

Yeah, we're fine. I shouldn't have snapped at her. It was stupid.

Does that mean you are going to sing?

Of course. I was never not going to sing. I just wanted to be asked.

Excellent. I'm glad it's all resolved. ☺

Unusually for Bethany, I did not get a smiley face back.

The carol service took place a week later, on the Sunday evening before Christmas, and a favourable tide meant that the church was full almost to capacity, with a couple of hundred visitors from the mainland supplementing the local congregation (which was most of the village, excluding Daddy, because of his dislike of singing, and Mrs Frost, because of her dislike of people). Bethany and I sat side by side in the right-hand central pew, a couple of rows back from the front. The front pew, as always, was reserved for the hard-of-hearing, and the second was occupied by the children from the village infant school, along with their parents and Mrs Atkins, who was still the island's lone teacher. As always, Mrs Atkins had greeted me and Bethany as soon as she saw us.

'My goodness,' she said. 'You look so grown-up! I almost didn't recognise you.'

I deduced that this was aimed mostly at Bethany, since I looked the same as I always did, in jeans and a loose-fitting cardigan. Bethany, in contrast, was wearing a long cream-coloured dress with embroidered curlicues on the hem. Her hair was shiny and held back with a thin silver headband. She looked extremely pretty, and had clearly gone to some effort. I wondered if it was in light of her small rebellion during our journey back from Berwick station. Perhaps her dressing up for the carol service was a way of making amends with her parents? In any case, I surmised that the problem really had been laid to rest, as Bethany was here, and I didn't, at first, detect any indication that she was unhappy to be so.

This illusion started to fall apart approximately half an hour into the service, during 'O Little Town of Bethlehem'. I noticed that Bethany had stopped singing. I was probably the only person who noticed because she was on the very end of our pew. When I turned my head to check if she was OK, she was staring absently ahead, not even mouthing the words. By the middle of 'Silent Night', she had started crying. Subtly. Or as subtly as one *can* cry.

I didn't know what to do.

'Are you OK?' I asked. It was difficult to pitch my voice at a level that was audible over the singing without drawing anyone else's attention to the situation, and after a single, failed attempt, I realised it was a stupid question anyway. I abandoned the endeavour and instead reached for her hand. It was not an action that came naturally to me, but I couldn't think of an alternative, other than pretending not to notice; and it seemed I'd made an acceptable choice. Bethany didn't turn to look at me, but she squeezed my hand as it found hers, and she did not let go when we sat back down.

Reverend Collins started reading from Luke, Chapter Two, his voice clear and resonant, but I paid no attention. My brain was working overtime until the end of the service, by which time Bethany was calmer, though still visibly upset. As soon as the last note of the last carol had faded, she released my hand, slipped out of the pew, and exited the church. I didn't know if she wanted me to follow, but I did. Even though I had very little to go on, I'd managed to formulate a fledgling hypothesis – the only one I could think of that made sense in the immediate context. And, if I was correct, it was a big enough issue to also explain Bethany's erratic moods and behaviour over the last month or so.

She walked out of the churchyard and down towards the sea. It was a clear night and the moon was only one day past full, so there was plenty of light to negotiate the stony path down to the beach; and although she'd put on her dark jacket, the hem of Bethany's dress was still easily visible at a distance of twenty metres. I caught up with her near the old lifeboat station, and we sat on the bench overlooking the bay. There was only a thin ribbon of distant water separating the island from the mainland, with the exposed sand stretching darkly before it.

Neither of us spoke for a while. In hindsight, I should have waited longer; she might have told me everything there and then if I had. Instead, I blurted out the question that had occurred to me at the end of the church service.

'Have you lost your faith?' I asked.

Bethany made a noise somewhere between a sob and a laugh. 'I don't believe a word of it. I haven't for a long time.'

I nodded but, in truth, I was a little surprised. Not at having my theory confirmed, but because she was so unequivocal about it. I had expected an admission of doubt, a creeping uncertainty. Not this. As I'd intimated to Will earlier in the term, Bethany and I had not spoken about religious matters for a while, and not properly since the infamous Easter of 2015. *Don't try to convert Bethany.* That had been Daddy's advice afterwards. In the meantime, she had apparently managed to convert herself, despite her upbringing.

'How long are we talking?' I asked. 'When exactly did you stop believing?'

Bethany shrugged, as if the details weren't all that important, which was confusing, given that she'd been so distressed in the church. 'I've been doubting for at least a year. But it was over the summer that I basically stopped believing.'

'Why didn't you tell me?'

'I almost did. Do you remember the last day of the holidays? I came over to see you but you were out. I texted afterwards but you didn't want to talk.'

I did remember, obviously. It was the evening of the car in the sea.

'You could have been a bit more persistent,' I pointed out. 'I mean, you know I would have dropped everything if I thought it was something serious.'

'I know. But it's . . . it's just difficult to talk sometimes, isn't it? You sort of ball up all your courage, then the moment doesn't quite pan out the way you're expecting . . . You end up telling yourself that it's not the right time after all, or that it's just something you need to deal with yourself.'

'Is that what happened? You thought you could deal with it by yourself?'

'More or less.' Bethany shivered, hugging her jacket more tightly around her chest. 'I had this . . . moment, that afternoon, when I just felt like I was seeing everything clearly for the first time in ages. I was praying – trying to pray – and it was the first time I'd tried properly in ... I dunno. Maybe a month or something. My dad had been talking about prayer in his sermon that morning, and he finished with these famous lines from Matthew: "Ask and it will be given to you; seek and you will find; knock and the door will be opened to you." Well, that's what I thought I was doing. I was alone in my room, and the house was completely quiet. And I sat with my eyes closed, and I . . . sought.'

I nodded, waiting for Bethany to continue.

'That's it,' she said. 'I just sat there, seeking, for however long, and it was just me in my room talking to no one. It was exactly the opposite of what I'd been promised. I've always been told that God wants to have a personal relationship with us, but if that's the case, you'd think He'd do a better job introducing himself.'

Bethany looked at me, and after a moment, shrugged again. 'Well, you pretty much know the rest. I decided I'd go and talk to you, even though I thought I knew what you'd tell me. That I was one hundred per cent right – of course there's no one there listening to the thoughts in my head.'

'Yes,' I said. 'I mean, I hope I would have phrased it better, but other than that . . .'

Bethany nodded. 'Right. But you were out, obviously, and it was clear you didn't want to talk later on. So I thought, OK, leave it until tomorrow. Then the next day, the urgency wasn't really there anymore. I told myself that I should wait a little longer. I suppose I had it in my head that I wanted to be absolutely sure about what I thought, and I wanted to get there on my own. Does that make sense?'

I nodded. 'Perfect sense. You wanted to be free of outside influence. You wanted to make up your own mind without me telling you the hundred reasons you're right.'

Bethany gave a very small smile at this, though her expression had not otherwise changed; she still looked very subdued. 'Right.'

'What about your parents?' I asked after a moment. 'Have you spoken to them? Are you going to?'

'What do you think?'

'I don't know. That's why I asked.'

'Of course not. It's not the sort of conversation we could have.'

'Oh.' I thought for a while. It was difficult for me to relate to Bethany's situation as nothing remotely similar had ever happened to me. Daddy and I had the same worldview on most philosophical issues, and when we did disagree, it was never a big deal. I couldn't imagine our basic relationship changing all that much in the unlikely event that he suddenly became a devout Christian, or in the unlikelier event that I did. Clearly, it was different for Bethany, but it still seemed to me that the fundamental issue was indisputable. 'You're allowed to make up your own mind,' I told her. 'I don't see how they could possibly object to that.'

Bethany didn't say anything. I tried to press the point, as gently as I could.

'It's obviously causing you significant distress. It must be difficult sitting in church every week, with all these thoughts going round your head.'

After a few moments, she started sobbing again. I put a cautious hand on her shoulder, not knowing what else I should do. It took her a long time to calm down.

'I'm not telling them,' she said eventually. 'It would ruin their life. It would ruin *my* life. Hopefully, they'll never need to know.'

I was used to Bethany being somewhat dramatic, but this seemed excessive. I'd say it felt out of proportion to what we were talking about, but perhaps that's just hindsight. I still didn't have all the facts at the time, so it was impossible for me to have that clear a picture of what was going on.

'We should probably be getting back,' Bethany said. 'Mum and Dad'll send out a search party otherwise. Plus it's freezing.'

'Well, it *is* winter,' I said.

It wasn't a very profound note on which to end, but that's where the conversation did end. Bethany took my arm and we walked back to the church, neither of us saying a word.

It was two weeks before I had the full story. In the meantime, the Christmas holiday passed quickly and unremarkably. Daddy took a week off work, but as always our celebrations were low-key, with minimum disruption to my usual holiday routine. We made and ate a small Mushroom Wellington for Christmas dinner, and afterwards we Skyped Gee. We opened a tin of chocolates and watched some festive films, such as *It's a Wonderful Life* and *Die Hard*. Daddy drank some beer. I read and wrote, working out further details for the backstory to my parallel Earth – the historical events that would feed into the main plot. On days when I was struggling for ideas, I spent my time revising for my mock GSCE exams, which were scheduled to start the second week back. On days when the weather was good enough, I took Gladys for long walks around the island, which was mostly deserted.

During this time, I texted Bethany frequently, but it was clear that she was not yet ready to discuss her loss of faith in further depth. The messages I got back weren't dismissive as such, but they were terse and guarded, and I got the strong impression that I shouldn't push her too far at the present. It was frustrating as I kept thinking about what might have been if we'd started this conversation back in September, when Bethany had come to me of her own volition, actually wanting to talk. If it hadn't been for the car in the sea and that first missed opportunity, then maybe the whole autumn term might have played out more smoothly. In retrospect, it was hard not to think that several pointless arguments could have been avoided if I'd known about Bethany's crisis of faith, and the strain it had obviously caused.

In the present circumstances, though, I thought my best course of action was to give her space, while at the same time making a greater personal effort to understand what she was going through, so that when she was ready to talk, I'd be ready to help. It was difficult because I had been brought up without any religious beliefs; I couldn't really imagine what it was like to have faith in the first place, let alone have it and lose it. I had not held any supernatural beliefs since I was six, when careful questioning of you and Daddy had exposed the truth about the Tooth Fairy. And this had come as no great shock. It was more the gradual realisation that a particular idea was unlikely, given how the rest of the world seemed to work.

I suppose this was also my default attitude when I tried to analyse Bethany's situation. She'd reviewed the evidence and come to the only logical conclusion – that the universe doesn't look like the creation of an all-powerful and benevolent God. It looks like animals eating other animals. It looks like natural disasters and periodic mass extinctions. And if you extend your horizon beyond Earth, it looks mostly empty and uninhabitable.

This was the attitude – the logic – that I had to work very

hard to suppress. Because, clearly, it was not helpful when it came to understanding Bethany's current feelings. She was experiencing a high level of distress – far higher than I would have expected, given her claim that she hadn't believed for several months. My conclusion was that she was still struggling to adjust to her new way of thinking, which did make sense, from a psychological standpoint. Bethany had grown up believing. She had presumably been told things that were not easy to relinquish: that God had a plan for her; that life on Earth was just a temporary phase in her existence; that she had a soul that would live forever. And now she had to confront the likelihood that none of it was true. From this perspective, I could start to see why she was so upset.

When we returned to school in January, I felt that I had reached a position where I would be better able to support her, and I did not have to wait long to do so. On the first day back, I returned to our shared room after lessons to find Bethany curled in the foetal position on her bed. She glanced up for only a moment when I entered, but I could see at once that she had been crying again.

I hadn't planned a speech, but I did have a broad idea of what I needed to say to help her through this. I had been talking for approximately three minutes when she told me to 'shut the fuck up'.

I did, but not for long. I figured that if Bethany needed to vent some of her emotions in a safe space, I'd be here for that too. After a few moments of silence, I said: 'Bethany, I don't mind if you need to swear at me. It's fine to be scared and angry. What you are experiencing is a major paradigm shift – an existential crisis, really – and this isn't something you should try to suppress. Honestly, I think it's best if—'

'I'm not having a fucking existential crisis!' Bethany shouted. Or rather, she did that weird thing where someone shouts but doesn't actually raise their voice. If anything, her voice got quieter.

I waited. Calmly. Patiently.

'I think I'm pregnant,' Bethany said.

I sat down on the floor.

16

Holding it Together

I didn't say anything for a while. There was too much to process, and Bethany had started crying again. I stared at the small gap underneath her bed as question after question raced through my mind. How had this happened? *Where* had this happened? And when?

I realised, quite swiftly, that none of this was of immediate, critical importance; and the first question was just idiotic. I knew *how* this had happened.

When Bethany was no longer crying, I asked: 'Is Will the suspected father?'

'Of course Will's the fucking father!' Bethany hissed. 'How many boys do you think I've been sleeping with?'

'Until a few minutes ago I assumed zero. Now I assume one. I just wanted to make absolutely sure I've got the facts straight.'

Bethany didn't respond to this. She had wriggled into bed while I was sitting on the floor and now had the duvet pulled up over her face. For me, this made it somewhat easier to think.

'Have you taken a test?' I asked. 'You said you *think* you're pregnant. You don't know for sure?'

I had to wait for a while, but eventually Bethany lowered the duvet and said: 'I've missed a period. At least one.'

'Possibly more than one? You're not sure?'

'I had some bleeding but it was very light. I don't know anymore.'

I nodded, slowly. 'You need to get a test.'

'I know I need to get a test!'

Bethany was getting worked up again. Which was understandable, all things considered. I gave her a few more moments, then said: 'You know I'll help you, don't you? I'll help however I can.'

So far, I'd had zero success at helping Bethany, so I thought her response to this offer was justified: she started crying again. But when she spoke, I was surprised to hear something else. Relief. Relief and gratitude.

'Thank you. God, *thank* you!'

I didn't know what else to do, so I got up from the floor and sat on the bed next to her. I put my hand on her back as she continued to cry. There was one more question I thought I needed to ask. I didn't see how it could be avoided. 'Does Will know?'

Bethany shook her head. 'Phoebe, you can't tell anyone about this. You understand that, don't you?'

'Of course.'

'You're the only person who knows. The *only* person.'

I nodded, and for the first time in the conversation I felt like I was standing on solid ground. As a friend, I knew I had many shortcomings, but untrustworthiness was not one of them. If Bethany needed me to keep a secret, I would keep it forever. Barring torture, or her life being in jeopardy, it really was that simple.

*

Bethany fell asleep just before five. I reasoned this was a good thing. She was emotionally exhausted and would probably find it stressful going to dinner. I found Suzi in the common room and told her that Bethany was ill and had gone to bed. It was not even a lie, really, so I had no difficulty sounding convincing.

'You probably shouldn't disturb her,' I said. 'She has a headache, but she doesn't think it's anything major. Mostly, she's just tired. I can look in on her again as soon as I'm back from dinner.'

Suzi thought about this and then nodded. 'Has she got plenty to drink?'

'I left a glass of water on her bedside table. She said she'd come and get some aspirin if it gets any worse.'

This was enough to placate Suzi and I went down to the dining hall reassured that she would not be waking Bethany.

Needing as few distractions as possible so that I could recharge and reflect, I sat on my own, away from the other boarders. So it was somewhat ironic that this was the day that Hu attempted to sit down next to me and strike up a conversation about *Red Rising*, which he'd finished over the holiday.

I cut him off mid-sentence. 'Hu, I'm afraid this is not the best time for me. I need to be alone with my thoughts. Perhaps we could discuss the book on a different occasion?'

'Oh . . . OK, sure. I just wanted to say thanks, really. I enjoyed it a lot.'

I felt bad; Hu's cheeks looked red, and I suspected I'd managed to offend him. But I couldn't change my mind. I really did need time out.

'I'm glad you like it,' I told him. 'And I honestly would like to talk about it with you. Just not now. Please?'

Hu nodded. 'Yeah, of course. Not a problem.'

He left and joined another table. It was unfortunate, but I thought I had handled the situation as well as I could in the circumstances. My self-improvement plan was of secondary importance now; the best thing to do was to put it out of my mind and focus on the matter at hand.

Bethany was pregnant. Or possibly pregnant. And now that I'd got over the initial shock, and was no longer having to deal with the immediate emotional fallout, I felt weirdly calm about that fact. In some ways, it was easier to deal with than the existential crisis I'd misdiagnosed, in that it was at least less abstract. There were practical things I could do to help, things that Bethany would obviously struggle with in her current mental state. We'd agreed that she needed to take a test, but if this was going to happen without delay – as it definitely should – I was going to have to take charge of the logistics.

Back in our room, Bethany was still asleep. I placed a sandwich I'd collected from the canteen next to her water on the bedside table, adding a quick note.

Sandwich – in case you're hungry when you wake up. It's cheese so it shouldn't deteriorate too much. I told Suzi you have a headache. If I'm asleep and you need anything, you can wake me up at any time. I honestly don't mind.

I went to the common room to reassure Suzi that Bethany was still soundly asleep, and then excused myself for the rest of the evening, on the pretence that I was going to revise in bed while keeping vigil. In reality, I rescheduled revision for nine o'clock, after the phone curfew, and spent the next two hours on Google.

*

I was awake at six the following morning. Bethany was also awake by then, but she wasn't up. She was propped against one of her pillows, still wearing her school uniform from yesterday. She did not look good. Her blouse was crumpled, her eyes were red and puffy, and her hair was all over the place. The cheese sandwich hadn't been touched, though I saw that the note had been removed. She smiled weakly.

'Thanks for covering with Suzi,' she said.

'Not a problem.'

'Did she ask a lot of questions?'

'A few. I managed to convince her you just needed some rest. It wasn't that difficult.'

'Right . . . thanks, again. I don't know what I would have done otherwise. I wasn't really in a good state for . . . well, I wasn't in a good state for anything.'

I nodded. 'How are you feeling now?'

'I'm feeling . . . Christ, I don't know . . .' I stayed quiet while Bethany searched for her words. 'I'm feeling like I want the ground to open up. I'm feeling like I can't possibly cope with this and my life is basically over. But a tiny bit less than yesterday, so I suppose that's something.'

'I'm sure you can take a sick day if you need it. Suzi and Kevin already think you're ill.'

Bethany thought about this for a moment, then shook her head. 'No. I can't be stuck in here all day. It'll drive me nuts. I think I need to . . . Fuck, I don't know. I just need to get through today, somehow.'

'You need to do the test,' I told her. 'The sooner the better.' Bethany paled noticeably. But I'd already made the assessment that tough love was needed here. Further delay would make matters worse. 'I've been doing some research,' I said. 'There

165

are three basic options for you to choose from. The first is the simplest and the quickest, and I know your impulse will be to reject it out of hand, but please don't. Hear me out.'

I waited for Bethany to give me some cue that I should proceed. She was still looking extremely pale, even in the dim light of the bedside lamp, and she had her fists clenched tight. But eventually she nodded.

'The school nurse,' I said. 'I know you've already indicated that you—'

'No. No, Phoebe. Are you completely insane? I've told you! No one knows, no one is going to know! What do you think—'

I spoke over her. It wasn't difficult because she was again using her whispered shout. 'It would be one hundred per cent confidential. I found numerous reliable sources, *including* the school's own policies on medical confidentiality and the sharing of personal information. If you ask the nurse to keep something private she has to respect your wishes. It's that simple.'

Bethany snorted at this. 'Phoebe, it's not that simple. It's definitely not that simple.'

'OK, it's *almost* that simple. Technically, she's not bound to silence if your life is at risk, or if you've committed a serious crime or are planning to do so. Or if she deems you mentally incompetent. None of which applies, in this case.'

'Right. Until I have a complete breakdown in her office. At which point she decides that I'm mentally incompetent and calls my parents.'

'That's not what mentally incompetent means. You're not mentally incompetent in the technical sense.'

'I am not going to the school nurse!'

'There are several major advantages. One: it's by far the quickest and easiest option. Two—'

'Phoebe, stop. Just stop. No school nurse. What are the other options?'

I suppressed the urge to continue arguing my case. Because the school nurse was definitely the best option; this was why I'd mentioned it first. But I'd been prepared for the fact that Bethany might prove intractable on this point. I took a breath and moved on.

'The second option is that we book an appointment at a clinic in Berwick. Obviously, it would have to wait until Saturday, so you'd have the stress of not knowing for another five days, but the same confidentiality rules apply. And you'd be with a trained professional who'd be able to offer further advice and emotional support, whatever the result.'

Bethany nodded silently. She didn't look convinced, but she was at least willing to consider this option; she hadn't rejected the notion of professional help entirely. 'What's the third option?'

'Home test. We'd still have to wait until the weekend to do it, but we can pick one up from any pharmacy. Or I suppose—'

'OK. Home test. If it's negative then that's the end of it. All I have to do is keep it together for a few more days.'

I didn't say anything for a few moments. I'd been pretty certain this would be the option Bethany would pick, even though it was the worst option in several respects. But I'd already decided that I'd support her, whatever her choice. The only thing I had to address was her last point. '*Can* you keep it together for a few more days?'

'I think so.' She put her head in her hands. 'Fuck. I don't know. I'll have to, won't I?'

I nodded, trying to project a sense of confidence that I absolutely did not feel. In theory, four days was not that long

167

to wait, but in practice, I feared another breakdown, and by midmorning, my doubts had only grown. Bethany looked extremely uncomfortable and distracted in class. I hoped, at first, that this was only obvious to me – that I might be in the unprecedented situation where I was picking up subtle behavioural signals that everyone else had missed. But after our English lesson, just before lunch, Mrs Harris asked Bethany to stay behind for a 'quick word'. This was not surprising as Bethany had failed to respond to a very simple question about *To Kill a Mockingbird*; she didn't even know which page we were on.

I decided it would be safest if I stayed behind too, for moral support, but Mrs Harris clearly had other ideas. 'Phoebe, you don't need to be here,' she said. 'I just want a quick chat with Bethany.'

'I don't mind waiting,' I replied.

'OK. But maybe you'd like to wait outside? It won't take long.'

'No, I'm happy here, thank you.'

Mrs Harris pursed her lips. 'Phoebe, *I'd* like to talk to Bethany alone. Please wait for her outside.'

'Oh . . . OK.' It was a good job that Mrs Harris was looking at me in this moment, as I could see rising alarm on Bethany's face. I decided to go all-in with my emergency intervention. 'It's just that Bethany was feeling a little bit under the weather yesterday. I promised Suzi I'd keep an eye on her.'

Mrs Harris turned at once to Bethany. 'You're ill? You should have said something. Do you need to see the nurse?'

'I'm feeling a lot better today,' Bethany told her, not looking or sounding at all better. 'I'm just a bit tired. I didn't sleep well.'

Mrs Harris took a moment before nodding. 'Maybe you should get some fresh air? You look like you could do with it.'

'I think fresh air is a very good idea,' I told Bethany, once we were back in the empty corridor. 'I'm scheduling an emergency walk. We can pick up a sandwich *en route*.'

'I'm not sure I can manage anything. I feel like I'm going to be sick.'

'You can attempt a sandwich,' I told her. 'Take it slowly. We'll make sure we're well away from anyone else in case it comes back up.'

We walked across the yard, past the sports hall, and all the way to the athletics track at the southern boundary of the grounds. As I'd predicted, it was deserted. It was 8th January, it was cold and grey, and nobody was using their second lunchtime back at school to practise the 400 metres.

'I don't think you're going to last until Saturday,' I told Bethany. 'I think we need to reconsider the options.'

I saw her tense up immediately. 'I'm *not* going to the school nurse. Seriously, Phoebe, you can forget it. If I have to pretend to be ill and hide in my room for the rest of the week then that's what I'll do.'

'I'm not suggesting the nurse. You've made your feelings about the nurse very clear. I've been considering another possibility.'

'What possibility?'

'The Tesco Superstore has a pharmacy, and it's only two point eight miles away. I think the best window would be after dinner, some time between six and eight. If we plan it properly, I shouldn't get caught. I'll be back before anyone knows I'm gone.'

'Christ, Phoebe. You can't walk several miles to the supermarket and back. It's insane!'

'Agreed. I've already ruled that out based on the lack of street lighting, pavements and pedestrian crossings. I'll get a taxi. The only real risk is that someone sees me leaving or returning to the school grounds, but the risk is minimal. Kevin and Suzi will be busy after dinner, and most of the teachers will have left by then.'

'Shit, Phoebe. I don't know. What if you *are* caught? You shouldn't even be the one going.'

I shrugged. 'You can't go. You're in no fit state.'

Bethany looked at me but didn't say anything.

'I need you to be here to cover for me,' I told her, 'just in case. It probably won't even come up, but if Suzi or Kevin asks, you can say I'm in our room doing more revision. Or I'm in the shower. We've got the rest of the afternoon to get our story straight.'

'Shit. Shit, shit, shit. Are you sure you want to do this?'

'Definitely. Not knowing is having a serious impact on your mental health.'

'Yeah, and knowing might be even worse. Fuck.'

We walked on in silence for a while. As far as I was concerned, knowing was always better than not knowing. You needed accurate information to make good decisions – or, in this case, any decision. But obviously Bethany had to make the call here. I wasn't going to proceed without her permission.

'OK,' she said eventually. 'Let's do it.'

17

The Test

I left our room at 6.15 p.m., carrying my laundry bag and walking completely normally. I passed Natasha Tomashevsky coming out of the bathroom, and she nodded and said 'hey', and I smiled and nodded back, but said nothing, because there was nothing that needed saying. I'd seen her at dinner, as usual, and now I was just heading downstairs to the laundry room. To do my laundry.

Apart from Natasha, the corridor was empty, as was the stairwell. On the ground floor, I removed my bundled coat from the laundry bag, folded the bag into my pocket, and exited the building. I didn't hesitate because I knew this was the moment of greatest risk. It was like flying in an aeroplane: seventy-one per cent of accidents happen during take-off or landing; once you're airborne, the risk drops significantly, and at cruising altitude, it's practically zero.

I walked at a steady pace past the chapel and the junior school, slowing only as I approached the car park. There were a handful of vehicles parked up, but none had their lights on. I'd phoned for the taxi just before leaving our room, and had been given an estimated wait time of five to ten minutes. I didn't know if the car park had CCTV, but I assumed it had, since this is a sensible precaution for any car park. I also assumed that no one would be monitoring the CCTV, as that would be overkill; logic told me that no one would check the recordings unless there was some obvious reason to do so. Nevertheless, I had no intention of waiting in the open for up to ten minutes. I stood in the trees at the edge of the car park with my hands pushed down in my coat pockets. The sky was still cloudy but no rain was forecast. It was cold, though; I could see my breath in the night air. I was very glad that I wasn't walking to Tesco.

The taxi service sent a message just before the car arrived. This was extremely useful as it meant I did not have to emerge from the trees like a serial killer. When the taxi's headlights lit up the car park, I was waiting on the pavement like a normal human being.

My heart was pounding as the taxi sped down the pitch-black road leading to the A1 roundabout. Needless to say, it was the first time I had ever had to sneak out of school, and I'd be lying if I said I didn't find it somewhat exhilarating. My senses felt heightened, my mind was clear, and my usual, day-to-day anxieties had all but disappeared. Adrenaline was obviously a major factor here, but I was also aware of something else going on, something more interesting and noteworthy. I was experiencing an unfamiliar feeling of competence. The situation I was embroiled in was utterly, utterly alien, and yet, I had skills, I realised, that were surprisingly suited to it. Research, planning, logistics – these were the things I was good at! Furthermore, it turned out that I *could* cope in a crisis, just as long as it wasn't my crisis.

In that moment, I felt a brief but intensely satisfying sense of being in control – as if I actually knew what I was doing.

There was only one other customer in the pharmacy, a middle-aged woman browsing the vitamins. I'd already decided that I wasn't going to waste time hunting through the family planning section. The taxi was waiting in the drop-off zone, and there was zero sense in being coy. I walked straight to the counter and made eye contact with the pharmacist.

'I require a pregnancy test, please. The cheapest you've got.'

The pharmacist gave me a strange look.

'The expensive digital ones are a scam,' I explained – though there was a good chance she understood this already, being a pharmacist. 'They contain the exact same urine test, just wrapped up in some needless electronics to justify the inflated price.'

She continued to look at me, her mouth slightly open.

'If anything, they're less reliable than the basic models,' I added. 'They have more components to go wrong. I did some product research this morning.'

'I'm sorry,' the pharmacist said, after another puzzling hesitation, 'is this for a science project or something?'

'No. It's for the usual purpose. To investigate a potential pregnancy.'

'Right . . . I think the cheapest are two for a pound? Is that OK for you?'

'Yes, that's perfect.'

I removed a pound coin from my purse and completed the transaction with all possible haste.

Ten minutes later, I was back at school. I got the taxi driver to let me out just before the turn-off, as an extra precaution, and then sent a message to Bethany: *Got it. I'll be back outside in 5 minutes. Can you let me in?*

Her reply was almost instant. *Be right there.*

I started walking, keeping my ears pricked and my eyes trained on the darkness ahead. There was no flash of headlights, no noise except the wind, and when I got back to the car park, there was still no one there. I walked past the junior school and the chapel, as quickly and quietly as I could. My contingency plan, should I see or hear anyone approaching, was to run and hide in the trees. And, thankfully, this was not a plan I had to enact.

I made it all the way back to Boarding, before I encountered a problem. I'd hoped that Bethany would have already released the latch on the door, but a gentle push revealed that it was still locked. I waited for a minute, completely exposed, my heart thudding faster and faster. I checked the messages on my phone, but there was nothing; it had now been seven minutes since our last exchange. The only logical conclusion was that something or someone had delayed her on her way down. Even with Bethany's long history of being late for everything, I knew this was the one instance where her punctuality should have been a given.

I didn't know what to do. I couldn't call her in case she'd been waylaid by Suzi or Kevin. It would look extremely suspicious if I called her while I was supposedly in the shower, for example. I was just considering crossing the yard and hiding in the bushes when the door suddenly swung open. I almost jumped out of my skin, before relief brought me crashing back to earth.

Bethany was there, looking pale and scared and nauseated. As soon as I was inside, I removed my coat and folded it back in my laundry bag. 'What kept you?' I whispered.

'I'm sorry! I got halfway here, then realised I was going to throw up!'

'Are you OK? Did you make it to the toilet in time?'

'Barely! And luckily it was empty.'

'Suzi and Kevin already think you're ill,' I reminded her. 'It wouldn't have been a disaster.'

'Phoebe, I can't keep my head straight at the moment! If anyone had seen me, I think I'd just have broken down in tears. You'd still be waiting outside.'

I nodded sympathetically. 'It's OK. It didn't happen. If anyone sees us now, you're just helping me with my laundry. Let's go.'

We made it halfway back before bumping into Suzi, who was coming out of the common room. I didn't wait for Bethany to panic or start crying. 'Laundry!' I said, perhaps a little too enthusiastically. 'We're on a revision break!'

Suzi glanced at my laundry bag, then at Bethany, then at me. Fortunately, I didn't think I could detect any suspicion in her eyes; if anything, she looked amused. 'I'm not sure laundry counts as a break, Phoebe. You're supposed to do something relaxing.'

'I find laundry relaxing,' I countered. 'Bethany's just here for the gentle exercise and conversation.'

'Right. You're feeling better, Bethany? You still look very pale.'

Bethany managed to shrug. 'Better than yesterday, I think.'

Back in our room, Bethany had to spend a lot of time calming down, and then even more time 'psyching herself up' for the test.

'Do you want me to talk you through a breathing exercise?' I asked.

'No. I just need a moment. That's all.'

So, while Bethany sat on her bed with her eyes closed, I sat on my bed and read through the instructions and supplementary information. It seemed straightforward enough. Urinate on the stick, wait two minutes, observe the result. According to Google, the test was 99 per cent accurate when used correctly. A false positive was slightly more likely than a false negative, but neither was probable; and if we repeated the test, we could reduce the chance of an erroneous result even further – to one in ten thousand.

I relayed this information to Bethany as soon as I'd finished reading, but I'm not certain she was listening. She stayed silent, her eyes still closed.

I tried to think about what I could say to help her, what I'd like to hear in her position. What *I'd* like would be for someone to give me all the relevant information and statistics. Clearly, I was going to have to dig a little deeper.

'Do you want me to come with you?' I asked eventually.

'What . . . to the toilet?'

'Yes.'

'It's going to look weird, isn't it? If someone sees us going into the toilet together. Or coming out.'

I shrugged. I was more used to looking weird than Bethany was. 'It will look worse if you come out in floods of tears. Anyway, Suzi's right: you're extremely pale. You've already thrown up once this evening, so there's our excuse. If anyone sees us coming out, we'll just say I was there to keep your hair out of the toilet bowl while you vomited. Simple.'

Bethany smiled. It was a forlorn smile, but still a smile. 'You're getting good at this. The whole deception thing.'

'Thank you. It's been a steep learning curve.'

Bethany had some trouble urinating, which wasn't all that surprising in the circumstances. I turned to face the door, and after a few moments, she managed to get two samples – one on each stick. We wrapped them in a paper towel and returned to our room, having already decided that checking the results in the toilet was a terrible idea. We passed no one in the corridor, so the vomit story was unnecessary.

'You look,' Bethany said. 'Please. I can't.'

I unfolded the paper towel and saw the results, which were identical, unambiguous.

'You're pregnant,' I said.

I didn't think there was much point trying to soften the blow.

18

A Lack of Sleep

Bethany was calmer than I'd expected her to be. She needed holding for a while, in the aftermath of the test result, and spent some time crying soundlessly on her bed, but later she seemed more in control of her emotions. Mostly, she was just quiet and still; she said she needed time to think, and wasn't ready to talk yet. I used the remainder of the evening, before the phone curfew, to undertake further research online. When Bethany *was* ready to talk, I wanted to ensure I'd gathered all the relevant facts.

As it happened, it was close to midnight the next time she spoke, at which point I was settling down for sleep, having concluded that my support would not be required until the morning. 'Are you still awake?' she whispered. 'I don't think I can sleep. I don't know what to do.'

'You could try imagining a relaxing scene. Or you could—'

'No. I mean I don't know what to *do*. I'm completely lost.'

I was not altogether surprised by this. I switched my bedside lamp back on. 'We should talk about it. Talking about it will help to clarify your thoughts.'

'Are you OK with that? It's pretty late.'

'I don't mind. But you'll have to speak up a bit. I can barely hear you.'

'Phoebe, it's nearly midnight. I'm not speaking up.' Bethany got out of bed and came over. 'Move up.'

I wasn't certain how I felt about this. Bethany *had* got into my bed before, but that had been in junior school, when we'd been away from home for the first time. It hadn't been so awkward then. For a start, she hadn't taken up so much space. My bed was only just able to accommodate both of us.

I waited until she was settled next to me, then said: 'Are you going to tell Will?'

'I have to, don't I?'

'Technically, no. There's no legal requirement for you to inform him.'

'Jesus, Phoebe.'

'That doesn't mean you shouldn't tell him,' I clarified. 'You probably should. It's his problem too, and it's certainly not fair for you to go through it on your own.'

We were both silent for a while.

'What about your parents?' I asked.

'They'd make me have it. You know that, don't you? If I tell them, my life's basically over.'

I was shocked by this. Not by Bethany's parents' stance on abortion, since I knew this was the general stance of the Church of England, but by Bethany's belief that they could force her to continue a pregnancy against her wishes. 'No one can make you do anything!' I told her. 'There's only one person who gets a choice here. One and a half if you include Will.'

'Phoebe, please. Will isn't half a person.'

'That's not what I meant,' I said, even though it was, to a small extent. 'My point is that he doesn't get to decide either, not in the same sense that you do. Legally and morally, your choice is the one that matters.'

'You don't understand,' Bethany said, very quietly. 'They might not be able to literally force me, but . . . fuck, as far as they're concerned, I'd be committing murder. They'd disown me.'

'I don't think they can do that until you're eighteen.'

'So they'd just never talk to me again. It amounts to the same thing. Our relationship would be over.'

I didn't know if this was true or not. In usual circumstances, I'd have assumed that Bethany knew her parents and their opinions far better than I did, but it was possible that her judgement was being clouded by emotion. Bethany's parents weren't monsters – they were pleasant people who held some common but erroneous beliefs about the nature of reality. And however strong their convictions were, I couldn't envisage them ever disowning her. Nevertheless, I thought it better to guide the conversation back to firmer, simpler ground.

'Do you want to have a baby?' I asked.

Bethany didn't hesitate here. 'Of course I don't!'

'Do you believe an embryo has a soul?'

'I don't think *I* have a soul.'

She was getting agitated. I reached across and put my hand on her arm. 'You do have a soul, just not an immortal soul. You have a soul in the sense that you're a human being with a subjective experience of personhood. The thing that makes you *you*. But an embryo doesn't have this. The scientific consensus is that consciousness doesn't arise until the later stages of pregnancy. Even basic experiences like pain don't exist until after twenty-four weeks. The necessary brain structures and connections don't exist before then.'

'You're saying I should just get rid of it? Just like that. Like it never happened?'

'I'm not saying you should do anything. But you can't make

an informed decision unless you understand the science, and the science says an embryo has less capacity to suffer than a farmyard chicken. Probably zero capacity. From a moral standpoint, early term abortion should be less controversial than eating a KFC.'

From the silence that followed, I suspected that Bethany was shocked by this statement. But it was the logical conclusion to draw once you'd discounted all religious objections. I started to elaborate on this point, but didn't get very far before Bethany cut me off.

'Phoebe, I understand what you're saying, and it's not that I disagree with you. It's just . . . You weren't raised on this stuff. The soul, sin, Judgement Day – these are completely abstract concepts to you, aren't they? Trust me, it's a bit different when you've spent most of your life believing in them. I mean, really believing.'

'Yes, but you don't believe anymore. That's what you said: you don't believe a word of it.'

'No, I don't. I honestly don't. And I'm still scared – that's the ridiculous thing. I'm scared of things that I don't even believe in. Does that sound completely insane?'

I didn't have to think about this too long. 'No. You can be scared of something that poses no rational threat. Like house spiders, for example. I think the important thing is not to be ruled by those fears. You can't let a phobia influence a decision this big.'

Several more minutes passed before Bethany said: 'You know what you told me earlier, about medical confidentiality?'

'It applies for as long as you want it to,' I told her. 'A doctor might encourage you to tell your parents, but they can't force you. No one can.'

Bethany sat up in bed, holding her head in her hands. 'I can't actually keep this from them, can I? I can't. It's impossible.'

'It will be difficult,' I told her, 'but it's not impossible. It just requires careful planning and execution. We should contact a medical professional for further advice. We can do it tomorrow if you like, after school.'

'Slow down! I need time to think. I can't make a decision just like that.'

'This isn't a decision,' I pointed out. 'It's information gathering. And the earlier you do it, the more time you'll have to consider every option.'

We continued talking for some time after that, but mostly, it was just covering the same ground again and again. Bethany needed a lot of reassurance. Eventually, though, the gaps in the conversation grew larger. Her breathing became more regular, and she fell asleep, still in my bed. I briefly considered moving to hers, before realising Bethany might sleep better if I stayed put. Moreover, I'd got used to her being there. It no longer felt so uncomfortable; all things considered, it felt strangely pleasant.

The next morning was predictably intense. Having advised Bethany that she probably shouldn't, I fuelled up on an insane amount of coffee. In the end, I'd slept for less than three hours, and this had left me edgy, irritable, and in desperate need of some time out – which I knew I wasn't going to get. Bethany was still holding herself together, but her uncharacteristic behaviour was starting to draw a lot of attention. Twice that morning, I found myself cornered by our peers: first by Jessica Chapman at break time, and later by Emily McPherson, as I tried to retrieve books from my locker. Both wanted to know if something was 'up' with Bethany. I didn't have the capacity to allay their concerns, and simply told them that I'd noticed nothing unusual in Bethany's demeanour. They seemed to find my claim plausible. It was an unusual but welcome payoff of being seen as socially useless.

By lunchtime, I could no longer cope without ten minutes on my own. I took my sandwich outside and put my headphones on, having been assured by Bethany that she could survive without me in the dining hall. I listened to the first six minutes of 'Ghost Love Score' with my eyes closed, at which point, someone started tapping me on the shoulder. It was Will. I considered shutting my eyes again – just blanking him completely. But Will was the kind of idiot who'd remove my headphones himself, and if he touched me, I thought I might have a meltdown.

I stopped the music. 'What do you want? What do you *want*? Make it quick!'

Will held up his hands. 'Jesus! Is there something going round at the moment?'

'I don't know what you mean. Tell me what you mean or leave me alone.'

'Bethany's acting weird,' Will said. 'And now you're biting my head off for no reason.'

'You've just ruined an otherwise perfect song,' I told him. 'That's my reason.'

'Well, I won't bother asking what you were listening to,' Will sneered.

I glared at him. 'Shut up, Will. What's wrong with Bethany?'

'You tell me. She's been super-distant all week. If I try to talk to her, I'm lucky to get a one-word response.'

'She's recovering from a minor illness. Apart from that, she's been completely normal.'

'Bullshit. She's been anything but normal.'

I shrugged. 'We'll agree to disagree.'

'Don't you care? You're supposed to be her friend.'

'I *am* her friend. And I know her far better than you do. She's been ill, she's otherwise fine. Just get off her case!'

'What's that supposed to mean? I'm not on her case! Is that what she's said?'

'She's said nothing. We spend zero time talking about you.'

Will spluttered theatrically. 'Right. *Right.* So why are you both being so moody? What is it, synchronised periods?'

'Fuck you, Will! Firstly, that's a myth. Secondly . . . fuck you!'

I walked away.

Once I was sure he wasn't following, I messaged Bethany: *I need to see you. Athletics track – it's urgent! Use the side exit to avoid Will.*

Bethany caught up with me at a jog, a few minutes later. 'What happened?' she asked, breathlessly. 'What's the matter with Will?'

'He came to talk to me. I shouted at him. Then I texted you.'

'You shouted at him? Why did you shout at him?'

'He was being a dick. That's not important. I think you need to tell him.'

'I know I need to tell him. It's just . . . shit! How do I even start that conversation?'

'He knows something's wrong. He's not a *complete* idiot.'

We'd stopped walking. Bethany looked at me but didn't say anything.

'Just text him,' I said.

'Text him? Are you insane? I can't tell him I'm pregnant by text!'

'Fine, so tell him to meet us here now. I can tell him for you.'

'No! No, no, no. Absolutely not! It has to be me. I just need some more time.'

'I don't think you've got much more time. You have to tell him *something*.'

'I know!'

'At least if you do it now it will be over with. And it will be on your own terms. He won't force it out of you five minutes before double Maths. This way you'll both have some time to recover before lessons.' I checked my phone. 'Half an hour, to be exact.'

'Half an hour? Shit, Phoebe!'

'It's not ideal,' I admitted. 'But what is right now?'

'Fuck! Fuck, fuck, fuck.' Bethany took her phone out and spent thirty seconds jabbing at the screen with a shaky finger. We waited until it buzzed. 'Oh, crap! He's coming.'

I put my arm around Bethany's shoulder. Will strode into sight a few minutes later. Fortunately he was walking quite quickly, so the wait wasn't as horrendous as it could have been.

I rotated Bethany so that she was facing me, with both my hands on her shoulders. 'OK. You're just going to tell him. No hesitation, like ripping off a plaster. You can do this.'

I turned to face Will. 'Bethany has something to tell you. You need to be quiet and listen.'

True to form, Will started talking straight away, so I raised my voice and spoke over him. 'Will, shut the fuck up! You don't get to talk right now. Bethany: go!'

'I'm pregnant,' Bethany said.

Will didn't say anything. Bethany slumped, then sat down on the damp grass. I crouched behind her and hugged her, because clearly she needed it. Eventually Will sat down too. He leaned forwards and put his head in his hands. 'You're sure?'

Bethany nodded.

'We did a test yesterday,' I told him.

'Fuck,' Will said.

I couldn't think of anything to add to this, and it seemed Bethany couldn't either.

'What are you going to do?' Will asked.

This was the point at which Bethany started sobbing. It was the first time that morning, even though she'd been continuously stressed. I realised that she wasn't going to be able to answer Will's question, regardless of whether or not she knew the answer.

'We're considering the options,' I told him. 'But we'll be sure to keep you informed.' I don't think I said it in a particularly harsh way, but he gave me a look as if I'd spat at him. He got to his feet and took a single step back.

'Look, I need some time to . . . Jesus fucking Christ! How am I supposed to deal with this right now? I can't. It's fucking insane.'

'Well, I'm sorry it's so fucking inconvenient for you!' Bethany screamed.

Will just stood with his mouth open. I hugged Bethany tighter while she continued to cry.

Will tried again. 'Beth, I'm sorry. We can talk . . . later. I'm just . . . I can't think. I need time. So do you.'

He turned and walked away. After a few metres the walk

became a jog, then a sprint. It wasn't a graceful exit, but Bethany did start to calm down once Will was out of sight.

'I'm sorry,' I told her. 'I'm not sure how I thought that was going to play out. But better than that, obviously.'

'No, you were right,' Bethany muttered. 'It was the only way. Like a plaster. At least I know where I stand now.'

'What do you mean?'

She sniffed. 'You heard him. What are *you* going to do? Not we. You.'

'Oh, I see . . . Well, it is your choice, like I've said. Maybe he was just acknowledging that.'

'Is that what you think he meant? Honestly?'

'No. Probably not.'

Bethany shook her head. 'Fuck him. I'm not sure I even want him involved in this. If he wants to run away . . . maybe it's for the best.'

It was hard to argue with this analysis; Will had literally run away, and the situation had improved. The evidence suggested that he was worse than useless, and I did not foresee this changing any time soon. 'I'm still here,' I told Bethany. 'I'm not going anywhere.'

19

Responsible Adult

Having kept his head down for the rest of the afternoon, Will wasn't at school the next two days. Nor had Bethany heard from him. All things considered, this was an excellent outcome, at least in the short term. With Will temporarily out of the picture, Bethany seemed both calmer and stronger. I could tell she was still angry, not far below the surface, but this, too, was an improvement. To my mind, her anger was cleansing; she was no longer continually on the edge of tears, and this meant that she was far more able to think and talk about what came next.

I used my free time to source as much information as I could regarding the abortion process, including several videos made by clinicians, which were readily available online. I made a comprehensive playlist, which Bethany and I were able to watch together on my laptop across consecutive evenings, during the time set aside for homework or private study. There were a few instances when I had to pause so that Bethany could 'take a moment', but mostly, she was composed and focused. By the time we'd finished all the videos, her mind was made up.

There was a clinic in Newcastle within walking distance of the train station and open seven days a week. The website indicated that, for early pregnancies, it was usually possible to arrange a consultation and treatment on the same day, and the whole appointment should take only a few hours in most circumstances. This, of course, was crucial information, and did much to reassure Bethany. I think she was starting to believe, for the first time, that there really was a way to do this – a way that would not wreck her life. All that remained was to speak to a clinician.

Bethany arrived at my house just after nine o'clock on the Saturday morning, by which time, Daddy had left for work and I had finished reading through a 145-page PDF entitled 'The Care of Women Requesting Induced Abortions'. Since it was aimed at medical personnel, it was extremely thorough, and I now felt confident that I had educated myself as much as I could, given the time constraints.

I made her a decaffeinated coffee and then debriefed her in the living room. Gladys was there and, as always, was tremendously excited to have a visitor. She wagged her tail non-stop for about ten minutes, before settling on the sofa next to Bethany. I think it helped to reduce the tension somewhat.

'The clinician will try to persuade you to talk to your parents,' I told Bethany, as she stroked behind Gladys's ears. 'It's best practice, as advised by the British Medical Association, and she's obliged to do it. However, you are *not* obliged to accept her recommendation. And it won't affect anything going forward. Remember that. She cannot refuse you an appointment.'

Bethany nodded, and I continued.

'She'll advise you that you can and should bring someone with you to the appointment, and she'll probably tell you this should be a trusted female adult. She'll say—'

'Phoebe! What the hell? She'll tell me I have to bring an adult?'

'No. She'll tell you that you *should*. It's not the same. It just makes things far simpler for them if there's a responsible adult involved. It solves a lot of potential issues, such as who's going to look after you and take you home after the treatment.'

'But you'll be there with me, won't you?'

'Of course. But I'm not an adult. They won't automatically accept that I'm able to provide adequate support.' Bethany was looking increasingly anxious, but unfortunately there was more. 'I won't be allowed to go with you into the clinic either,' I told her. 'I can stay in the waiting room, but they'll only let an adult accompany you for the assessment and procedure. I'm sorry. It's not a legal requirement, but it seems to be a red line for the clinic. If you want someone with you throughout, it can't be me.'

'But it has to be you! I want you there!'

'We can ask. But it seems highly unlikely that they'll allow it.'

Bethany sat with her head in her hands for a few moments, then said: 'What if you *were* eighteen?'

'Then it would be fine, obviously. Everything would be much easier.'

She gave me a look which I failed to interpret, before rolling her eyes. 'What if we say you're eighteen? Are they going to demand proof?'

'Oh . . . I don't know. But they might. I mean, I don't think I look eighteen.'

'It's just presentation. Seriously, give me half an hour to do your hair and makeup. You can pass for eighteen, no question.'

'But it isn't necessary. You do understand that? There's

nothing legally that means you need to have an adult with you.'

'Phoebe, I want you to be there. Do you think I'll be better off on my own?'

'No, obviously not.'

'And do you think it's a good rule? The one that says you can't be with me in the clinic because you're not eighteen?'

I didn't have to think about this. 'No. It's arbitrary and illogical. Ideally, these things would be judged on a case-by-case basis.'

Bethany gave me another meaningful look and, this time, I got the point.

'You're right. It's a rule that deserves to be circumvented.' I took a big gulp of coffee and reconfigured my mindset. 'OK. So I'm eighteen. No other details have to be significantly changed. We live in the same village and have known each other forever. We go to the same school, but I'm in the Sixth Form. I'm responsible and reliable.' I drained the rest of my coffee, set the cup on the table, and took out my phone. 'That means I should be the one to make the call. Assuming you're ready?'

'You're sure? I mean, I can do it. It's just . . .'

'I think it makes more sense for me to do it. I'm the responsible adult. I'm sure she'll want to talk to you as well, but I can just pass the phone over when the time comes.'

Bethany closed her eyes and nodded.

'It's not going to be that difficult,' I told her. 'They'll want some background information. They'll want to make sure you understand your options. Remember: their job is to help you, not to throw up barriers.'

'How are you so good at this?' Bethany asked.

I shrugged. 'I've done my research and know what to say.

It's like following a script. I'm only likely to get into trouble if she tries to make small talk.'

This last was a small joke, intended to help Bethany relax, and it seemed to fulfil its purpose. She gave a tiny smile.

'Are you ready?' I asked.

Our advisor was called Michelle and she was professional, kind and easy to talk to. I summarised the situation and she took some notes on Bethany's date of birth, location, general health and so forth, along with some more basic information about me. I confirmed that we had done a pregnancy test and the result had been positive. No problems occurred until we got on to the subject of Bethany's parents.

'Do you think she'd be willing to speak with me about it?' Michelle asked.

'Yes, but she won't change her mind. Her parents are religious and hold views incompatible with abortion.'

'Her parents can't force her to have the baby. It's very important that Bethany understands that.'

'She does understand.' I didn't want there to be any doubt about this, so I quoted for Michelle the relevant section from the British Medical Association guidelines. '"A parent's refusal to give consent for a termination cannot override the consent of a competent young person." Correct?'

'Yes, that's it exactly. Are you a medical student?'

'No. I did some background reading.'

There was a short pause down the line. 'You said Bethany's parents have religious objections to abortion?'

'Yes.'

'And these objections would prevent them from supporting Bethany's decision?'

'Yes. Absolutely. Bethany believes that telling them would cause irreversible damage to their relationship. She thinks it would ruin her parents' lives. It's quite possible she's right.'

'Phoebe, I can honestly say that things are almost never as bad as that. The number one concern for most parents is their daughter's wellbeing. Everything else is secondary.'

'Bethany's father is a Church of England vicar,' I told Michelle. 'So things might be different in this instance.'

There was another notable silence.

'Would it be OK if I spoke to Bethany?' Michelle asked. 'Does she feel ready to do that?'

I looked at Bethany, who gave me the smallest of nods. I handed the phone over.

Bethany spoke to Michelle for another ten minutes, and during that time, she started to look noticeably calmer. The conversation was mostly about Bethany's feelings. There was some further discussion about the circumstances with Bethany's parents, but once Bethany had reiterated that she had no intention of telling them, the subject was quietly dropped. At the end of the call, an appointment was made for the following Saturday at 10.30 a.m. An initial consultation, followed by treatment if Bethany decided to proceed. I would be allowed to accompany her.

After we'd hung up, Bethany cried for at least ten more minutes. But this time, they were definitely tears of relief.

20

The Plan

I don't usually nap, but that afternoon I did. I slept for two straight hours, and when I woke up, I felt refreshed and alert. I started working on a checklist of all the things that had to happen before next weekend's appointment. My revision schedule was of course taking quite a big hit, and had been all week, but there wasn't much to be done about that. At the moment, helping Bethany was pretty much a full-time project.

The following morning, I collected her from her house and we walked up to the castle. It was closed because it was out of season, and it was early enough that there weren't a lot of people out walking; many of our neighbours would be at the church, listening to Reverend Collins's Sunday service. Bethany still attended most weeks, but she assured me that her parents did not mind her missing the odd one, and it wasn't going to arouse any undue suspicion. This was good as we were both keen to press on with our planning at the earliest opportunity. I had spent the time since breakfast working out a mental agenda for the various issues we needed to discuss.

'First, we need a viable excuse,' I told Bethany. 'Something that's going to give us the flexibility to be away all day, and possibly into the early evening. Obviously, the cinema is a tried and tested alibi. Unless you can think of something better?'

'Cinema and shopping,' Bethany said. 'My parents think I'm too stressed out over my exams, so I doubt they'll object to me taking a day off. They'd probably encourage it! We need to pick you up some clothes too. Nothing drastic. I'm thinking smart jeans, a top that isn't a hoodie. Do you own any normal shoes?'

'You know exactly what I own. I have my school shoes, my running shoes and these.' I gestured at my walking boots. 'I'd classify all three as perfectly normal.'

'You don't own any casual shoes,' Bethany said. 'That's all I meant. We'll be able to pick up something suitable for under twenty quid in Tesco. It doesn't have to be high fashion. It just has to work with what we're going for: you need to look like a normal eighteen-year-old girl who buys her own clothes.'

'I *do* buy my own clothes!'

'Phoebe, I'm not having a go, honestly. In usual circumstances I'd say wear whatever the hell you want to and good for you. But these aren't usual circumstances. Trust me. You need to look a couple of years older and different shoes will help. And a handbag. I'm guessing you don't have a handbag hidden away somewhere?'

'You know I don't! Anyway, how are we going to have time for shopping? We need to get to the train station by nine o'clock. Michelle said we should be prepared to be at the clinic all day if necessary. All day! We do not have time to buy me clothes!'

Bethany didn't reply to this straightaway. Our walk had taken us around the north face of the castle and towards the walled garden, which appeared similarly empty. We went inside and sat on the bench.

'OK, I have an idea,' Bethany said. 'We have to get the train at, like, nine o'clock, right?'

'Twelve minutes past nine,' I said.

'Whatever. We have to be at the station *early*. That's already going to look suspicious. So, what if we stay at school on the Friday evening, instead of going home? Think about it. We say we want to go to town the next day, get permission to leave Boarding on the Saturday morning. My mum can pick us up from Berwick later on in the afternoon. What time's the tide?'

I still found it astonishing that Bethany didn't know the tide times, having lived on Holy Island for fifteen years. Surely everyone else did, since the tides had such a big impact on our daily lives? Plus, they followed a fortnightly pattern that was extremely easy to memorise!

'One twenty,' I said patiently. 'The causeway is clear at four.'

'Perfect. So we can't get picked up any earlier than four thirty, anyway. We can leave school early, go to Tesco before the station, and have a legitimate reason to be away all day. We just have to get my parents to agree.'

I nodded. 'OK. It's a good plan. Have you heard from Will?'

I knew it was a problematic question, but I couldn't see a way to broach it delicately. Better just to blurt it out.

Bethany's face darkened. 'What do you think?'

'I think you should send him a message. Tell him to get his act together and get back to school tomorrow. He at least needs to know what's happening, even if he's not directly involved. Otherwise he's a liability.'

After a moment, Bethany nodded and got her phone out. The message she typed was short and angry.

'How do you feel?' I asked, once she'd hit send.

'Weirdly better,' she said.

Will *was* at school the next day. We had a mock Maths exam in the morning, but the three of us met up at lunchtime at the athletics track, which was predictably deserted. I'd reached the conclusion that no one at school was interested in athletics, at least not in January.

Bethany gave Will a brief synopsis of her intentions, and he became immediately less tense.

'I think you're doing the right thing,' he said. 'I mean, you can't keep it, obviously.'

'You can keep it if you want to,' I told Bethany. 'You can change your mind right up to the procedure.'

'Whoa, hang on a second!' Will stopped walking and made the Time Out signal with his hands. 'What are you saying? You're not seriously suggesting she does? It's insane!'

'Of course it is. But it's Bethany's decision. It's not your place to tell her what she can or can't do.'

'It's not your place, either! This doesn't even involve you.'

It was gratifying that Bethany intervened at this point. 'Will, you don't get to shut Phoebe down. *She*'s been here for me from the start. She's involved and she stays involved. It's what I want.'

'But you're not actually thinking of keeping it, are you? You're not changing your mind?'

'Of course I'm not! That wasn't the point Phoebe was making. Can we just try to get through this without you two tearing each other apart?'

Will exhaled noisily, then held up his hands. 'Look, I realise I've been a bit useless. I know that, OK?'

Bethany stayed silent.

'You've been worse than useless,' I said.

'Fine! I've been worse than useless. I think it's kind of understandable in the circumstances, but let's forget that for now.' Will closed his eyes and took another deep breath. 'Do you want me to come with you?' he asked.

'No,' said Bethany.

'Definitely not,' I agreed. 'I imagine you'd be in the way.'

Will did not look offended. Mostly, he looked relieved. 'What about money?' he asked.

'What about money?' Bethany replied flatly.

'Well, someone has to pay for it, right?'

'Will, it's not 1946,' I told him. 'The NHS pays, obviously. It's healthcare.'

'All right. It wasn't obvious to me.'

'We don't need money,' Bethany said.

'He could cover travel costs,' I pointed out. Bethany gave me a look. 'What? Frankly, it's the least he can do.'

Bethany shrugged and turned back to Will. 'You can pay the travel costs.'

'Right, good. Great. How much?'

Bethany didn't answer. For some reason, she looked extremely upset again. To my mind, this was the first instance of Will actually being helpful.

'It's probably easiest if we just invoice you afterwards,' I told him.

Will shook his head and muttered something inaudible. I don't know why. His father worked in finance, so presumably he understood what an invoice was. He looked at Bethany. 'You will tell me if there's anything else you need, won't you? I realise this situation is completely fucked up, but . . . Well, I am still here. I'll do what I can.'

Bethany nodded but said nothing. She still looked upset, but as far as I was concerned, things had gone quite well. Certainly better than the last meeting.

21

Cinema and Shopping

It was a strange week, though not as strange, nor as difficult, as the one before – not by a long stretch. We weren't boarding again until Friday, which meant that I got some respite every evening, with access to my punch bag and trampoline, and Gladys and the garden, and all the other things that helped me to stay on an even keel. It was somewhat harder for Bethany, of course, being at home with her parents and trying to act normally, although the fact that we were in the middle of our mock exams did help, in all sorts of ways. Not only did it provide the justification for her appearing stressed, but it also gave her a ready-made excuse to lock herself away in her room for hours on end. Nevertheless, by the end of the week, the cumulative pressure was clearly taking a heavy toll. Shockingly, this was one context where Will proved himself to be not one hundred per cent useless. At the very least, he was another person to mouth the lie, when anyone at school asked, that Bethany was completely fine. It was just exam stress, nothing more.

We were awake before six on Saturday.

'When's the earliest we can leave?' Bethany asked.

'It will be light enough around quarter to eight,' I told her. 'I mean, it's still going to look weird that early, but less weird than if we tell Suzi we're leaving while it's still dark.'

Bethany nodded. 'We might as well get you ready, then.'

She started by ironing my hair with straighteners and putting it back in a simple black band. This was the easy part. Afterwards, she made me sit in my desk chair and angled the lamp at my face. The atmosphere was that of an interrogation.

Despite her claim that I had 'good skin', Bethany applied cosmetics across the full surface of my face. And not just once; there were multiple layers.

'What on earth are you doing?' I asked, after the first ten minutes. 'Why is it taking so long? Your makeup doesn't usually take this long!'

'Relax. I'm contouring. It will bring out your cheekbones.'

'My cheekbones? Bethany, that's absurd! We're attending a medical procedure, not a beauty pageant.'

'You need to stay still. Otherwise it will take even longer.'

'But you're losing sight of the goal! I'm supposed to look like a responsible adult. What kind of responsible adult wears a tonne of makeup to the abortion clinic?'

'Phoebe, relax – seriously! You're not going to look like you're wearing a tonne of makeup, not if you stay still and let me blend. You have to trust me on this. I know what I'm doing.'

I stayed in the chair for another twenty minutes. My eyebrows were darkened and filled in with a pencil. My eyes themselves were subjected to four different cosmetic procedures, with Bethany insisting that the overall effect would be subtle. Subtle! My several requests for a mirror were ignored until Bethany had painted my lips, at which point she decreed that I was finally ready.

It's hard to explain what had happened.

The face looking back at me in the mirror was *my* face, but it wasn't a face I'd ever seen before. My skin looked warmer and my cheeks less rounded. Astonishingly, my eyes did not look overdone, but their shape had been subtly altered and better defined. My whole face was better defined – cleaner and sharper, as if I was suddenly seeing myself in a higher resolution.

'I look . . .' I didn't have the words to finish.

'You look great,' Bethany said.

'I wasn't expecting it.'

'Yeah, thanks. I got that.'

'I look like a woman.'

'That's the general idea.'

'I mean, I always thought makeup served no practical purpose, but this is actually . . .' My stomach suddenly lurched. 'We should leave as soon as possible. No one can see me like this! People will stare!'

'Phoebe, it's not even seven yet. Who gets up before seven on a Saturday? We can have breakfast and leave in forty-five minutes. Stick to the plan.'

'Suzi will see me. Suzi's always up early. Plus, we have to tell her when we're leaving. It's a fire regulation!'

'OK, calm down. Honestly, it's just a bit of makeup. I doubt she'll even say anything.'

'Phoebe, you're wearing makeup!' Suzi said, when we went through to the common room ten minutes later. This was the first thing she said. Not good morning. I couldn't think of a sensible response, so I said: 'Yes. I wear makeup now.'

Bethany laughed, and it wasn't even a fake laugh. It was the first genuine laugh I'd heard from her since before Christmas.

'It looks nice!' Suzi added quickly. 'I'm sorry, I didn't mean to embarrass you; I just wasn't expecting it. You look so different!'

'Older,' Bethany said. 'She looks older, don't you think?'

'She does, definitely.' Suzi's expression turned more serious. 'What is it you're seeing at the cinema?'

I didn't wait for Bethany to fail to remember. 'We're seeing *The Favourite*. It's a dark historical comedy about Queen Anne. Olivia Colman's performance is supposed to be outstanding.'

'Right. And what rating has it got?'

'Ninety-one per cent on Metacritic. The *Telegraph* said—'

Bethany interrupted. 'It's a fifteen, Suzi. You can check if you like.'

'And it's just the two of you going?'

'Yes, of course,' Bethany said.

Suzi held up her hands. 'I'm not accusing you of anything. And I certainly don't want to pry . . .'

At this point I caught up with the subtext. 'You're not prying,' I told Suzi. 'You're *in loco parentis*, and entitled to ask. But I can confirm the film we're seeing is age-appropriate.'

Suzi nodded, apparently satisfied. 'When are you leaving? You'll stay for breakfast?'

'We'll probably just grab some toast and leave early,' Bethany said. 'Phoebe wants to walk to the station.'

Suzi did a double-take. 'You're walking? Isn't it a bit of a long way?'

'It's three and a half miles,' I told her. 'It will be good exercise.'

'Jesus Christ,' Bethany said, once we'd eaten our toast and left the building. 'We're walking for an hour to catch a train to see a film about Queen Anne. Do you realise how ludicrous that story is?'

'Suzi believed it,' I pointed out.

'Suzi believed it because it came from you,' Bethany said. 'From anyone else it would sound completely insane.'

We weren't really going to walk all the way to the station because, unfortunately, we didn't have time. I'd called a taxi from our room and it drove us to the Tesco Superstore.

In the clothing department, Bethany picked me out some black calf-length boots with a faux-fur trim to go with the skinny jeans and winter coat she'd lent me. She found a crossbody bag for five pounds and a ribbed grey top reduced to nine, which she insisted would work better with my new look than my perfectly serviceable jumper. And when I viewed myself in the full-length mirror, I had to concede that she was right.

For the first time in my life, I looked sophisticated. I was a version of myself I barely recognised.

We arrived in Newcastle just before ten and followed Google Maps to a left luggage facility not far from the station. Here I deposited a carrier bag containing my running shoes and old jumper, since we'd agreed it would be a hindrance at the appointment and might look incongruous.

The abortion clinic was located on the third floor of an unattractive building on an unattractive road crammed with noisy traffic and squat, uniform office blocks. After speaking to the receptionist, we went through to a small waiting room, where Bethany completed her medical history form with a slightly shaky hand. There were three other women already in the room, along with two male support persons. I placed the women's ages at approximately twenty-two, twenty-seven and forty. Bethany was the only teenage pregnancy.

'I feel like everyone's looking at us,' she whispered. 'Or at *me*.'

I doubted this was actually the case, but glanced around again to check. One of the women had her eyes closed, one was gazing at the door back through to reception, and one was reading a magazine. Both of the men were staring fixedly at their shoes. 'No one's looking at us,' I whispered back. 'If anything, I'd say they're actively avoiding looking.'

The initial stage of the consultation, in which Bethany discussed her options with the pregnancy counsellor, lasted about ten minutes, and much of this involved talking about appropriate emotional support, which was a euphemism for telling her parents. After Bethany had laid out the facts in sufficient detail, the counsellor conceded that her family situation was somewhat unusual, and the argument for disclosure was not straightforward.

A medical assessment followed, in several stages and involving three different clinicians. A nurse went through Bethany's medical history, ran a blood test, swabbed for STIs, and discussed the pros and cons of various contraceptives. A sonographer did an ultrasound to confirm the pregnancy and estimate the gestational age, which was approximately nine weeks – consistent with Bethany's belief that her last period had occurred in the third week of November. Finally, a doctor assessed her to make sure that she understood the treatment options and was capable of giving informed consent.

The two treatment options were familiar to both of us from the videos we'd watched the previous week. Bethany could either take the 'abortion pill' – actually two sets of pills, one in the clinic and one at home – or she could have a vacuum aspiration, where the foetus would be removed by suction using a small vaginal pump. On the face of it, the first option sounded preferable, but we'd already discounted it since it meant Bethany would have to manage her induced miscarriage at home, which would be an additional stress. The vacuum option may have been more invasive, but it did mean Bethany could go home this afternoon knowing that it was all over.

The process began as soon as Bethany had signed her consent form. She was booked into theatre, given a pre-operative medication to dilate her cervix, and we were taken through to a new waiting room. She had to change into a hospital gown, but after that, there was nothing else to do. We sat and we waited for Bethany's cervix to dilate.

The ninety minutes passed remarkably quickly, given that there was nothing to fill it. My memory is that Bethany had her eyes closed almost the whole time. We didn't speak, and I decided that I didn't want to do anything else. I left my book in my bag and my phone in my pocket.

Bethany had opted to have the termination awake – not because she wanted to be awake, but because we couldn't risk missing our train home. All things being equal, I'm certain that she would have preferred to have been completely oblivious while the abortion was performed. Instead, she had to settle for a local anaesthetic and sedatives, though the doctor had assured us that this would take away any anxiety during the procedure; there was even a chance that Bethany would not remember it afterwards, as some short-term memory loss was a known side-effect of sedation. This was clearly the ideal outcome as far as Bethany was concerned. Then it really would be like it never happened.

She was taken away for less than twenty minutes. I had enough time to lose a game of chess against my phone before a nurse took me through to the recovery lounge. Bethany was there already, in a reclining chair, looking relaxed. That was the first thing I noticed; I hadn't seen her looking relaxed for at least a fortnight. I went over and sat on the arm of her chair, before realising that I didn't know if I was allowed to, and then realising that I didn't care. Bethany kind of flopped her head against my shoulder, as if I were a pillow, and I stroked her hair, thinking this was probably what the situation called for.

'How are you feeling?' I asked.

'Happy,' she said. 'I feel happy.'

22

Not Normal

Half an hour later, she was discharged. She was no longer groggy, no longer slurring her words, and no longer pregnant. It felt like a small miracle, even to me. It was eleven days ago that she'd had the positive test result, but it seemed like a month.

We walked back to the station via the left luggage facility, arm in arm. Bethany still felt happy, even after the drugs had worn off.

'I feel light,' she told me. 'Honestly, I feel as if I've been carrying a literal brick around in my stomach for the last month. And now it's gone. That's how I feel.'

It was curious. Under normal circumstances, I'd have queried the use of literal in this statement. I'd have told her that a nine-week foetus was about the size and weight of an olive, so the suggestion that it had felt like a literal brick was dubious at best. And yet I said none of this. Not out of tact, but because in that moment, I could see how it might even be true.

'Have you texted Will?' I asked.

'Not yet. I just want to enjoy not thinking about him for a bit longer. Anyway, it won't hurt him to sweat for a bit.'

While I could see the appeal of this, I told Bethany she should do it sooner rather than later. For some reason, I had in my mind the story of Theseus and his father: Theseus sails to Crete on a ship with black sails, but promises his father that he'll replace them with white sails on his return. That way his father will know that his son has survived the Labyrinth, killed the Minotaur and is coming home. Except the inevitable happens. In the chaos of his escape, Theseus forgets to change the sails. His father sees the black sails from the cliff top and throws himself into the sea.

I did not think Will was likely to throw himself into the sea, but it would be wrong to make him suffer just for the sake of it.

'I'll text him when we get to the station,' Bethany told me. 'Then he can forget this ever happened.'

'What about you?' I asked.

'I can forget *Will* ever happened.'

'Oh.' I didn't know what else to say to this. It was a policy I was delighted to support, but it seemed a little optimistic, given that she was still going to see him at school five days a week. 'Is it definitely over, then? Is that how Will feels, too?'

'What do you think?'

'I don't know. That's why I'm asking.'

'Well, he's not here, is he? I think that says it all.'

'You did tell him not to come,' I pointed out.

'If he cared about me, he'd be here. He'd have *wanted* to be here. Like you did. Seriously, what would you have done if I'd told you not to come? Would you have just accepted it?'

'No. I'd have written you a ten-page essay arguing my case. But I'm possibly not normal in this respect.'

Bethany looked at me for a long time. 'I'm glad you're not "normal". You're perfect the way you are.'

I blushed, obviously.

*

The train back was much busier, but because it was the service that ran almost the full length of the country, from Penzance to Glasgow, it had about ten carriages and plenty of spare seats. Bethany and I found two next to each other and I spent the first portion of the journey removing my makeup with a pack of wipes.

'You don't have to if you don't want to,' Bethany told me. 'You can leave it on.'

'Aren't you worried about your mum asking questions?'

'I'm not really worried about anything anymore. I can just tell her I gave you a makeover.'

'I think she'd find that highly suspicious. You shouldn't get complacent.'

'I'm not. It's just . . . God, it actually feels like this is over now. I'm still getting used to that. It seemed impossible a few days ago.'

The clinic had provided Bethany with information and contact numbers to take away with her, in case she needed any follow-up counselling or other aftercare. It seemed unlikely, but I made her copy the numbers into her phone, under a fake contact name, in case of an emergency. I did the same, and the paper copies went into the rubbish bin. I put the condoms she'd been provided with in the zip pocket on the inside of my new bag. Bethany insisted that she wasn't planning on needing them any time soon, but I thought it was best if I had them ready to dispense in an emergency.

'Will they be safe there?' Bethany asked. 'I mean . . . well, you know what I mean.'

'They'll be safe. There's no likely scenario where Daddy would be rummaging through my bag. And, anyway, I can't imagine it being a big deal if he found them.'

'Wouldn't it raise a few questions? I mean, I thought you told him you might be asexual.'

'*Might* be. He knows I like to be prepared for every eventuality.'

Bethany shook her head. 'You know, I envy what you've got with your dad. It's ... so honest, so straightforward. I don't think I'll ever have that with my parents.'

I didn't know how to respond to this statement. It made me sad on Bethany's behalf, but I couldn't think of anything to say to make her feel better. I appreciated that I was very lucky with Daddy; he was perfect and our relationship was perfect. But acknowledging this out loud wasn't going to help much in the circumstances.

After a while, Bethany reached out and placed a hand on mine. I wondered if all this physical contact was going to be a permanent feature of our friendship now; it seemed like it might be. 'Do you know one of the worst things in all this?' she asked.

I shook my head.

'As much as I feel like I've betrayed my parents, gone against their values and everything they tried to teach me . . .' She had to stop for a moment to brush a tear from her eye. 'As much as I feel that, there's another part of me that feels like I'm the one who's been betrayed by them. And I know that makes no sense on the face of it, because if I'd just stuck to their rules, I wouldn't have ended up in this colossal mess, but . . . God, I don't know. Maybe it's wrong to think like this, but it's as if my life has been confined to this very narrow channel and I've never been allowed to step outside of that. But perhaps if I had, everything would have been different. I'd have been able to find my own way a bit better. Does that make any sense to you?'

There was a lot to consider here, so it took me a while to unpick. 'I think so. You're saying that if your upbringing had been less prescriptive, if you'd been given a bit more freedom, then the situation with Will might have played out differently. You'd have been in a better position to make good choices?'

'Yes! That's it exactly! At the very least, I'd have had the chance to do things differently, without all the lies and sneaking around, without feeling so unsure of myself all the time.'

This came as a big surprise. 'That's how you felt? Unsure of yourself?'

'Next to Will, I did.' Bethany gave a small shrug. 'Well, you know what he's like. Mr I've-lived-in-New-York-and-Singapore-and-had-all-these-experiences-you-can't-even-imagine. Meanwhile, I've done precisely nothing. I suppose it just made me feel like I had something to prove – that I wasn't just this . . . child who's led the most boring and sheltered life ever.'

Bethany broke off, blushing deeply.

'Did you ever tell Will any of that?' I asked after a moment.

'Of course not. That's the point, isn't it? It's hard to be open like that when you're so afraid of being judged. Of failing to meet someone else's expectations.'

'You told *me*.'

'That's because you're the one person I know won't judge me. Or not like that. You just accept me as I am and don't ask for anything more.'

I didn't know what to say to this either. But in this case, I think saying nothing was OK. It felt like the conversation had reached its natural conclusion.

We arrived back in Berwick about half an hour later. Before we went through the ticket barrier, Bethany stopped to give me a hug. It lasted approximately two minutes, with neither of us saying a word, and it wasn't even a little bit uncomfortable. I closed my eyes and, in all honesty, I felt as good as I'd ever felt.

Mrs Collins was waiting for us in the car park. Bethany spoke to her and laughed and smiled. I gave her a brief synopsis of *The Favourite*, based on what I'd read about it online. In the back of the car, Bethany reached over and slipped her hand into mine. And on the surface, everything remained completely innocuous.

On the Monday after the abortion, I delivered Will his invoice. It was lunchtime and he was kicking a rugby ball around with some friends, acting pretty much as Bethany had predicted he would: as if he didn't have a care in the world. I was quite prepared to march into the middle of the game, but I didn't have to. As soon as he saw me, he came over.

We walked a short distance away, out of earshot and using the trees as a screen. From the whispering going on in the corridors, I'd deduced that most people realised that Bethany and Will were finished, and those who didn't would know soon enough. Yet the need for discretion had obviously not disappeared; I did not plan to go waving the abortion invoice around in a public setting.

As far as I could see, there was now only one path to the truth coming out, and that was through one of us saying something – me, Bethany or Will. I was sure about me and Bethany, and Bethany was sure about Will. 'Trust me,' she'd said earlier that morning, 'Will can keep his mouth shut when it's in his own interest. He's already proven that.' On reflection, I thought this was likely correct. Will had been running from the consequences of his actions from the moment he learned of them; I assumed his number one goal was still to get out of this with as little fallout as possible.

He looked at the invoice for just a few seconds before nodding and putting it in his pocket. It contained only the figures alongside one-word summaries of what they were for: train, taxi, lockers. I hadn't charged him for my new clothes (even though one could argue they were an allowable expense), and I had the relevant receipts and tickets at the ready should he ask for them. Which he did not.

'Listen, Phoebe,' he said. 'Thanks for helping out with this.'

'Oh, you're *welcome*,' I told him. I'm not usually adept at projecting sarcasm in my voice, but on this occasion, I must have succeeded.

Will held up his hands. 'All right. Let's just leave it there, shall we? It was a shitty situation for all of us, and now it's over. Finished.'

I found I couldn't leave it there. He was being too much of a dick. 'For all of us? Was it as shitty for you as it was for Bethany?'

He scowled at me, but said nothing.

'It was a shitty situation for Bethany, one that you made worse.'

'Well, thank God *you* were there to rescue her! And now she can see how great you are and how shit I am. So it's worked out well for you, hasn't it?'

'Yes, it has. It's worked out well for me and well for Bethany.'

It seemed that Will didn't have anything more to say at this point, so I turned and walked away.

As I approached the main entrance to school, I noticed Hu sitting on the steps, reading. I had spoken to him in passing since the incident in the dining hall, when I'd rebuffed his attempt to sit with me, but I knew I hadn't done enough to set things right between us. Now seemed the perfect time, given that it was a day for resolving long-standing issues.

Oddly, I didn't fret about what I was going to say. I did what I suspect Bethany would have done in a similar situation: I just walked over and sat down beside him, without any plan or script.

'Hi, Hu.'

He placed his book open in his lap. 'Hi, Phoebe. What's up?'

'Not much anymore. I just wanted to apologise if I've been a bit standoffish over the last couple of weeks. I had some personal issues I was dealing with and . . . well, I'm not very good at multitasking. I tend to focus all my attention on one area at the expense of everything else. I know it can make me seem aloof and disinterested, but it doesn't mean that's how I actually feel.'

I was aware that it was quite a broad apology, but I hoped that Hu would see it was heartfelt and this would offset any deficiency in my words.

He looked confused for only a moment, then said: 'Anything you want to talk about?'

'Excuse me?'

'The personal issues.' Hu blushed a little. 'I'll understand if you don't, obviously. But I don't mind listening if it would help?'

I was quite taken aback by this. I suppose it just felt very kind and genuine, especially after dealing with Will and his two-facedness. 'Thank you. I appreciate it, honestly, but the matters have been resolved. I just wanted to . . . clear the air.'

And even as I said this, I felt much lighter.

'What are you reading?' I asked after a moment.

Hu showed me the cover. It was a pristine copy of *The Dispossessed* by Ursula K. Le Guin. 'A present from my mum,' he told me. 'She saw that I'd started reading more again and was on it straightaway. Have you read it?'

'No, not that one. I did read *The Left Hand of Darkness* – it's another of hers, about an alien race that can change biological sex, and the implications that has for the society. It's a fascinating concept. There's a copy in the school library, if you're interested . . .' And we sat and talked about books for the next several minutes. The previous term, I'm sure I would have viewed this interaction through the lens of my self-improvement plan – as a notable success to be recorded and filed away for safekeeping. But now, with everything that had happened since Christmas, I found the urge was no longer there. For some reason, it just felt easier to enjoy the conversation in and of itself, without the need to see it as an achievement to be checked off a list.

23

The Mystery Woman Returns

For a while, normality returned.

We finished our mock exams, and when the results came through, they were not disastrous by any means – a little down on what might have been expected by our teachers, but certainly not bad enough to sound any alarm bells. The revision I'd managed to do over Christmas (and in between researching abortions) was sufficient for me to maintain my grades in most subjects, with only Maths, History and Computer Science suffering to any significant degree – Maths and History because they had come on the back of a very intense weekend, and Computer Science because I simply didn't care that much about it, and decided to focus my efforts elsewhere. As for Bethany, there was a more noticeable and general dip in her grades – entirely understandable to the two of us, but a mystery to everyone else, given how hard she'd apparently been working. I think in other circumstances, her parents might have been more concerned than they were; but they knew that Bethany had been stressed during the exam period, and could see how much happier she was now. They were quick to accept her explanation that she'd 'just got a bit too worked-up about everything'.

Bethany and I had always spent a lot of time together, but

it was in the aftermath of the abortion that we started seeing each other every weekend. The fact that we had drawn closer through the ordeal was, I think, obvious to both of us. But beyond this, I also felt that the nature of our friendship had changed significantly over the past few months. It now incorporated a lot more physical closeness – the hugs and hand-holding and arms round the shoulder that had become a feature of our relationship during the period when Bethany had needed so much extra emotional support. This wasn't new ground for Bethany, who already had that sort of relationship with some of her other friends – Jessica and Emily in particular, who had always been quite tactile with her. But for me, it was a novelty. I had never been one for hugs (or not with anyone who wasn't you, Daddy or Gee), so the fact that I could actually enjoy sharing this sort of bond with Bethany, too, was a surprising discovery. Equally surprising was how quickly this started to feel like a natural part of our friendship – something done intuitively, unthinkingly. By the February half-term holiday, I found that I had got so used to being physically close to Bethany, that I missed her when she wasn't there.

Although I continued to attend Chess Club every week, at some point I stopped thinking of it as being part of my self-improvement plan. I suppose my feeling was that I'd taken my self-improvement plan as far as I needed to. My friendship with Bethany was secure, and I felt once more that this was all I really needed. I'd proven to myself that I *could* do things differently, that I could step outside of my comfort zone and explore new social strategies if I chose to. But after months of disruption, months of effort, I decided, for now, I'd rather just enjoy my life as it was. I'd continue to play chess, I'd continue to talk to Hu and exchange books with him periodically, but these things did not have to be part of some overarching scheme to better myself. Since we had our actual GCSEs coming up at the end of spring, this should clearly be my focus.

With this in mind, I suggested to Bethany that our revision should start early this time round – at least two months before our first exam.

'Two *months*?' she queried.

'Yes. I'll draft us a timetable with plenty of built-in breaks and rewards to keep us motivated.'

Bethany looked at me incredulously.

'I'm thinking coffee and cake,' I told her. 'My dad will be happy to donate both. I was also hoping to re-watch all sixty-seven episodes of *Game of Thrones* before Season Eight drops in April.'

'Again? You must have watched them all, like, a hundred times!'

'Four times. They're very compelling. You should watch them too! Honestly, you'll enjoy it. It will make the nine weeks of revision fly by.'

This was (eventually) a winning argument. I drew up our shared timetable, and halfway through March, we put it into action. Bethany complained at first, but I could tell that she wasn't very serious – spreading the revision over such a long period meant that it never felt pressured or intensive, and after the first couple of episodes of *Game of Thrones*, it was obvious that she was hooked. She said that she was happy to keep watching as long as we kept this component of the timetable secret from her parents; she doubted they'd approve of the violence, language, nudity and incest.

This was probably a sensible suggestion, because as things stood, Mrs Collins was a strong and vocal supporter of my quest to get Bethany revising early, especially when I reassured her that my timetable took into account the need for plenty of rest periods to de-stress and avoid burnout. It was the last Sunday of March when she spoke to me privately about how relieved she was that Bethany appeared to be so much happier and calmer this time round.

'You've been a really good influence on her over the past few months,' Mrs Collins said.

'Thank you,' I replied. I was making coffee in the vicarage kitchen at the time, and I didn't know what else to say.

'To be honest, her father and I were more than a little concerned back in January,' Mrs Collins continued. 'She wasn't acting at all like herself.'

'How so?' I asked, being careful to keep my voice steady and my eyes on the task at hand – pouring boiled water over ground coffee beans.

'She seemed very distant,' Mrs Collins elaborated. 'Lethargic, irritable. I mean, I realise that exams can be stressful, but she's never been like that before.'

'Year Eleven has been extremely challenging,' I said. No word of a lie. 'But I think we're very much on top of things now.'

Mrs Collins nodded, beaming at me. 'Yes, I can see that. Just keep on doing what you're doing. It's obviously working.'

'Absolutely,' I agreed.

At the time, it was a nervy conversation to have, but once it was over, I felt reassured that I had handled it well, and whatever worries Mrs Collins had had, they were now in the past. As far as she and Reverend Collins were concerned, their relationship with Bethany was the best it had been since before Christmas.

As for Bethany herself, I suppose there was only one dissatisfaction that persisted in her life – the fact that she couldn't be open with her parents about her loss of faith. Of course, our exam preparation meant that she had an acceptable excuse not to attend church on Sundays for a while, but even with this, the need to pretend was an ongoing struggle. She had admitted this to me on numerous occasions, and most notably on her sixteenth birthday in April, when her parents had bought her a new gold cross to wear around her neck.

'It was hell!' Bethany told me that evening in her room. 'I don't want to be horrible to Mum and Dad, because I know they thought it would be this beautiful, meaningful present that I'd be able to keep forever. But it was so *so* difficult! I just had to sit there with this big grin plastered on my face, hoping they wouldn't see through the lie.'

'It looks nice on you,' I said, trying to help Bethany focus on the positives. 'Honestly, it's very pretty. Can't you just view it like any other piece of jewellery?'

Bethany shook her head sadly. 'It's not just the cross. It's everything. I mean, I still have to pray three times a day, before every meal. I have to take my turn saying grace. It feels like such a sham.'

'Well, at least it doesn't take long,' I reasoned. 'We're talking about seconds, really, aren't we? It's not like it makes up a huge part of your day.'

'Phoebe, you're missing the point. It's not the time it takes. It's the fact that it's always there. I feel like I'm living a lie, day-in, day-out.'

'Oh.' I thought about this statement for a while. 'If it bothers you that much, you should probably tell them. I mean, it's the only alternative, isn't it?'

'I'm not telling them. Do you honestly think it would make things any better?'

'I don't know.'

'It wouldn't. That's what's so frustrating! I can leave things as they are or I can make them worse. Those are my options.'

I didn't know if Bethany's assessment was correct – it was hard to judge from the outside looking in – but I could see why she was reluctant to disrupt the status quo. Given how things had been back in January, her fear of making a bad situation worse was quite understandable.

But at that point, neither of us knew that we were facing a ticking clock. We didn't know that everything was about to fall apart, in a way that neither of us could have imagined.

The beginning of the end was, in retrospect, the day I bumped into Mrs Frost. It was Easter Sunday, just after ten a.m., and I was walking Gladys, taking advantage of the fact that many of the island's visitors would be in church, leaving the lanes and beaches quiet. Bethany, too, had insisted this was one day she absolutely *had* to attend her father's morning service. Easter was by far the most important date in the Christian calendar, and missing it was simply not an option. She'd said that I could come over to hers after lunch, but before then, she'd be gritting her teeth and putting on her 'pious face'.

I'd been walking for about fifteen minutes, contemplating the situation with Bethany and her parents, when I encountered Mrs Frost at Emmanuel Point. She was sitting on one of the benches at the base of the obelisk, looking out to sea. She didn't say anything as I approached, or when I sat down at the other end of the bench with Gladys at my feet. Mrs Frost glanced at Gladys, Gladys wagged her tail, and I decided I wouldn't be the one to break the silence. If Mrs Frost wanted to talk to me, she could. If she didn't, I'd get on with my walk. I discovered, to my surprise, that I did not really mind either way. It was five months since we'd last interacted and I was just interested to see what she'd do.

'Well, Phoebe,' she said after a minute or two had passed, 'how are you?'

'I'm well, thank you.'

'And the writing?'

'It's been on hiatus for a while now. I've had a lot of other stuff going on: Chess Club, exams. Friendship stuff.'

'You didn't strike me as a girl with many friends.'

I hesitated for a moment, wondering if I could legitimately claim that I had friends, plural, now. Hu was sort of a friend, I thought, but it seemed disingenuous to place him in the same category as Bethany, at least as far as this conversation was concerned. 'No. Just the one, really,' I said. 'But we're very close. Her friendship's important to me.'

'More important than your writing?'

'I don't think they're mutually exclusive. The friendship's just taken up more time over the last few months. I plan to get back to the writing with a vengeance come the summer.'

Mrs Frost sniffed but did not enquire further. She glanced at Gladys again and said: 'Does it have a name?'

'Gladys. She's Welsh.'

'I'd have thought you were more of a cat person.'

I shrugged. 'I like cats. I like dogs. I never really got why so many people feel like they have to pick a camp.'

'It's because they have radically different characteristics,' Mrs Frost told me. 'Dogs are pack animals, loyal and eager to please, but requiring continual attention to thrive. Whereas cats are independent and self-contained. They give their affection sparingly and on their own terms. And if they think they can get a better deal elsewhere, they'll up and leave. Just like that.'

I thought about this for a few moments. It was possible that Mrs Frost was being poetical, that her words had layers of meaning beyond the superficial – like when she'd said that most of my classmates would end up as prostitutes. Or it was possible she was just making an accurate observation about cats and dogs. Either way, she was still fun to talk to.

'Dogs were domesticated approximately thirty thousand years before cats,' I told Mrs Frost. 'I saw a documentary about it once. It's thought that their wolf ancestors were attracted to the smells of cooking meat at campfires. So people started feeding them the scraps and bones, and they gradually grew tamer and started living and hunting with the humans. But cats didn't come until people settled down and started farming. Food stores attracted rodents and the rodents attracted the cats. Some anthropologists say the big difference is that while humans domesticated dogs, cats domesticated themselves. I suppose that fits quite well with your thesis. Basically, we invited dogs into our lives, but cats chose to live alongside us of their own initiative.'

Mrs Frost smiled at this. It was notable because Mrs Frost seldom smiled. After a moment she got up from the bench and smoothed out her long skirt. 'Feel free to come over for a coffee sometime,' she said, 'once you're done with the exams.'

That was all.

I watched her walk away, and then I continued down to the beach with Gladys. It was nice to be invited back, but I didn't think I'd go. I didn't think I'd have any real cause to.

I was wrong.

*

It was two weeks later, Sunday 5th May, around ten a.m. Ten days before my first exam. I had just left the coffee shop and was heading home when I saw her. She was coming the other way down the street but was looking at her phone, which was why I thought she hadn't noticed me – although I knew it was also likely that she wouldn't have recognised me anyway. Why would she? We'd talked once, for a couple of minutes almost six months ago, and though it had been memorable for me, on account of her odd behaviour, there was no reason to believe it had been equally memorable for her.

The Mystery Woman.

I didn't think about what I was doing, and I certainly didn't have a plan. I turned and followed her, at a distance of ten metres or so, my heart skipping erratically. Now that tourist season had started again, and since it was a bank holiday weekend, the streets were thick with people, and following her unobtrusively was not difficult. She stopped at the window of the craft shop, but only for a minute, during which time I stood across the lane and waited. It was a sunny morning, cloudless and windless, so I took the opportunity to put on my sunglasses, after which I could stare at her with impunity.

She continued to the next corner and took a right, then another right at the next corner, then another. It obviously made no sense, as she was walking in a circle at this point. But I didn't have time to figure it out. I followed her around the third corner and found her stopped dead, a bare metre away, leaning against the wall with her arms crossed. Looking me straight in the face.

'Are you following me, Phoebe?'

'Yes. I'm following you.' My throat was extremely dry, and my voice sounded strange in my ears, and I didn't know what else to say. I was unprepared, obviously, and in a state of shock.

'Why are you following me?'

I took a deep, shaky breath. 'Because I want to know who you are. You apparently know who I am. And you know my father. You said you were going to wait to talk to him and then you disappeared and never came back. It was an odd thing to do.'

'It was half a year ago,' the woman said, 'and it was nothing. It's certainly not important anymore.'

'Why did you leave?' I pressed. 'You sat down, I asked how you knew my father, and then you left, without any explanation. It was extremely confusing.'

She spoke slowly, in a voice that seemed carefully measured: 'I'm sorry I confused you, Phoebe. I didn't mean to. But it's not something you need to concern yourself with. I used to know your father, I thought it would be nice to catch up, and I changed my mind. That's all.'

'How did you know my father?' I asked. 'How do you know me?'

The Mystery Woman didn't say anything for a few moments. It looked as if she was weighing her options, but it was difficult to be sure.

'Let's go for a walk,' she said eventually. 'If we have to do this, we can do it somewhere that isn't the middle of the street.'

I'd have preferred that she gave me the answers there and then, but I didn't want to argue. We walked in silence past the village green, through the churchyard, and towards the sand dunes, with her leading the way. This was the point at which I realised she knew exactly where she was going; she was familiar enough with the island to walk directly from the shops to the stretch of dunes that was least likely to be swamped with tourists. Past the old lifeboat station and northwards, away from the priory and the harbour. It was the place *I'd* have chosen if she'd asked me to find somewhere we could talk uninterrupted.

'You're local,' I told her. 'Or you used to be. You're not anymore or I'd know who you are.'

'My parents live here,' she said. 'I lived here until I was twenty-one. That was eight years ago.'

'Who are your parents?' I asked.

'Graham and Jane Tibbet. I'm Rachael.'

Everything clicked into place. Almost everything. 'You worked in the coffee shop. Not for very long, just a few months, I think. *That's* how you know my father.'

Rachael nodded slowly, hesitantly. 'I'm surprised you remember. You would have only been seven or eight at the time. I worked for Stuart . . . for your father the summer after I finished university. Three months – not long at all.'

It made sense now: why she looked familiar but I'd been unable to identify her. I have an excellent memory for facts and dates and events, but it's not so easy to remember the face of someone you knew for only one summer when you were eight years old, and had probably seen only once or twice. Most of that summer I would have been home with you, Mum, or else with Bethany and Mrs Collins, if you were having a bad day and could not look after me. There were a lot of bad days during that period; it was the end of that summer when the cancer was diagnosed.

This thought jolted another one. Mr Tibbet – Rachael's father – was currently ill. He'd had heart surgery approximately six months ago. I remembered that Reverend Collins had been visiting the Tibbets as part of his pastoral duties.

The dots were now easy to join: Rachael, the Mystery Woman, had presumably come back to the island because her father was ill. While she was back, she decided to pop into the coffee shop to say hello to Daddy, because she'd worked for him eight years ago. But instead of waiting for him . . . she'd changed her mind and left. It made sense. So why did I still feel weird, as if I was missing a key part of the puzzle?

'I heard about your father,' I told Rachael. 'I'm sorry he's been ill.'

She shot me a look that I diagnosed as surprised, and then gave a short, sharp laugh. 'Of course you heard. That's how this place works, isn't it? Everyone knows everything, the second it happens.'

'Is he feeling better?'

'No. He's dying. Slowly, but still dying.'

'Oh. That's terrible.' I felt suddenly sick and looked away. 'Obviously that's terrible.'

I thought I saw Rachael shrug, in my peripheral vision, but she didn't say anything. I heard a clicking noise and smelled cigarette smoke. I still didn't want to look up. 'My mum died when I was ten,' I told her.

'I know. I'm sorry.'

I did glance up now, and I was surprised to see that Rachael had tears in her eyes, despite her flat tone. This didn't help with my queasiness. I felt awful, like I'd made a mistake that I couldn't rectify. And at the same time, the overarching *weirdness* had not gone away.

'I'm sure that Daddy wouldn't mind talking to you,' I told Rachael. 'If you wanted to stop by the shop again.'

She gave me another look, but this one was impossible to interpret. She sucked and exhaled from her cigarette, then dabbed at her eyes with her other hand. Her fingers were shaking.

A minute passed, maybe two. I was on the verge of walking – offering my condolences and getting out of there, just to be away from the situation. But if I left, I'd still be missing something, something important. So I stayed rooted to the spot, looking at my shoes, with no idea what would come next.

When Rachael finally spoke, I couldn't detect any trace of emotion in her voice. She was no longer crying. 'I think it would be better if you didn't mention this chat to your father,' she told me. 'I don't feel like seeing him anymore. It was a whim and it wasn't important. So you can stop being confused now, can't you?'

'I'm still confused,' I said.

She looked at me and remained silent.

Rachael shook her head. Her expression was still impossible to read. 'I've got nothing else to tell you,' she said. 'Please don't follow me again.'

And she walked briskly away.

I sat down on the dry grass at the top of the dune and tried to understand what had just happened. I was emotional. I knew I was experiencing some unusually intense emotions, but I didn't know what they were. In that moment, if I'd been asked to explain how I was feeling in anything but the broadest terms, I'd have been utterly defeated. I didn't know.

So I stayed where I was for five, ten, twenty minutes, not really thinking, but just waiting for my mind to settle, waiting for any coherent thought to come.

My mind didn't settle. But slowly, very slowly, I was able to sift through the conversation, identifying one salient detail.

Rachael Tibbet had visited Daddy on a whim, and she'd left on a whim. It was unimportant. Yet she didn't want me to tell him about the conversation we'd just had. I didn't know why this was. She'd sort of implied it would be pointless, but, then, what did it matter either way?

I got up, having reached an apparent brick wall. Then I sat down again. Something else had just occurred to me, and it caused the sick feeling in my stomach to intensify.

Rachael had known who I was today, but she hadn't on the day she came into the coffee shop. And why would she? She hadn't seen me for eight years either, and it was a safe assumption that I'd changed more than she had in this time. Added to this, it was a weekday, so under normal circumstances, I should have been at school.

She'd asked for Stuart, and had said she'd wait for him to get back. Then I'd said: *How do you know my father?* That was the point she must have realised who I was, and it was the exact point she decided to leave.

The conclusion I had to draw was this: Rachael Tibbet left because of me. She wanted to see my father, but she did not want to see him while I was there.

I got up and started walking back towards the village. My limbs felt heavy and uncooperative, as if caught in a dark numbing fog, and at the same time, my surroundings no longer seemed quite real. I passed chattering families and groups of tourists without being able to discern anything they were saying. I passed through the churchyard like a ghost, over the green, past the *Crown and Anchor*. By the time I realised where I was heading, I was almost there. I jogged the last fifty metres of Mrs Frost's lane and pounded on her door until she answered.

'Phoebe,' she said. 'I thought I'd have longer to brace myself. Don't tell me your exams are over already?'

'I need you to tell me the truth about something,' I said.

'The truth? About what? What's got you so agitated?'

'You once told me that you couldn't avoid the gossip on this island, even if you wanted to.'

'I don't remember,' Mrs Frost said flatly.

'I do. I don't forget conversations.'

'Well, I'll be careful what I say in the future. Does any of this have a point?'

'Did my father have an affair?'

Mrs Frost didn't miss a beat. And she didn't answer the question, either. 'What makes you say that?'

'I just met a woman named Rachael Tibbet who used to work for my father, eight years ago. There's something weird going on. She was the Mystery Woman who came into the shop and then left and didn't return, and you said she sounded like an old girlfriend, and I told you that was absurd because I thought it *was* absurd, but I don't think that anymore because now I think—'

'Phoebe, you're incoherent. Furthermore, this has nothing to do with me! I have better things to do than involve myself in the island's gossip. Far better things.'

'Does that mean there *was* some gossip?'

Mrs Frost looked at me, her face expressionless.

'Was there some gossip. Was there? Was—'

I didn't get to ask a third time, as Mrs Frost cut me off. 'Phoebe, I wouldn't tell you even if I knew. It's absurd. If you have an issue with your father, talk to your father.'

She shut the door.

There was an empty milk bottle on the doorstep and I kicked it and it fell over and smashed. Then I ran back into the village.

I had no intention of talking to my father. I went to Bethany.

24

Managing Difficult Emotions

'Jesus, Phoebe. What's the matter?'

It was Bethany who answered the door, and I quickly established that her parents weren't in. They were at church, because it was still Sunday morning. I was shocked to learn this. It seemed like half the day had passed since I'd been talking to Rachael Tibbet on the sand dunes, but in reality it had been less than an hour; when I looked at the clock in the vicarage hallway, it had only just gone eleven. It was the time I should have been arriving at Bethany's door with my laptop and revision notes.

'I've discovered something awful,' I told her.

She didn't ask what the something awful was straightaway. She took me through to the living room and I sat on the sofa and bit my fingers while she insisted on getting me a glass of water.

'OK. What's happened? Tell me everything.'

And I did, starting with the Mystery Woman's first appearance back in November and ending with Mrs Frost refusing to answer my questions, which I took to be some sort of answer in itself. Because I'd never known her to lie, and if she'd heard nothing, I was sure she'd have told me outright;

she obviously didn't want to have the conversation, and that would have been the simplest way to end it.

'You don't know that for sure,' Bethany said. 'I mean, there could be all sorts of reasons she didn't want to talk to you. It doesn't mean she's keeping something from you.'

'That's exactly what it means!' I said, my heart still thumping. 'Unless you have a better explanation for all of this? If you do, I need to hear it.'

Bethany didn't say anything for a few moments. She picked up my glass of water from the coffee table and pressed it to my lips, pretty much forcing me to sip. It was probably a sensible thing to do. My throat ached and I was finding it difficult to speak.

'I don't have an explanation for you,' Bethany said. 'There's only one person who can give you a proper answer. I honestly think Mrs Frost's right about that.'

'I'm not talking to my father! I can't even think about that right now!'

'It's the only way to clear this up. I know it's hard, but you should hear his side of things.'

'His side of things? He doesn't get to have a *side* of things! He either did it or he didn't.'

'I don't think it's always that straightforward.'

It wasn't what I wanted to hear from Bethany at that moment. I wanted her to agree with me. Or I wanted her to tell me I was absolutely wrong and explain why. Not make excuses for the inexcusable.

'My mum was ill. She was dying! How could he do that to us? How could he?' I was aware that I was becoming increasingly shrill, but I couldn't help it. I just kept going, talking louder and less coherently. Because all I could think was that he'd betrayed us, betrayed you, when you were about to be handed a death sentence. 'He was supposed to love us! He was the one person who could never let me down!'

My voice gave out and I was crying uncontrollably, and the next moment Bethany was beside me on the sofa. I collapsed into her. She put her arms around me and I shook and cried; and for the longest time I didn't have a thought in my head. There was only emotion, pure and relentless, like a tsunami wave that just keeps on coming, drowning everything.

You'd think that was the end – the catharsis, with nothing left to pour out of me. But you'd be wrong. The worst was still to come.

I was aware of wetness. My cheek was pressed against Bethany's right breast and I'd pretty much managed to drench that side of her top. My first detached thought was that I should be embarrassed. But I wasn't; I felt safe. I felt warm and comforted. As my tears subsided and I stopped shaking, I realised that Bethany was stroking my hair and making soft shushing noises. I stayed still and closed my eyes and allowed myself to drift. Bethany kissed the top of my head.

And that was the moment.

I opened my eyes and tilted my face towards hers. She was smiling very gently. I put my hand on her cheek and pressed my lips against her mouth. And for a fraction of a second it was perfect.

Then she pushed me away. I looked directly into her eyes, and what I saw there was horror. Horror, shock and bafflement.

I got up and I ran to the door.

*

I got up and I ran to the door. Bethany was shouting at me, but I couldn't make any sense of the words. I was in freefall, air rushing in my ears as I sprinted up the lane, aware of the people around me only as blurred obstacles to be dodged.

I ignored Gladys when I got home. I walked straight past her and into my room, closing the door behind me. My phone had started ringing and it was Bethany, so I did the simplest thing and blocked her number. Then I blocked Daddy's number as well. That was half my contacts blocked in the space of thirty seconds. I flopped onto my bed and buried my face in my pillow to the point where it was hard to breathe. I thought about what I had to do next.

The first thing was to check my bank account: I had £480, which was plenty. Next, I searched for flights and found one leaving from Edinburgh Airport that afternoon, at 16.50. I booked it. It was an easy decision to make because I had so few options open to me. I didn't want to be home when Daddy returned in approximately five hours. I didn't want to see Bethany again. There was only one person left to go to. The tide would be out for another two hours, so I had exactly that long to escape.

I shoved what I needed into my rucksack, which was very little. My passport. My laptop and headphones and chargers. Some underwear and my toothbrush. I found the ring you'd given me for my sixteenth birthday – the One Ring – in my bedside drawer and put it on. After a brief hesitation, I also packed *The Ninth Rain*, which I was currently halfway through. Reading, at the moment, was unthinkable – I knew I would not be able to concentrate. But I had enough foresight to see that it might be a comfort eventually. At the very least, I would not have to face the distress of having left a half-read book behind, which I knew would play on my mind.

I made sure that Gladys had food and water down and took her to the garden for a wee. I gave her a goodbye cuddle. She knew something was wrong because I was crying again and she started whimpering.

I phoned the taxi company as I walked north out of the village and arranged for them to pick me up at the end of the causeway. I didn't want to get into a taxi outside my house in case any of the neighbours saw and asked where I was going, or just came over to talk to me while I was waiting. But if anyone saw me hiking out of the village with my rucksack, this would look like a perfectly normal occurrence.

The taxi took around twenty minutes to arrive. I waited off the road in the long grass until I got the text message saying the car was approaching. The taxi driver asked if I was going anywhere nice and I told him I was going to see my grandmother. Then I put my headphones on because I didn't want him to talk to me again. And I closed my eyes behind my sunglasses and sat on my hands to stop myself from biting my fingers, and as long as I didn't think, everything was OK.

The key was to keep things simple and break the journey into small, practical steps, like following an algorithm. This was easy at first. The taxi took me to Berwick train station. The train took me to Edinburgh Waverley. From there, I had to walk a short distance to catch the tram to the airport. I'd done all these things before, most recently two years ago when we'd last visited Gee. But I'd never done them alone, and I find airports difficult at the best of times because they are crowded and over-stimulating, with fluorescent lights and signs and advertisements everywhere and continual announcements through the loudspeakers, which are also everywhere. And they usually have a one-way system that forces you to walk through the duty-free shopping area on the way to the departure lounge, and the duty-free shopping area has an unbearably strong and confusing smell from all the perfume that people are sampling.

So when I arrived at the airport, I headed straight for the Special Assistance counter, which is where you go if you have mobility issues or are blind, or if you have a hidden disability, like me. The interaction with the woman behind the counter was made easier because I knew she'd have had special training to deal with irregular customers, and I didn't need to worry about where my eyes were pointing or whether my tone of voice was correct.

'I have ASD and require a hidden disability lanyard,' I said.

And she smiled and didn't say anything stupid or ignorant or condescending. She said: 'There you go,' and slid the lanyard across the counter.

I felt much safer once I was wearing my lanyard because it no longer mattered so much if I had a meltdown. If I suddenly started crying or shaking, or acting abnormally in the Security queue, the staff would see that I needed special assistance and come to help me. They wouldn't shout at me or interrogate me as a potential terrorist.

I did not have a meltdown. I joined the express queue at Security and was waved through the metal detector and body scanner without incident. I held my breath through the duty-free and went to the Bureau de Change to purchase euros. Then I found the quietest corner of the departure lounge and sat wearing my headphones and sunglasses, waiting for my flight to be called.

Even though I'd only booked my ticket a few hours ago, I'd still been able to reserve a window seat on the plane, because most people don't want to pay the extra charge for an allocated seat and would probably rather spend their money on perfume or alcohol. This was a big relief as it meant I only had to sit next to one other person and I wouldn't have to get out of my seat every time they needed the toilet. My hidden disability lanyard meant that I was able to board the plane first along with two families with pushchairs and a woman with a cane. As soon as I found my seat, I squashed myself against the window and made sure the armrests were down and the air conditioning wasn't aimed at my face. Then I fastened my seatbelt, put my headphones back on and closed my eyes. Aside from the safety demonstration, I kept my eyes closed for the entire three-hour flight. I pretended I was alone, floating.

The plane landed at nine p.m., Central European Summer Time, and the temperature in Alicante was 19° Celsius, 66 Fahrenheit. This was good as I hadn't brought a coat.

Once I'd made it through Passport Control, I realised that I hadn't had anything to eat or drink for about ten hours. I wasn't even a little bit hungry, but the air-conditioning on the plane had left me extremely dehydrated. I didn't have any coins for the vending machines so I went the shop in Arrivals and bought a litre bottle of water, which I drank immediately.

Next came the hard bit. I turned my phone back on and sent a message to Gee, which said: *Hello, Gee. It's Phoebe. I'm at Alicante Airport. I'm coming to visit you if that's OK. I don't have anywhere else to go. I'm going to find a taxi and I should be at your house in approximately 90 minutes.*

And I hit send and waited for a message to come back, but it didn't. Instead, my phone started ringing.

'Hello, Gee,' I said.

And she said: 'Phoebe, thank God you're all right! Your dad's frantic!'

'I don't want to talk about Daddy,' I said.

'What on earth's happened?' Gee asked.

'I don't want to talk about that, either.'

'Phoebe, you have to call him. He's worried sick!'

'I don't care. I'm not talking to him. Can I come to your house?'

'Of course you can. I'm not going to leave you stranded at the airport! But I am going to call your dad, to let him know you're safe. You have to let me do that.'

I thought about this. 'OK. You can tell him I'm safe, but that's all. I don't want him to try to contact me.'

'I won't do anything you don't want me to,' Gee said.

'I'm going to get a taxi now,' I told her.

'Are you sure you're OK doing that? I can call one for you if you'd prefer? It might take a little longer, but—'

'I don't want to wait, and I know where to go. The taxis are clearly signposted.'

'What about money? It's going to be expensive.'

'I know. I have money.'

'You need to call me if you get into any difficulty. In fact, call me when you're in the taxi. Call me straightaway.'

'I can send you a message.'

'No. *Call*. It's safer.'

I didn't ask why it was safer. I promised that I'd call when I was in the taxi and said goodbye and hung up.

I didn't have to queue for long. I got into a taxi and gave the driver the address, which he repeated back to me before inputting it in the sat nav. He turned in his seat to look at me and said something I was unable to decipher.

So I said: '*Más despacio, por favor*,' which means 'Slower, please.'

And he said: '*Es – un – camino – muy – largo*,' which means 'It's a very long way.'

I said: '*Sí, claro*.' ('Yes, I know.')

And he said: '*Cuesta mucho*.' (It will cost a lot.)

So I said: '*Sí, claro*.'

And he didn't say anything, so I got my purse out and made a fan of my euros. There were two fifties, ten twenties and six tens.

And the driver shrugged and turned back to his wheel and we started moving and I called Gee to let her know I was on my way.

Most of the journey was fine. We were on the *autopista* for forty minutes and then turned off into the mountains. I only started to get worried when we had reached the last village before Gee's. Because soon I'd have to tell her. I'd have to talk to her about Daddy, and before that, I'd have to tell her about me, what *I'd* done; I didn't think I could give her an adequate explanation of why I was here without including all of it. The alternative was to refuse to say anything.

And this was the alternative I thought I was going to go for, right up until the moment I saw her. I planned to tell her that I was exhausted and could not speak until the morning. But she was waiting for me in the car port when I arrived; she'd probably been alerted by the taxi lights illuminating the drive.

I looked at her and she looked at me and opened her arms.

I threw my rucksack on the ground and ran to her. Then I

broke away from the hug and took a large step backwards. My throat was choked with tears, but I still managed to sob the words out, before I lost my voice forever: 'I think I might be a lesbian and I sexually assaulted Bethany!'

I don't know what I'd expected to come next, but Gee's reaction wasn't it. She gave a small shake of her head and said: 'Come inside. I'll put the kettle on.'

25

No Plan

It was close to midnight, far too late for caffeine, but Gee made me a hot chocolate all the same. I had stopped crying. I sat on the sofa under the ceiling fan, with no idea what to say.

'You can start with Bethany or you can start with your dad,' Gee suggested, setting my mug down on a coaster. 'You'll feel better once you've talked about it.'

'I won't feel better,' I told her. 'I'm never going to feel better.'

Gee smiled gently at this. 'I can remember you telling me something like that once before. You asked me if it would ever stop hurting. Do you remember?'

I nodded. It was six years ago, but I remembered very well. 'You said that all pain fades over time, but some never goes away entirely. But you said I would learn to be happy again in spite of it.'

'And was I right?'

'Yes. You were right. But . . .' I couldn't think of a good but. Instead I asked: 'Aren't you upset by what I told you? By what I did?'

'No, love. I'm not upset. If you're a lesbian then you're a lesbian. It doesn't make a blind bit of difference to me. As for the other . . . well, why don't you just tell me what happened? I very much doubt it was how you think it was.'

'You don't believe me?'

'No, I don't believe you. I *know* you. The idea that you assaulted anyone is frankly ludicrous.'

I felt myself blushing. 'I kissed her, on the lips. She didn't want me to. She pushed me away.'

'I see. And you continued anyway, did you? Once she'd made it clear she didn't want you to?'

'No, of course not! I ran out of the house.'

'OK. So it wasn't assault. Just put that out of your head right now. It was a misunderstanding. They happen. I take it you haven't spoken to her since?'

'No. She was disgusted with me. I could see she was.'

'I doubt that, too. Granted, I don't know Bethany all that well, but . . . Well, you tell me. Is Bethany a bigot?'

'No, of course not!'

Gee nodded. 'Which makes it unlikely that Bethany would be disgusted with you. Correct?'

'But she was! It's not to do with being homophobic. It's because . . . because of the way it happened. Because . . .' I trailed off briefly, not knowing how to continue. Gee had said that it wasn't an assault, but that was still how it felt. The shame of it made Bethany's reaction justified in my mind. 'She was horrified,' I said quietly. 'I saw she was!'

Gee waited a moment, then put her hand on mine. 'Phoebe. Is it possible that you're wrong? If you look at it logically, given what you know about Bethany, and what you know about yourself. I mean, you don't always get these things right, do you? I think you'd be the first to admit that.'

I thought about this for a long time. Gee was obviously right in one regard, although I was better at interpreting Bethany's expressions than most other people's. But I had also been highly emotional at the time. It had been so difficult to think clearly! Even as I tried to remember now, to picture Bethany's face in that moment, I found that I couldn't determine exactly what it was that I had seen. All I knew for certain was how I had felt: pushed away, rejected, mortified. 'It's possible,' I conceded. 'But it doesn't make it any easier. I still don't know how I'm going to be able to face her again.'

'Of course you'll be able to face her again. She's your friend. It will probably be far easier than you think.'

'But how can it be? I've ruined it!'

'Why? It was a kiss, it's not the end of the world.'

I didn't say anything. After a moment Gee sighed and patted my hand. 'Phoebe, I'm not trying to belittle your problems, but I've been on this planet seventy-six years now. When you get to my age, you see things very differently. You haven't done anything wrong. Bethany's not going to think you've done anything wrong. We can't help who we're attracted to.'

I blushed again, very deeply. Because even after everything, it was very strange hearing it aloud. I was attracted to Bethany. I voiced the idea in my head, and I realised it was true. There had been plenty of times in the past when I'd struggled to untangle my emotions, when it had taken me a long time to understand precisely what I was feeling, but this was on a whole other level. I was attracted to my best friend, and it seemed unlikely that this was something that could develop in the course of a single day. My suspicion was that it had been there much longer – and I'd simply failed to recognise the signs for what they were.

'What do I say to her?' I asked. 'I've got no idea what to say.'

'You don't need to worry about that tonight,' Gee told me. 'But if you want my advice, it doesn't really matter what you say. You just need to talk to her. She's your friend and you can work this out together. Trust me, it's not going to be the huge trauma you think it is.'

I nodded and stayed silent. I didn't know if Gee was right – I didn't know how she *could* be right – but I did trust her. I trusted that she was going to help me, when no one else could.

As if sensing my thoughts, Gee said: 'Now we need to talk about your father, don't we? Tell me what's happened.'

It took a long time and Gee didn't say a word. She just let me talk, her face impassive. By the time I'd finished, I'd started to think that she didn't believe me about this, either. I told her everything I knew, and waited for her to tell me I was wrong, that she wasn't convinced.

'It was eight years ago,' Gee said, very gently. 'Your mum forgave him for it. Perhaps you should, too.'

I let this sink in, a cold hard stone, dropping to the bottom of a deep well. 'She knew? *You* knew?'

'Your mum suspected something was going on. Your father admitted it straightaway. By the time I knew, they'd already put it behind them.'

'Why didn't I know? Why didn't you tell me?'

'Phoebe, you were eight.'

'Not then. Afterwards, when I was older.'

'Because your mother asked me not to. Because it would have hurt you. Because it wasn't my place. You can take your pick, they're all true. I'm only telling you now because I don't have a better choice. I'm not going to lie to you.'

'Everyone's lied to me! My father's not the person I thought he was!'

'Phoebe, no one's the person we *think* they are. People are far more complicated than that. We rarely see more than a small part of them.'

I didn't know what to say to this, so I said nothing.

'It's OK to be angry,' Gee said. 'Your mum was angry. *I* was angry – just as much as you are now. She was my daughter, and when someone hurts your child it's no easy thing to forgive.'

'She was ill!' I spat. 'She was dying, and he betrayed her. How could he do that?'

I realised that I was sobbing again. Gee put her hand on my shoulder and didn't say anything for a long time. She waited until I'd stopped, and then said: 'Phoebe, love. I want you to think about the last eight years – really think about them. Now be honest. When has your dad not been there for you? How often has he put his needs ahead of yours? How often has he let you down?'

I stayed silent.

'You can see my point, can't you?'

'It doesn't change what he did. It doesn't make it go away.'

'No, it doesn't. And I think you know that's not what I'm trying to say. What I'm saying is that you need to weigh up this one thing against everything else you know about your father. He's not perfect because no one ever is. But that doesn't make him a monster. No one should be judged on their worst actions.'

I thought this was probably true. And yet my feelings couldn't be reasoned away so easily. They remained exactly as they were.

I wondered how it had been for you, Mum – how you'd felt, and how you had managed to forgive. I wondered, but I found no answers.

Gee got up from the sofa. 'Phoebe, I'm going to call your dad now. Relax – I don't expect you to talk to him. I'm just going to let him know that you're OK. He'll want to know.'

I looked at the clock. It was a quarter to one, quarter to midnight in the UK. 'He'll probably be asleep by now,' I said.

'He won't be asleep. Trust me.'

'I don't want you to call him.'

Gee sighed. 'I know you don't. I'm going to do it anyway. He deserves to know how you are.'

'What are you going to tell him? Are you going to tell him what we've talked about?'

'Do you want me to?'

'No.'

'Then I won't. I'll tell him we've spoken and you've got some issues that the two of you need to discuss together. Is that OK?'

'I don't want to discuss anything with him.'

'We can speak about it tomorrow. Right now you need to sleep. I've made up the bed in the spare room for you.'

'I don't think I'm tired.'

Gee shook her head. '*I'm* tired. And you probably will be, if you lie down and give yourself a chance. You look exhausted.'

She started to walk to the kitchen, where the phone was.

'Gee,' I said.

She stopped and turned.

'Thank you. Thank you for letting me stay. Thank you for talking to me.'

She dismissed this with a wave and continued into the kitchen. I went to my room with my rucksack. I didn't want to be there for the phone call.

I didn't expect to sleep, but I did. I didn't expect to feel any better in the morning, but I did. Because of the shutters on the window, the spare room was almost pitch black, and when I awoke, I only knew it was morning from the light seeping under the door. I had my headphones on; I'd fallen asleep listening to *Oceanborn*, which is Nightwish's second album.

There wasn't any disorientation. I was wide awake and I remembered everything that had happened the previous day, everything I'd said and done. The only thing that felt strange was that it had only been a day – less than a day. Twenty-four hours ago, everything had been routine.

I didn't feel like stretching or exercising. I showered, brushed my teeth, and went to find Gee, who was outside watering the garden. The morning was warm but not hot. There were low clouds and mist hanging over the mountains, obscuring their peaks.

'Hello, love,' Gee said. 'Did you sleep OK?' She sounded completely unrattled, as if my being there were the most normal thing in the world.

'I slept well,' I told her.

'Are you hungry? I can make you some breakfast in a minute.'

'Yes, I'm hungry.' I realised at once that this was an understatement. 'Actually, I'm ravenous. I didn't really eat yesterday.'

Gee immediately started tutting and went to switch off the

hose. 'You should have said. I would have made you something last night.'

'I wasn't hungry last night.'

Inside, Gee made toast and whizzed up some oat milk in the blender. She brewed some strong coffee and I sat and sipped it in the dining area. I had a small headache, but it disappeared quickly as I ate and drank. My diagnosis was insufficient caffeine the day before, combined with stress and a sleep deficit.

Gee waited until I'd finished, then said: 'Will you Skype your dad this evening?' She didn't preface it with any small talk.

'I still don't feel ready to talk to him,' I said. 'And definitely not on Skype.'

'You'd rather talk to him face-to-face?'

'No.'

Gee gave a large sigh. 'What about school?'

'It's a bank holiday.'

'I'm aware of that. What about school tomorrow?'

'I don't know . . . to be honest, I don't have a plan. I just needed to get away. I didn't have anywhere else I could go.'

Gee nodded at this. I suppose it was obvious that I didn't have a plan.

'Can I stay?' I asked.

Gee didn't answer this directly. She said: 'Your dad tells me you have exams next week.'

'Yes.'

'You're not going to miss them.'

I didn't know if this was a question or a statement. I decided the best thing would be to buy myself some time. 'I go on exam leave a week from now,' I told Gee. 'But my first exam isn't until the Thursday. That means I don't *have* to be at school for ten days. This week, we'll just be revising. I can do that here. I've brought my laptop.'

I had no idea what I'd do when I *did* have to go back for my exams. The thought still terrified me. I supposed I might be able to stay at school the whole time, and then, afterwards, I could come back to Spain. But I'd still have to see Bethany. I'd still have to share a room with her, which was unthinkable. I wondered if I could arrange to be moved. Or perhaps I could take my exams somewhere else, where I didn't know anyone. Perhaps I didn't have to take them at all; I could research the legalities over the coming days. But the most important thing, right now, was just to convince Gee to give me more time.

'How about we make a deal?' she said, after a few moments of silence had passed. 'You can stay here as long as you need to. I promise I won't put you under any pressure to leave. In return you have to agree to do just one thing for me.'

My stomach dropped, because I thought I already knew what the requirement would be. 'You want me to talk to Daddy?'

'I want you to do it face-to-face, as soon as he can get a flight.'

'I'm not ready!'

'Phoebe, you can't go on ignoring him indefinitely. He knows what this is about, and he's prepared to do whatever it takes to fix it.'

'He knows? You said you wouldn't tell him!'

'And I didn't. He's spoken with Bethany. She was the first person he called when you went missing – as you'd expect.'

I felt suddenly rooted to the spot. It was inevitable that they'd spoken – Gee was right – but that didn't do anything to negate the swirl of anxiety that again threatened to overwhelm me. All I could do was close my eyes and wait for it to pass.

'Phoebe, you just have to talk to him,' Gee said. 'That's all. That's my only condition. If you do that and it makes no difference, then I'm not going to make you leave. And I very much doubt your father would make you leave either. If it comes down to it, we'll work something out – the three of us.'

I didn't say anything. This was all happening far too soon, but I couldn't see any way out of it. The only comfort was that I trusted Gee; if I could get through this one meeting, then she'd keep her word. She'd let me stay.

'So what's it going to be?' she asked.

I don't like uncertainty. I suppose that's why things felt easier once I'd made my decision, even though I wasn't sure it was the right decision. I was still dreading the meeting; I still felt it was coming far too soon. But at least, now, I had some promise of resolution. I had a timetable I could focus on, and timetables always offer some degree of comfort.

Gee told me that Daddy had a flight booked to Alicante early the following morning. He was hiring a car to drive into the mountains and would be here around lunchtime. I would listen to what he had to say, and after that, if I wanted him to, he'd leave. There was a flight back to Edinburgh at 9.50 in the evening, so if necessary, he could be here and gone in a day – albeit a very long day. He'd be leaving and returning to Holy Island in the early hours of the morning.

'What about Gladys?' I asked.

'She'll have to go into kennels for a couple of days,' Gee said. 'Your dad's going to drop her off this afternoon and pick her up the day after he gets back.'

I nodded but said nothing. It was only two days, but it made me feel worse than anything else. Because Gladys wouldn't know it was only two days. She'd only know that she'd been abandoned, first by me and then by Daddy, for reasons impossible to comprehend. Gladys was the innocent victim in all of this.

The day passed quickly and quietly. I walked down to the village with Gee to buy bread and fruit from the shop, and she told me it was going to get hot at the end of the week. Maybe up to 28 degrees. Uncomfortably hot, as far as I was concerned. She asked me if I'd heard from Bethany and I told her that I blocked her number.

'Maybe you should unblock it,' she said. But that was all she said. She didn't bring the subject up again.

In the evening, I helped her make dinner, which was a vegan bolognaise made with fresh aubergines and courgettes and tomatoes. And of course it tasted far better than it would have done at home, because fruit and vegetables taste better in Spain.

When it got dark, I sat outside in the hammock and looked at the Milky Way arching like an impossible bridge in the sky. There was almost no noise from the road now, as few vehicles passed the village this late at night. All I could hear were the crickets and the wind.

I didn't think about tomorrow. I just focused on the stars and the wind, and the smell of the pine trees, and for a while, I felt peaceful.

26

A Walk up the Mountain

The hire car pulled into Gee's drive a little before one. I was in the garden, in the shade of the olive tree, and heard it crunching over the loose stones at the edge of the road, heard the engine cut out a few seconds later. Gee had said that she could stay with me and Daddy while we talked, or she could give us privacy – whichever was better. I still didn't know which was better.

I waited where I was, and I guess that Daddy and Gee spent some time talking inside, because it was another ten minutes before they came out. Daddy smiled weakly, and I didn't smile back. I looked away, towards the whitewashed wall at the edge of the garden. I'd expected to feel angry, but I found that I didn't anymore. I felt a weird hollowness in the pit of my stomach.

'Hello, Phoebe,' Daddy said.

'Hello, Daddy.' My voice sounded exactly how I felt. It was sort of flat and detached and thin, like a recording from the distant past.

'Can we go for a walk?' he asked after a moment of silence. 'It might be easier that way.'

I thought about this for a while and then nodded. It would be easier. If we were walking then we wouldn't be facing each other, and I'd have something mechanical to occupy my limbs;

I wouldn't just be cornered in the garden, full of pent-up energy. Even though it was irrational, I was a little annoyed that Daddy had thought of this – that he knew how to make things better for me. Three days ago, it would have felt reassuring, but now it seemed more like a cheap trick.

We walked out of the front gate, down the drive, and out of the village towards the mountains. It was cloudy again that afternoon, and comfortable weather for walking. It would have been nice, had I been on my own.

'I don't know where to start,' Daddy said. 'There are some things I have to tell you, but they can wait for now.'

I didn't say anything. We were crossing the bridge over the dry riverbed. The pavement was narrow so I walked in the road.

'Tell me what I should say,' Daddy said. 'What do you want to know?'

'Is Gladys OK?'

'She's OK. She misses you. I don't think that's the most important thing right now.'

'It's important to me.'

Daddy sighed and shook his head. 'I'm sorry. It's important to me, too.'

I waited until we'd crossed the road and were heading up the stony path that curved towards the mountains. 'Why did you do it?'

'I'm not going to make excuses.'

'I don't want you to make excuses. I just want you to tell the truth.'

I could sense that Daddy was looking at me, but he didn't say anything for some time. I don't know why. Telling the truth should not have required this much thought.

'*Are* you going to tell me the truth?' I asked. 'Because it's just occurred to me that you might not, even now. I can't take it for granted anymore, can I?'

'Phoebe, that isn't fair. Yes, there are things I haven't told you. That doesn't mean I've been lying to you for the last eight years. It isn't that simple.'

'You haven't been honest with me, then. We can agree on that.'

'No. You're right – I haven't always been honest with you. I've concealed things. I've kept things back, usually because I thought I had a good reason to. That's how I would have justified it, anyway. Have you always been honest with me?' The question caught me off-guard, but fortunately I did not have to answer it; Daddy immediately backed down. 'I'm sorry – that isn't fair, either. We're talking about me, not you. And you're right: I've given you ample reason to distrust me. All I can say is I'm going to do everything I can to regain your trust, starting now. I'll answer any questions you have, and I guess you'll have to make up your own mind whether you can believe me.'

I waited. Daddy took a deep breath before continuing.

'The truth is I was unhappy. I was angry, frustrated. I resented the way my life had turned out. Your mum and I . . . well, we had our fair share of problems by then.'

'You're being vague. What were the problems? Didn't you love her anymore?'

'Of course I loved her. I didn't stop loving her.'

'If you loved her, you wouldn't have betrayed her.'

'Phoebe, things aren't always that black and white. You have to understand that.'

'Some things are black and white,' I told him.

255

And he didn't say anything for some time. We continued walking, and the path got steeper, and we didn't see anyone else on the mountain. There were no farmers working on the terraces because it was lunchtime and they'd all have gone home for their siesta.

'Phoebe, I don't want to upset you,' Daddy said eventually. 'It's the last thing I want to do. But just because you love someone, it doesn't mean the relationship is perfect. No relationship is. With your mum and me . . . well, the truth is that we hardly *had* a relationship at the time. I was working six days a week, and there were plenty of days when your mum couldn't even get out of bed. And when she was well enough, every bit of her energy she gave to you. Which is how it should have been. You were her priority. You were the priority for both of us. But you needed a lot of help back then. You weren't . . . Christ, Phoebe. I don't know how I can put this. You were hard work sometimes. Something would go wrong in your day – the smallest thing, and you'd blow up. You wouldn't be asleep until midnight, or you'd wake up at two and need one of us to be with you for the next hour. The net result was that your mum and I spent less and less time together. I was stressed and tired, she was exhausted, and there was basically never any respite from it. It wasn't the life either of us had pictured for ourselves. Can you understand that?'

'I understand,' I told him. 'I was difficult. I was a *problem*.'

'Phoebe, you were never a problem! That's not what I meant at all!'

'You said I was hard work. Your words.'

'That doesn't mean I ever thought of you as a problem. You were the most important thing in the world to me. You always

have been. But you can ask anyone who's ever been a parent –
it's not always easy. At times it's the most physically and
emotionally demanding thing you can imagine. And it can feel
utterly relentless when you're in the thick of it. You don't get
any days off, no matter how tired or unhappy you are. You just
have to push all that to one side and get on with it.'

'You said you weren't going to make excuses.'

'I'm not making excuses. None of this changes how badly I
acted. But you wanted me to be honest, and that's what I'm
trying to do. I'm trying to tell you how I felt at the time.'

'Unhappy?'

'Some of the time, yes. Unhappy, self-pitying, selfish – take
your pick.'

'So you decided to have sex with a twenty-one-year-old to
make yourself happier?'

To my surprise, Daddy did not try to dispute this analysis.
He nodded and said: 'Yeah. Put bluntly, that's exactly it.'

'And meanwhile Mum was at home, dying. It was the time
she needed you more than ever, and you betrayed her.'

'Yes. She was dying and I betrayed her. And I've had to live
with that ever since. I didn't know about the cancer at the
time, but that doesn't really change anything. She deserved far
better – and so did you. I don't know what else I can say.'

I didn't know what he could say either. I didn't know how I
felt. There was still the same sense of hollowness inside me. It
was as if the anger and sadness had been burnt away, leaving
nothing in their place. Just this pervading grey fog.

'Would you have ever told me?' I asked.

'No. I wouldn't. What good would it have done?'

'It would have been the truth.'

'It would have caused you pain. It *has* caused you pain.

Seriously, Phoebe, what good would have come of it? Sometimes telling the truth comes with a very high price. I think you understand that.'

'What about in November? You lied to me then, too. I told you about her coming into the shop, I described her. You must have known. You must have known there was a chance I'd find out about her.'

'It's been eight years, Phoebe. I always knew there was a *chance* you'd find out. And I hoped to God you wouldn't. And in November . . . well, I still hoped you wouldn't. Was it the right decision? In hindsight, no. At the time . . . I honestly don't know. Perhaps it was a bad decision, but I chose the path that I thought was best at the time.'

'Best for whom? Me or you?'

'Best for both of us. If I could have kept you from finding out about this forever, then that's what I would have done. I still think it would have been a far better outcome. You said you wanted the truth, and that's the truth.'

We walked on in silence. I don't know how long it lasted, but quite a long time. There was the sound of the wind and the far-off traffic from the road below, but nothing else. Then Daddy said: 'Listen, Phoebe. There's something else I need to tell you. It's not to manipulate you, and it's definitely not to excuse my own behaviour. But . . . Well, I'm just going to tell you. You're not a child anymore, obviously. You know I've spoken to Bethany?'

My stomach dropped, instantly. 'I don't want to talk about Bethany.'

'We have to.'

'I can't think about what happened. I can't face it!'

Daddy stopped in his tracks. It was difficult, but I forced

myself to stop too. I glanced up at him, almost for the first time since we'd set out from Gee's.

He held up his hands. 'Phoebe, it's not an issue. Bethany's already told me that. She just wants to know that you're OK, so please put it out of your head for now. That's not what we need to talk about.'

I didn't know how to respond to any of this, but Daddy didn't give me much of a chance anyway. I was still processing what he'd said when he continued with the next part.

'Bethany told me what happened in January. She told me everything.'

I was stunned. 'She told you? Why?'

'I found condoms in your bag. I'm sorry – I wasn't snooping. I was just worried about you. You'd been missing for two hours at that point, with no note to say where you'd gone or that you were going to be late home. You weren't answering your phone, and when I tried Bethany, I couldn't get through to her either. I started looking for anything that might give me some clue about where you'd gone. The bag was stuffed at the bottom of your wardrobe. It didn't look like something I'd seen you with before. When I found the condoms in one of the pockets . . . well, I didn't know what to think. The only thing I was sure of was that something was going on. You usually let me know if you're going to be five minutes late, Phoebe. It was just so unlike you.'

I nodded. This was true, obviously. I remembered telling Bethany that there was no likely scenario where Daddy would go rummaging through my stuff, and in a sense, I had not been wrong. It was an unlikely series of events that had led to this outcome. 'You called Bethany again?' I surmised.

'Yes. I called Bethany again. I told her that you were

missing and weren't answering your phone. I told her I'd found the condoms in your bag and needed to know what was going on. And she told me. Straightaway.'

'Straightaway? She didn't try to lie?'

'Of course she didn't. She was hardly going to throw you under the bus, was she?'

'What bus?'

'It's an expression. It means—'

'I know what it means! My point is there *wasn't* a bus. We'd already agreed that I'd say they were mine if you found them. There was absolutely no need for her to tell you everything. She was terrified of anyone else finding out!'

'Yes, I'm sure she was. She was very distressed on the phone. And yet she told me anyway.'

'Why?'

Daddy shrugged. 'You'd have to ask Bethany that. But I suspect she decided that you were more important. You'd disappeared. You weren't answering either of our calls. I think her priority was just to tell me anything that could shed some light on your state of mind.'

I digested this, slowly. Bethany had told Daddy about the abortion. And she'd done so because she was worried about me. She was more worried about me disappearing than she was about protecting her secret – the secret she was going to take to her grave.

'What are you going to do?' I asked. 'Will you tell her parents?'

Daddy didn't say anything for a moment. He looked me in the eyes, his face expressionless. 'You tell me what I should do. What's going to cause the least damage here?'

I thought about what he'd told me a few minutes ago.

Sometimes telling the truth comes with a very high price. I think you understand that. I'd missed the point then, but I didn't miss it now. 'They won't find out if you don't tell them,' I said. 'They'll never find out.'

'They might find out. You can't be certain they won't.'

'Almost certain. But that's not even the point. Bethany hasn't done anything wrong. She hasn't betrayed anyone.'

'I agree. But that's not how her parents would see it. And they certainly wouldn't want me to keep this from them. They'd want to be told, and they'd view it as a betrayal if I didn't tell them. There's no doubt about it.' Daddy gave me a questioning look. 'So whose trust should I break? Which is the good option?'

'There isn't one,' I admitted. 'There are two bad options. But I still think one of them's worse.'

Daddy looked at me for another moment, then nodded. 'So do I. I'm not going to say anything to Bethany's parents. I've told her I won't. But I've also told her that perhaps *she* should. It's something she needs to think about.'

'She has thought about it. She's not going to change her mind.'

Daddy shrugged. 'Maybe not. But it's a big secret to carry forever, and she *is* thinking about it. I wouldn't assume that this is over yet.'

Neither of us said anything for a while. We walked higher up the mountain path, and as the silence stretched, I became aware of a subtle shift in my mood. I no longer felt hollow; I felt conflicted.

'Do you think I'm a hypocrite?' I asked. 'Because I've kept things from you too?'

'No. I don't. I think you've done as well as you could in the circumstances. I think that's always true of you.'

I didn't know what to say to this. It was so contrary to how I viewed myself most of the time. I was used to obsessing over all the things I got wrong – all the things I should have done better.

We carried on to the top of the mountain. It wasn't planned; in fact, it wasn't even discussed. We just kept walking until the path ran out and we stood at the highest point – a narrow, treeless plateau overlooking the broad valley below. The last couple of hundred metres had been steep and rugged, and we'd completed them without speaking a word. Nor had I been thinking about anything in particular; there were loose rocks underfoot, and I'd had to concentrate hard to avoid slipping

Now, at the summit, Daddy was hunched with his hands on his knees, breathing heavily. I stood a few metres from him, looking across the cascade of pine trees that tumbled to the valley floor. I traced the winding mountain road to the village, to the red roofs and whitewashed walls of the houses, as small as Monopoly pieces. My pulse was throbbing and my calves ached, but for the first time in two days, my mind felt clear. I made a decision.

27

Return

It took about an hour to walk back down the mountain, which meant Daddy still had plenty of time to make his flight in the evening. I told him that I was going to phone the school office to advise them that I'd be taking three more mental health days, in addition to the one I'd already had.

'I'm not sure they'll be too happy with that,' Daddy said. 'I mean, it's a little unorthodox. It might be easier if I just tell them you have tonsillitis or something.'

I considered this. 'You're saying that they'll take a problem with my tonsils more seriously than a problem with my brain?'

'Well, it sounds a little ridiculous when you put it like that. But yes – that's what I'm saying. It's how the world works, I'm afraid.'

'It shouldn't be the way the world works. I'm going to tell them the truth.'

I called up from the phone in Gee's kitchen and, as Daddy had predicted, Sandra on reception was not convinced.

'You want to take *three* mental health days?'

'That's correct.'

'Phoebe, has something serious happened? It's just that . . . Well, are you OK? Are you ill?'

'I'm physically well, but mentally unwell. I'm at my

grandmother's house in Spain. I require a few days to relax and reset.'

'Your exams start next week.'

'Exactly. My exams start next week and I'd like to go into them feeling at my best. I'm not going to perform well if my head's a mess.'

There was a long pause down the line, then Sandra said she'd have to call my father to sort this out.

'He's here,' I said. 'I'll pass you over.'

Daddy spoke to her for another ten minutes or so before hanging up. 'Well, it's approved,' he said. 'I had to be put through to the headmaster, but he accepted your reasoning. Eventually. Well done.'

'Thank you for helping.'

'You're definitely coming back at the weekend?'

'Definitely. I'll book the flight before you leave.'

Daddy smiled. 'I'll pay. Is there anything else? Would you like me to say anything to Bethany?'

I took a deep breath. 'You can tell her I'll see her on Sunday. Assuming she's OK with that.'

'She'll be OK with that. I guarantee it.'

So Daddy flew home that evening, and I stayed in Spain for three more days, doing as little as possible. I drank iced coffee with Gee in the garden. I napped in the hammock. At night, I stayed up late and looked at the stars. Daddy was right: it was not an orthodox reason to be absent from school; the Local Education Authority would probably have labelled it as truancy. But as far as I was concerned, it was time well spent.

On the third day, the Friday, I lay in the shade of the olive tree and gazed through the gaps in the branches at an almost cloudless sky, my thoughts drifting. I suppose it was inevitable, but eventually I started thinking about you, Mum, and the last time we were in Spain together. It was the October I turned nine, just after your diagnosis but before you started chemotherapy. What I remembered first was this: I hadn't wanted to go to Spain because it meant taking time out from school, and this was unacceptable to me. It didn't matter when you and Daddy explained that it was OK because of our circumstances, or when you said that it was something we really needed as a family. I couldn't stand the thought of everything suddenly changing, even if it was 'only' going to be for a fortnight. What *I* needed was for everything to stay as normal as possible, as routine and predictable as the tides.

Of course, this wasn't something I was able to articulate well at the time. I had a meltdown and said I wasn't going to go and you couldn't make me, and then you lost your temper and shouted at me. You told me we *were* going because there were more important things than my routines at the moment, and I'd just have to put up with it.

It's the only time I can ever remember you shouting at me.

Almost immediately afterwards, you came to my room and said that you were sorry and if I really couldn't stand the idea then we didn't have to go. You said that you understood how scary and confusing it was for me at the moment, and you were scared and confused too, but that was one of the reasons you wanted to spend some extra time with me and Daddy and Gee. Life wasn't going to feel normal for a little while, and that was why we all had to look after each other. Now was the time to be extra close as a family.

You hugged me and I calmed down, and over the next few

days I came to terms with the idea of being taken out of school for a fortnight so that we could go to Spain and spend time as a family. And when we did, it was far better than I could have imagined. October in Spain was like a hot August in Britain. We spent a lot of time outdoors, in the garden with Gee or going for short walks in the village. Most afternoons, we went to the community swimming pool. You had packed your copy of *The Lord of the Rings* as I'd finished *The Hobbit*, and you thought I'd probably manage to read the whole book in two weeks in Spain, which I did. I was completely immersed, and we spent a lot of time lying on sunbeds next to each other reading. I remember Daddy saying we were a pair of bookworms.

Now, as I lay under the Spanish sun in May 2019, I realised that there had been a lot going on that autumn that I was unaware of. It wasn't just about your diagnosis and coming to terms with that. It was also about what had happened over the previous summer, Daddy's infidelity, and recovering from *that*. And even as I had this thought, I was surprised to find that I could now hold it in my head quite calmly, without recoiling, without the overwhelming sense of betrayal and panic I'd experienced only a few days ago. It wasn't that I didn't feel hurt or angry anymore, because these feelings were still very much there, not far below the surface. But somehow my perspective had shifted enough to accommodate them. I could see that my feelings were just one element in a much larger picture.

I thought about the things Gee had told me: that people were complicated and should never be judged only on their worst actions. Then I thought about Daddy, and having to offset this one awful thing I knew about him against everything else: all the times he'd been there for me in the last sixteen years, the way he was willing to protect Bethany's secret, the fact that no relationship was ever perfect, and it was obviously possible to love someone and act in a way that ran counter to this. I thought, again, of you losing your temper and shouting at me, and all the times I must have shouted at you or Daddy when I was younger, because I felt scared or frustrated. I thought, finally, about how I'd left home without leaving a note, and making sure that I was impossible to contact, causing Daddy significant worry and distress. It wasn't something I'd consciously considered at the time, but if I had – and if I was being honest with myself – I knew exactly how I would have felt about that. I would have felt it was what he deserved. I would have *wanted* him to be scared and upset.

Needless to say, it was not easy to acknowledge this, even to myself, but it was probably beneficial in the long run. I've known for some time that it's often difficult for me to pinpoint what emotions I'm feeling at any given moment, but the realisation I came to then, under the olive tree, was that emotional states aren't always one thing or another. Sometimes, they're one thing *and* another. Sometimes, they're muddled, or self-contradictory.

I thought about Bethany, then, and my very muddled feelings with regard to her. I don't know how long I spent thinking, and I don't know that I made any real progress. But, again, the most significant thing was perhaps that I was now able to think about Bethany, and the kiss, without experiencing the same crushing anxiety I'd felt in its aftermath. I wasn't calm, exactly; there was still some level of agitation as I lay there and considered what had happened and what it might mean – whether it was just a fleeting moment, born out of the highly charged surrounding circumstances, or if it held some deeper significance beyond this. But after a while, the tension started to abate. My chest felt less tight and my breathing slowed, and at some point, I just accepted that this issue with Bethany wasn't going to be solved through introspection alone. I'd have to wait a couple of days until I could see her, and hopefully that would bring some clarity. In the meantime, I decided to seek further advice online.

I went to Bethany's late on Sunday afternoon, one week after I'd been there last. One week after the kiss. My mind was considerably clearer than it had been, but I was nervous, nevertheless. As I rang the doorbell, I still didn't know what I was going to say. But I clung to what Gee had told me: *It doesn't really matter what you say . . . She's your friend and you can work this out together.* Gee had been right about seeing Daddy and she would be right about this, too.

I didn't say anything at all when Bethany answered the door, and neither did she. There was a small flutter in my stomach. Then she stepped forward, into the porch, and put her arms around me. We hugged. And right then, it was all I needed. I didn't feel the urge to kiss her. I just felt happy that I was back, when a week ago that had seemed so utterly impossible.

'Come on,' she said. 'Let's go for a walk.'

The island was busy again, as it would be every weekend until the autumn, so we ended up walking to the north beach, which was usually the quietest. We talked along the way, and it wasn't awkward. Bethany asked me about Spain; I asked her about the last week at school.

'It was weird, you not being there,' she said. 'It made it less . . . Well, it made it *less*. In general.'

'What did you tell your mum and dad? I assume they asked why I'd disappeared to Spain.'

'They did. I told them you were having an existential crisis.'

I felt myself smiling at this. 'Did they believe you?'

Bethany shrugged. 'They found it completely plausible. Anyway, I didn't know what else I *could* tell them.'

'You could have told them that I kissed you and immediately fled the country.'

'That's your truth to tell, if you decide to. But just so you know, I'm fine with it – honestly.'

'I thought you were horrified,' I said, blushing a little.

'Of course I wasn't horrified! I was shocked. It was . . . well, it was a shock.'

I nodded. 'I realise that now. I didn't at the time. I thought I'd ruined our friendship. Permanently.'

'Phoebe, you can't ruin our friendship. It was a kiss. It's not a big deal.'

'It's kind of a big deal,' I said. 'For me, anyway.'

'OK. It *is* a big deal. Of course it's a big deal. But you're still my best friend. I don't want anything to get in the way of that. Do you understand?'

I nodded again. I did understand, but it was still a relief to hear the words. A huge relief.

'So how long have you known?' Bethany asked.

I didn't need a clarification. Nor did I need to calculate. 'A week.'

Bethany actually laughed at this. 'Seriously?'

'I've known precisely as long as you have. Except *known* might be the wrong word. I'm still not sure exactly what it is I know. It's been a confusing week; I'm still trying to work through my feelings.'

269

'Have you talked to your dad about it?'

'No, not properly. I think he's giving me some space until I'm ready. I talked to Gee about it, though.'

'And what did she say?'

'She said we can't help who we're attracted to.'

'Well, she's right. But . . .' Bethany waited tactfully as a gaggle of tourists passed us on the other side of the narrow lane, heading back towards the village. 'Phoebe, you know I don't feel that way about you, don't you? I mean, I love you like a sister, but it's never going to be anything else for me. I'm sorry – I'm not sure if I even need to say it, but—'

'You don't need to say it. I know how *you* feel. I just don't know how I feel. That's the part that's going to take a bit of working out. I've started doing some basic research, though.'

Bethany smiled at this. 'Of course you have. Anything interesting?'

'Well, I'm probably *not* asexual, but I guess that goes without saying now. I think I might actually be demi.' I could tell from Bethany's face that she wasn't familiar with this term, which was not surprising. It was not particularly well known. 'Demisexual. It's where you have to form a strong emotional bond with someone before you start finding them physically attractive.'

'Right.' Bethany shrugged. 'Well, send me the appropriate TED Talk when you find it. I'll make sure I watch it.'

I searched Bethany's expression and tone of voice for sarcasm, and found none. She looked very serious.

'Here's a thought, though,' she said after a moment. '*Just* a thought. Perhaps you don't need to be in such a hurry to label yourself?'

I shrugged. 'I like labels. They help me to understand things better.'

Bethany smiled again. 'I know. All I'm saying is you're fine whatever you are. More than fine. You know that, don't you?'

'I do know that.' And what was surprising was that I meant it. For the first time in ages, I did think that I was fine. There was nothing I needed to change.

Bethany and I got to the beach and sat down at the base of the dunes. 'I've got a favour I need to ask you,' she said, 'before we go back. Actually, favour might be the wrong word. It's something big.'

'What is it?'

Bethany didn't say anything for a moment. She closed her eyes, breathed, and then opened them again. 'I want you to come home with me after this. I'm going to talk to my parents.'

I didn't need to ask what about. 'Are you sure? I don't want to put you off, but I can think of several reasons why you shouldn't. At least, not yet. There's our exams, for a start. Maybe you should delay for a month?'

Bethany shook her head. 'If I put it off, I'll never do it.'

I thought about this statement for several seconds. 'That suggests you still have doubts. If you're fully committed to this, then waiting for the appropriate time shouldn't be an issue.'

'The issue is me losing my nerve. If I don't do this, it will be because I'm afraid, not because I have doubts. Trust me, I've been thinking this through all week. I know it's the right thing to do.'

I nodded. I'd been somewhat prepared for this, of course, since my conversation with Daddy, but it was still a surprise hearing Bethany say the words aloud. 'What made you change your mind?' I asked.

'Lots of things. But mainly it was talking to your dad. It wasn't anything he said, more . . . I dunno. Just talking to him. Being *able* to talk to him.'

'What do you mean?'

Bethany shrugged. 'I was so scared at first. He told me he'd found the condoms and I just had this bolt of pure terror, as if my world was about to fall in.'

'You didn't have to tell him, you know. We had our story worked out and I would have gone along with it.'

'I know you would have. But you've told enough lies for me over the last six months. Plus your dad was frantic. He asked if you had a secret boyfriend. He asked if there was any chance the two of you had run off together! I think his head was just filled with all the worst stories you hear on the news. At that point, I realised that I couldn't lie to him. He deserved the truth, and he needed to find you. I figured that anything I held back was just going to make this even harder. I didn't want him to waste time on false suspicions.'

'You didn't know how he'd react, though. He could have told your parents.'

'Yeah, I realised that.'

'And you did it anyway.'

Bethany gave a small nod. 'I did. To be honest, I was pretty worried about you too. I guess I'd rung you a dozen times at that point, and I'd had a lot of time to think things through. My main thought was that I haven't always been a good friend over the last year. I've been so wrapped up in my own

272

problems. I didn't consider how much strain you must have been under too.'

'It wasn't why I'd run away, though. You must have realised that?'

'I thought it might be a contributing factor. But either way, it was another thing pushing me in the right direction. I told your dad, and it was definitely one of the better decisions I've made recently. He didn't judge me. He didn't make me feel like I'd made some unforgivable mistake. He just listened. Sympathetically. The same way you always have.'

'Because you haven't done anything wrong!'

'I've done plenty of things wrong. But that's not really the point.'

Bethany stared at the sea for a while. I didn't say anything. I waited for her to tell me the point.

'My parents *are* going to judge me. They are going to be appalled, at least at first. But I don't believe the same things they do, and I don't want to go on pretending. I want them to accept me as I am.'

This was not unreasonable, but that didn't mean it was going to be straightforward. I wanted to make sure Bethany knew this. 'What if they can't accept what you've done? Are you prepared for that possibility?'

Bethany shook her head, giving a very weak smile. 'I'm prepared for it. It doesn't change anything.'

'If your parents throw you out, you can come and live with me and Daddy. I'm sure he'd be OK with it.'

'Thank you. It's good to know I won't be homeless.' Bethany put her fingers to her temples and shook her head again. 'My dad gets back from church in about half an hour. I don't see any sense in dragging this out.'

'Do you know what you're going to say?'

Bethany laughed at this, somewhat hysterically. 'I haven't a clue.'

'Do you need me to say anything?'

'No. I just need you to be there. Same as always.'

28

Confession

We timed it so there was no waiting around. Once we were at the edge of the village, Bethany texted her father: *Are you home? I'm on my way back. I've got something I need to speak to you and Mum about. It's urgent. Phoebe's with me.*

A message came back a minute later. Bethany didn't tell me what it said, only that her parents were both home and waiting. I held her hand and we walked the rest of the way in silence.

Mrs Collins met us at the door with a worried face. 'Beth, what's this about? Is everything OK?'

Bethany shook her head. Her hand was trembling a little, and although she'd told me I didn't need to say anything, I thought this was one instance where I'd better. 'Bethany needs to talk to you and Reverend Collins at the same time. Please let her do that. It's extremely difficult for her, but important.'

Mrs Collins hesitated a moment, and then stepped aside so we could enter. Bethany squeezed my hand and gave me the shallowest of smiles.

We went through to the living room, where Reverend Collins was already waiting. Bethany and I sat together on the sofa.

'I had an abortion,' Bethany said.

Her voice didn't shake, and the words were perfectly clear – made all the clearer by the silence that followed. I let go of Bethany's hand and put my arm around her. I hadn't expected her to say it quite like that; I'd expected some build up. Mrs Collins seemed to agree that the lack of context was confusing.

'Bethany, I don't understand,' she said. 'Is this supposed to be a joke? Because it's not at all funny.'

Bethany didn't say anything. I'm not sure she was capable of anything more at that point; it had probably taken all her nerve just to get that one sentence out.

Reverend Collins was looking at Bethany with an expression that was difficult to read. In other circumstances, I'd have interpreted it as 'mild concern', but in *these* circumstances, that was not a reaction that made much sense. I had to conclude that he was probably in the same boat as Mrs Collins, waiting for the impossible punchline.

'Bethany, please tell me what's going on here,' Mrs Collins said, her voice becoming slightly shrill. 'You obviously haven't . . . You'd have had to have been pregnant. You'd have had to have had sex!'

Bethany still didn't say anything. Mrs Collins looked at me. 'Phoebe?'

'That's correct,' I said. 'Those are the things that happened.' I didn't know what else I could say in this situation. Bethany had told me I didn't need to do any talking, but it felt necessary now, and the simplest option was to restate the facts and wait for them to sink in. It did not take long this time. Mrs Collins's face collapsed. She started weeping into her hands.

Reverend Collins got up from his chair and left without saying a word. A moment later, I heard the back door open and close.

There wasn't anything to be done. I waited. I kept my arm around Bethany, who had finally stopped shaking. She was looking at her mother with an expression that was full of contradiction.

Reverend Collins came back in. He'd been gone maybe three minutes, and he looked as if he'd aged a decade. His face was taut and bloodless. 'Phoebe, I'd like you to leave now,' he said. 'We need to talk to Bethany alone.'

I looked at Bethany, who shook her head. 'I want Phoebe here.'

'It's not up to you,' Reverend Collins said flatly. 'This is my house and my decision.'

'Phoebe's been here for me from the start. If it wasn't for her, I'd have fallen apart months ago.'

'*Months* ago?' Mrs Collins said in a strangled sob.

Reverend Collins didn't seem to think this was a relevant detail. 'Phoebe, I've got no idea what your involvement in this has been, and right now I don't care. I'm telling you to leave.'

'If Phoebe goes, I go,' Bethany threatened.

It was an awkward situation, obviously, but I decided the best course was inaction. My allegiance was to Bethany, and however angry Reverend Collins was, I didn't think it likely that he would remove me by force.

I was right. After a ten-second standoff, he took out his mobile phone and called Daddy. 'Stuart, I need you to come and collect your daughter from my house. Right now. I want her out and she's refusing to leave.'

He hung up moments later, having uttered a curt *thank you*. I deduced that Daddy had figured out what was going on and hadn't wasted any time asking pointless questions.

Reverend Collins deduced the same thing, almost immediately. 'Does your father know about this?' he asked.

'He does,' I confirmed.

'He's only known for a few days,' Bethany said. 'He's pretty much the reason I'm talking to you now.'

Reverend Collins did not respond to this. The room stayed utterly silent until there was a knock on the door. Reverend Collins brought Daddy into the living room and said: 'Stuart, I've been informed you already know what's going on here. We can talk about that another time. Right now, Ruth and I need to speak with Bethany alone.'

Daddy nodded, then turned to me. 'Come on, Precious. Let's go.'

'Bethany wants me here.'

'Bethany isn't going to get what she wants!' Mrs Collins snapped. 'And you should never have been involved in this, Phoebe. I don't believe for one second that Bethany would have made this decision without you!'

'You don't get to talk to Phoebe like that!' Bethany said. 'All she's done is help me!'

'Help you *how*?' Mrs Collins said.

Daddy raised his hand, palms flat. 'OK, OK. I think everyone needs to calm down for a moment. This isn't going to solve anything.' Daddy turned back to me and spoke very softly. 'Phoebe, you need to come home with me now. Honestly, it's for the best. Bethany and her parents do need to talk in private. It's the only way through this.'

I looked at Bethany, who closed her eyes and gave a tiny nod. 'I'll be OK.'

We hugged again, then I drew back and placed my hands on her shoulders, looking her straight in the face. 'That was the bravest thing I've ever seen,' I told her, loud enough so that everyone could hear. 'You have nothing to be ashamed of. Nothing.'

Having maintained an icy calm throughout, Reverend Collins now raised his voice. 'Get out, Phoebe! Out!'

Daddy looked extremely tense as I went to him, and he was staring at Reverend Collins with barely suppressed anger. But he said nothing. He put a gentle hand on my back and guided me to the door.

'Are you OK?' he asked, once we were outside.

'I'm OK,' I told him. 'It's just the situation was impossible. I'm sorry if I was rude to Reverend Collins.'

'You were perfect,' Daddy said. 'I'm incredibly proud of you. Your mum would be too.'

For some reason it was this, more than anything else that had happened, that made me feel like I might cry. I swallowed heavily and said: 'I told Bethany that she could stay with us for a while, if she needed somewhere to go. Is that OK?'

'Yes, it's OK. But hopefully it won't come to that. Just give them some time.'

'How much time do you think they'll need?'

'A lot of time,' Daddy said.

29

Fallout

I was half-expecting Bethany to turn up at our house that night, but she did not. She didn't communicate with me in any way for over three hours, by which time I'd concluded that her phone might have been confiscated. This theory was debunked when a WhatsApp message finally came through at a quarter to nine.

They wanted to confiscate it, Bethany wrote, having established that she was OK and the preliminary talk with her parents was over. *It led to another massive argument. I had to tell them that I'd stay in the house, but only if they respected my right to keep my own property. Otherwise, I was prepared to leave.*

How did they react?

Not well! They don't want me talking to you or anyone else. But mostly you. I'm sorry. They'd figured out you probably went with me to the clinic and there didn't seem much point denying it. But now they're convinced you've put ungodly ideas into my head. As if I couldn't possibly have ungodly ideas of my own! I told them I'd stopped believing almost a year ago and it was nothing to do with you (I thought I might as well get everything out in the open!) but it didn't make much difference. I'm sorry. They shouldn't be blaming you for any of this.

You don't have to apologise. I assumed they'd be angry with me too. I'm just glad we're still able to talk.

Only because there's no practical way to prevent it. I told them that if they took my phone I'd still have my computer to talk to you, and if they took that I wouldn't be able to revise properly.

They accepted that?

We reached a 'compromise'. I get to keep my phone and my computer, in return they got to check through my messages first.

You let them read your messages??

I'd already deleted the ones I didn't want them to see. I got rid of Will's contact details yesterday, and I'll be deleting all this as soon as we're done. I'm not leaving anything for them to find. Not that it matters much anymore.

You haven't told them about Will?

No and I'm not going to. They want to call his parents. He deserves a lot of things but I'm not sure he deserves that.

I wasn't so sure, so I typed nothing and waited for the next chunk of text to come through from Bethany.

Whatever you think about Will he's stuck to his half of the bargain. He's told no one. You've got to give him that.

I suppose.

Phoebe I wanted to tell my parents. I did it for my own reasons and it's got nothing to do with Will anymore.

I had to concede that Bethany's logic here was sound, but I couldn't imagine that her parents would drop the issue so easily.

Are you still glad you did it? I asked. *Was it worth it?*

It was pretty horrible obviously. But I don't regret it. Yet. You should probably ask me again in a week.

I could see that Bethany was typing a new message, so I waited.

Mum cried for about an hour. I think my dad's still in shock. I've honestly never seen him like this before. He can barely look at me.

He might need a lot of time to process everything.

Maybe. I'm not sure.

It was a short message, but it had taken a long time to come through. I decided it was not an issue I should press any further.

What's happening next week? I asked. *Have you talked about it?*

A bit. I've agreed that I won't leave the house without permission. I'll make myself available to talk as and when. I'll respect the rules of the house etc. They're not forcing me to pray. So that's something.

What about Thursday? I asked. Thursday afternoon was when we had our first exam. In normal circumstances, Mrs Collins or Daddy would have been driving us both in that morning.

I've honestly got no idea. At the moment I can't see how the next month is going to work. They don't want me to see you but they can't pull me out of school in the middle of exams and I'm still going to have to stay there some nights. Basically it's a mess.

I had to agree. It was a mess.

Bethany continued to message me on and off over the next few days. Objectively, it didn't seem as if things were getting any better, but she appeared to be coping nevertheless. It was her parents who were struggling to function.

Her mother, she said, was still prone to tears throughout the day and without warning, with family meal times being particularly tense. Her father, meanwhile, was spending an increasing amount of time in isolation, either in his study or in the church in the early hours of the morning. On Wednesday, he had an emergency consultation with the Bishop of Newcastle, which Bethany only found out about from her mother, after he'd left.

He's going to discuss your abortion with the Bishop of Newcastle? I asked

I guess he is, Bethany replied.

Are you OK with that?

It would have been nice if he'd run it by me first, but my feelings obviously don't matter here.

Are you being sarcastic? I can't tell in text.

To be honest, I don't really care that much. If talking to the Bishop helps my dad feel better then he should do it. As long as I don't have to talk to her.

I deduced at this point that the Bishop of Newcastle was a woman, which added an interesting new dimension to the consultation, though Bethany assured me this was unlikely to affect her outlook on abortion to a significant extent.

I'd guess she's going to think the same thing my mum thinks. I've killed a baby and God will judge me for it.

Is that what your mum's actually said? I asked.

It's what she thinks. I know it is.

Things did not get better, but it was some time before they got markedly worse.

I saw Bethany for fifteen minutes before our Geography exam on Thursday; Mrs Collins had dropped her off as late as

283

she could while still complying with the school's guidelines on arriving in good time. Knowing that this would be our only chance to talk in person all week, we did not wait in the queue outside the exam hall with everyone else. We went for a fraught ten-minute walk around the yard.

'Did the Bishop of Newcastle help with your father's mental state?' I asked.

'In the short term, yes,' Bethany said. 'But in the long term, I'm not so sure. It's complicated.' She sighed deeply. 'My dad's *forgiven* me. My mum too. Absolutely and unconditionally.'

On the face of it, this was the best possible news, but I suspected from her tone that this wasn't the case. I was correct.

'It's bullshit. It's just a desperate attempt to make themselves feel better, and to try to bring me back into the fold. They want me to admit I've done something terrible and repent. That's the ultimate goal here.'

'Not necessarily. It seems clear that they want a reconciliation. Have they made your repentance a condition of this?'

'Phoebe, I know how this stuff works. It's been fed to me my whole life: admit your sins, ask for forgiveness and then everything will be perfect again.'

'I don't see the problem. That's what they believe, but they're no longer asking you to believe it, are they?'

'No, they're not explicitly asking. You're missing the point . . . OK, say, for example, you tell your dad that you're gay, and his reply is basically—'

'I'm not certain that I'm gay,' I pointed out. 'The situation might be a bit—'

'It's just a hypothetical! You tell your dad you're gay, and his response is: *OK, I'm devastated, obviously, but I'm able to forgive you* . . . well, you can see the problem with that. I know I don't have to spell it out for you.'

I nodded; the point was now obvious, especially in light of our previous conversations. 'You don't want them to forgive you. You want them to accept you.'

'Yes! They don't have to agree with me, they don't have to change their beliefs. But I need them to stop implying that my opinion doesn't matter. I'm not going to accept their forgiveness as some wonderful gift that I need but don't deserve. What kind of forgiveness is that?'

'Have you told them any of this?'

'I'm talking to a brick wall. We spent about an hour last night going over the same ground again and again. In the end, I just asked if I could leave the house for a bit, given that I was now *unconditionally* forgiven. So you can guess how that went. It's not a punishment, apparently; it's just a consequence of my actions. I need to regain their trust. Until I do, things are staying exactly as they are. Apart from being ferried to and from my exams, I'm basically under house arrest.'

I nodded. I had already deduced this was the case, based on today's transport arrangements. Yet I still had hope that things would improve with Bethany's parents, given sufficient time.

'They can't go on punishing you forever,' I told Bethany.

'It's not a punishment,' she said. Bitterly.

So what ensued, over the following weeks, was something like an impasse, or perhaps a standoff. She continued to be dissatisfied, her parents continued to be unhappy, and her father continued to receive spiritual guidance from God and the Bishop of Newcastle. In the short term, it would have certainly made Bethany's life easier if she'd accepted the forgiveness that was on offer, but I could understand why she refused to. Her goal had not changed since she'd first told her parents about the abortion. She didn't want her life to be easier; she wanted it to be better.

In support of this cause, she accepted every restriction that was imposed on her, in the hope that she'd eventually regain her parents' trust. She didn't leave her house unsupervised. Contrary to her earlier assumption, she was no longer permitted to stay at school overnight. On the couple of occasions when the tides were too inconvenient, Mrs Collins insisted they stay together in a hotel in Berwick. Consequently, the only times I saw Bethany were in the ten-minute snatches before or after an exam. We continued to message every day, but as time passed, it was only a small consolation. At a previous point in my life, I would have said that it was perfectly possible, and in some ways preferable, to conduct a friendship solely online. But now, I missed her physical presence very much. The strength of my feeling was a surprise, yet after some careful introspection, I concluded that I was not pining for Bethany in a romantic sense. My feelings, in this instance, were not at all confused. I simply wanted my friend back.

I comforted myself with books. When I wasn't revising or messaging Bethany, I spent my time re-reading *The Wheel of Time*, because it was familiar enough to feel reassuring and vast enough to get lost in. I didn't know if I'd manage to get through all fifteen books again, but the main purpose was just to keep myself busy and distracted, immersed in another world while I waited for something to change in mine and Bethany's.

And then something did change, and it was as if a chasm had opened beneath me.

In the final week of exams, I received a distraught phone call from Bethany.

'My dad's requested a transfer to a new parish,' she told me, in between sobs. 'He wants us to start afresh, as soon as we can.'

I waited for Bethany to catch her breath, but I already had a plunging feeling in my stomach. I knew what was coming next.

'There's nothing I can do,' she said. 'By autumn, we'll be gone.'

30

Perspective

I flailed on the brink of a precipice. The sensation was familiar because it was the same one I'd experienced a few weeks earlier, following the disastrous hour that had begun with the discovery of my father's infidelity and ended with the unplanned lesbian kiss. Immediately afterwards, I had gone into freefall, perceiving the situation as unsolvable – and this was the instinctive response I had to avoid this time round. Despair was not a useful reaction in this context, or perhaps any context.

Once I'd got off the phone to Bethany, I allowed myself ten minutes of deep breathing to regain my composure. Then I went through to the living room, swiftly summarised the phone call for Daddy, and asked if Bethany could still come to live with us. He took a surprisingly long time to answer. 'Poppet, I don't think it's that simple anymore. We're no longer talking about something temporary, are we?'

'You agreed that she could stay with us if her parents kicked her out. There was always the possibility it would be a longer-term arrangement.'

'Yes, but they're not kicking her out. As far as I can see, they still want to fix things.'

'It's a terrible way to fix things!'

'I agree. If anything, it's going to alienate Bethany even more. But her moving in here isn't going to solve the problem, either.'

'Could you talk to her parents?'

'I could, but I'm not sure it's my place. And I'm even less sure it would do any good. I might be one of the last people they want to discuss this with.'

'Will you try, though?'

Daddy didn't answer directly. After a few moments, he said: 'Phoebe, I know it's hard to understand, but you have to look at this from the perspective of Bethany's parents as well. I'd imagine they're every bit as scared and angry and confused as Bethany is right now. They've probably worked themselves into a position where starting again seems like the only option – the only way they can rebuild the relationship and do better.'

'But it isn't! It's probably going to make things worse for everyone. You've already said you agree about that.'

'I'm not saying it's a good decision. I'm saying you need to understand why they're making it. Approach the problem on their terms and encourage Bethany to do the same. Trust me: that's the only way any of this is getting resolved.'

Daddy had given me a lot of food for thought, and I immediately set my mind to the task he had suggested: I spent the next three hours considering and writing down everything I knew or could conjecture about Bethany's parents' motivations, assuming that their overriding objective was to 'fix' their family and protect Bethany from future harm. Needless to say, this was extremely challenging, and it led to some uncomfortable conclusions. Foremost among these was the fact that Daddy was probably correct in his initial assessment: Bethany couldn't live with us – it wasn't a good solution to her problems and it was unlikely that her parents would consent to it, given that she wasn't even allowed to be in a car with us at present. It was likely that Bethany's parents saw me, and perhaps Daddy, as a corrupting influence, and probably held similar views regarding school, since the unknown pregnancy culprit was still at large within that environment.

Working through these issues did not lead to a solution, or even an obvious plan, but it was helpful insofar as it cleared my head of clutter and got me to a point where I could see the broader picture of how this conflict was evolving. The process, and the intense concentration involved, had also made me very tired. I was in bed by eleven thirty, and deeply asleep soon after.

When I awoke, at the normal time, I found a message from Bethany on my phone, sent at 3.07 a.m. *This has all gone to shit. I wish I'd kept my mouth shut.*

This can be fixed, I replied. *Everything can be fixed.*

I waited but there was nothing back, so I got up and started my trampoline workout, and as I bounced, I repeated the same affirmation again and again. This *can* be fixed. Bethany didn't want to leave, and I doubted that her parents did either. The only thing driving them forward was their belief that it was the least damaging course of action. So if this reasoning was revealed to be spurious, there was every chance they'd be forced to reconsider.

It was the last day before our final exam, and aside from revision, I had a free schedule; I decided that I needed to talk to Reverend Collins as soon as possible. Due to tiredness, general despondency and the potential for the conversation to become heated, it was clear to me that Bethany might struggle to argue her case in the most effective manner. She needed an advocate and I was the best (and only) candidate.

I washed, dressed and fed Gladys. I left a note for Daddy which read as follows:

I've gone to St Mary's to see if I can talk to Bethany's dad. Don't worry: I've thought this through and I'm almost certain it's not a terrible idea. X

It wasn't the most elegant piece of writing I'd ever done, but it accurately reflected my mindset at that point. I was ninety per cent confidence, ten per cent I-don't-have-a-clue-what-I'm-doing. But if the last year had taught me anything, it was that you couldn't always plan for every eventuality; sometimes, you just had to make it up as you went along.

I was out of the house before seven, having skipped breakfast and coffee. Obviously, I didn't know for sure that Bethany's dad would be at the church this early, but she had indicated that it was a common occurrence, and when I got there, I found that the door was open.

It took a few seconds for my eyes to adjust to the interior, but when they did, I saw that Reverend Collins was sitting alone in a pew at the front of the building, directly opposite the pulpit. I had entered quietly and he did not look around or give any other indication that he was aware of my presence. He was sitting perfectly still and I assumed there was a good chance he was praying. I didn't want to disturb this, so I removed my shoes and crept to a pew at the back and sat down.

I was able to observe him for some time. The church was dark, cool and peaceful, and empty apart from the two of us. From a purely sensory perspective, I could see why church-going was appealing.

Eventually, Reverend Collins finished and got up. I don't know if he was startled to find me watching him – it was difficult to tell across almost the full length of the building – but he didn't hesitate in walking over.

He didn't say good morning. He said: 'Phoebe, I don't want to be rude, but I'm not sure I have anything to say to you. I can guess why you're here and it's not going to change anything. I have to do what's best for my family.'

'I understand that. Could we talk for a little while anyway?'

'I honestly think it will be a waste of time.'

'I don't mind risking that.'

Reverend Collins didn't say anything. I shifted over in the pew so that he could sit down if he wanted to, which he didn't. 'Where are your shoes?' he asked.

'I left them at the door. I wanted to sit down but I didn't want to disturb you with my footsteps if you were praying. It seemed the logical option.'

I wasn't certain, but I thought I saw the corner of Reverend Collins's mouth twitch at this. 'You can have five minutes,' he said.

I nodded my agreement and took my phone out so I could set the timer. Having five minutes was not a problem. In a sense, it was playing to my strengths, since a short and direct conversation suited me better. With five minutes on the clock, there could be no beating round the bush.

'Do you think Bethany's going to hell?' I asked, tapping the start icon on my screen.

'Phoebe, I can't answer that question in five minutes. It's

too complicated. I doubt that your notion of hell is the same as mine, for a start.'

'OK, but you think she won't be "saved". Is that correct? I mean, does she have to believe to be saved?'

'It's not that simple, but in brief, yes. That's the Christian teaching.'

'Can God choose to save her anyway, regardless of whether she believes or not?'

'He's God. He can do anything.'

'Yes, of course.' I decided this wasn't the time to bring up the standard paradox of omnipotence: i.e. can God create a dumbbell so heavy that even He can't lift it? 'So, you're saying it's not a deal-breaker? He can just—'

Reverend Collins cut me off; it was possible he was becoming impatient. 'Phoebe, you're a very intelligent girl, but these are complex issues that the Church has spent millennia considering. We can't adequately discuss Christian theology in five minutes, so if you have anything else to say, I strongly suggest you say it.'

I nodded. 'You want to take the course of action that's best for your family and for Bethany's spiritual health. Is that correct?'

'Yes. We've established that.'

'But what if you've got it wrong? What if moving isn't the best way?'

Reverend Collins sighed. 'If I'm wrong, I'm wrong. I can only do what's best according to my beliefs and conscience. The same as you.'

'And the same as Bethany,' I pointed out. Reverend Collins didn't reply, so I continued. 'She's very unhappy at the moment. You must be aware of that.'

'Yes, Phoebe. I'm aware of that. She's unhappy. We're all unhappy.'

'At the moment she wants the same thing you do. She wants a reconciliation. Aren't you worried that this course of action could make things worse? It could lead to a further deterioration in your relationship.'

'I'm aware of that too. I think it would save time if you assume that I've thought about these issues at great length – longer than you have. And I have to try something to bring our daughter back to us. I'm not prepared to simply wait as she drifts further and further away.'

To my great surprise, Reverend Collins sat down at this point. Closer up, I could see that he was tired. Tired and sad. Nevertheless, I saw little choice but to continue. A glance at my phone, which was resting on the pew between us, informed me that I had less than three minutes left to make my arguments.

I asked another blunt question: 'Do you think Bethany was responsible for murdering an innocent?'

'I can't answer that,' Reverend Collins said.

'Do you mean you can't bring yourself to answer or you don't know the answer?'

He was silent for a frustratingly long time. It might have been an uncharitable thought, but I worried he was trying to run down the clock. After all, whatever Reverend Collins's religious convictions, the notion that Bethany was a murderer was patently absurd. I decided a radical intervention was required, in the form of a thought experiment I'd encountered while researching the ethics of abortion.

'You're in a burning IVF clinic,' I told him. 'In the room with you are a newborn baby and a jar of one hundred refrigerated embryos awaiting implantation. You have time to save the baby or the hundred potential babies, but not both. Which do you choose?'

'Phoebe, that's ridiculous! The comparison isn't even—'

I spoke over him. 'It doesn't matter if the scenario is ridiculous. It's supposed to be ridiculous! The point is, it's not a question any sane person has to think twice about. The death of an embryo is a world away from the death of an actual baby, and abortion is not murder.'

'I see! Well, thank you for that moral instruction! This is the same advice you gave to my daughter, is it?'

'No. I listened to what *she* wanted and supported her decision. And I still think she had the right to make that decision for herself. You obviously disagree.'

Again Reverend Collins didn't say anything, and I couldn't afford to give him too much time before pressing the matter. 'What would you have done if you'd known? Would you have tried to persuade her to continue with the pregnancy?'

'Yes. I would have done everything in my power to persuade her.'

'I suspect that's why she didn't tell you. She knew it would be counter-productive.'

It was in the silence that followed that my alarm activated. I switched it off and stood. But Reverend Collins didn't stand. He shook his head. 'Sit down, Phoebe. I have something else to say to *you*.'

I sat.

Reverend Collins said: 'I realise that you can talk your way through this calmly and logically. It's not the same for me, and I don't think it should be the same. It's painful! I would have raised that child myself if it came to it. Do you understand that?'

I nodded. 'I understand. And I think Bethany did too. She understood and she didn't want to be forced into continuing with the pregnancy against her wishes.'

'I couldn't and wouldn't force Bethany to do anything!' Reverend Collins snapped. 'She has free will and she gets to make her own decisions. But she also needed to understand the full consequences of those decisions.'

'She did. I was there, and she underwent a thorough psychological evaluation before the procedure. She talked to a doctor and two trained counsellors.'

'I see! And what moral guidance did *they* give her? Since you remained completely neutral.'

'They also remained neutral. They only advised on the medical and emotional side of things.'

Reverend Collins snorted. 'So perhaps you can see my point? Bethany's *choice* was not made after a full consideration of what she was agreeing to. She deserved better!'

I could see that Reverend Collins was getting increasingly angry, and I wanted to diffuse the situation, if I could. The problem was, I didn't really know what else I could say to him. We were approaching this from very different angles. I think Reverend Collins recognised this too, as he'd started to get up.

'Can I tell you one last thing?' I asked, knowing that I was possibly just stalling the inevitable.

Reverend Collins looked at me for a moment, then nodded. 'One thing. After that, I'd like to consider the matter closed. You're always welcome in the church, obviously, but I don't want to have this conversation again.'

'We won't,' I said. 'I promise.'

Reverend Collins nodded again, indicating I could proceed. I didn't have time to pick my words carefully. But I understood, now, that there probably wasn't some perfect way of phrasing things, and there might not be any argument I could make that would change Reverend Collins's mind. I just wanted to finish the conversation on a less toxic note. I didn't want him to dismiss what I'd said out of hand, just because I'd upset him.

'I think you're aware that I suffered a minor mental breakdown about a month ago,' I told him, allowing the words to come as spontaneously as possible. 'Bethany may have informed you I was having an existential crisis, or something similar.'

Reverend Collins nodded, expressionless.

'Well, there were quite a few reasons for that, but the main one was I discovered my father had an affair eight years ago, the year before my mum died.'

The lack of any reaction from Reverend Collins suggested this was not new information for him, and supported what Rachael Tibbet and Mrs Frost had told me: that everyone knew everything on this island.

'I was extremely angry and upset,' I continued. 'I suppose it felt like my whole world had collapsed, because my dad had done this terrible thing, and all the ideas I'd had about him being perfect, about my family being perfect, turned out to be wrong. And I didn't have any way of reconciling all these contradictory ideas I had in my head, like I didn't know how you could supposedly love someone and treat them so badly, or how *I* could go on loving my dad when I knew he'd done this thing that seemed so selfish and cruel. Or how—'

Reverend Collins cut me off. 'Phoebe, I'm sorry you had to deal with all these things. But I'm not sure what point you're trying to make here. Is there supposed to be some obvious parallel to my own situation, or Bethany's? Because, frankly, I don't see it.'

'It's possible I don't have a clear point,' I admitted. 'But maybe that *is* the point. It's messy, and I still don't know how I feel about everything I found out. But I do know how I want the future to be, and I suppose I'm just prepared to work through the mess to get there. And I think it's more or less the same for Bethany. It's why she chose to tell you about the abortion when she didn't have to. She wasn't making her life any easier, obviously. But she wanted a chance to have a more genuine and truthful relationship with you.'

Reverend Collins started to walk away.

'Just one more thing,' I said.

'That was supposed to be the final thing,' Reverend Collins objected. 'We had an agreement.'

'This is closely related,' I told him. 'And it will only take ten seconds. If I could change one thing about my life – I mean *anything* – well, you can probably guess what that would be.'

Reverend Collins stared at me blankly for a few moments, then gave a small nod.

'I'd want my mum back,' I said. 'If I could have that, I don't think I'd care how difficult the circumstances were.'

I got up from the pew, collected my shoes, and left the church.

31

No Way Back

I'd done everything I could, and it had not been enough. That was the impression I left with, and there was nothing in the next twenty-four hours that changed my opinion.

On the Thursday, I saw Bethany for our final exam. As had been the case for the past few weeks, we had about ten minutes before and ten after, the narrow window in which Bethany was free from her parents' supervision and we could talk face-to-face. I had not yet told her about going to see her father, and I wasn't sure how she was going to react. But it turned out I needn't have worried.

'How did it go?' she asked – casually, as if she had no stake in this. 'Not great, I assume?'

'I think I made him quite angry,' I said, 'but I probably didn't make matters any worse.'

'I don't think that's possible anymore.' Bethany gave a smile that was not really a smile. 'Thank you, anyway.'

'Have you told anyone else that you're leaving yet?' I asked. 'Anyone from school, I mean?'

'I've not had much of a chance. If you add up all the time I've spent talking to anyone else in the last few weeks, it probably amounts to, like, ten minutes total. I swear, everyone thinks I've become an exam hermit.' Bethany smiled ruefully.

'I guess I'll end up breaking the news on WhatsApp. You know, I asked my parents if they'd let me go to the Leavers' Evening tomorrow. I thought there was *some* chance they'd allow it, to say goodbye to all the people I'm probably not going to see again.'

I'd not thought much about the Leavers' Evening. In reality, it was misnamed, and largely pointless, since most of our peers would be coming back in the autumn for Sixth Form. I could see why Bethany wanted to attend, though. She was actually leaving.

'Your parents said no?' I deduced.

'They said no. Same old thing: they're not punishing me, they just don't think it would be appropriate right now.'

I didn't say anything to this. It certainly seemed like a punishment.

'What about you?' Bethany asked. 'Will you go?'

'No chance,' I said. 'It's not my thing at the best of times, and I obviously wouldn't enjoy it without you. I'd just be there on my own, being weird and socially awkward. Also, I'm not sentimental – I don't put that much stock in ceremonies and significant dates and rites of passage. I'm happier just ticking along without the fuss.'

I thought it was a fairly innocuous statement, and consistent with everything Bethany already knew about me, so I was surprised that she seemed so upset when she responded. 'Phoebe, you're going to be without me for the next two years. What are you going to do with that time? Are you going to spend it all hiding, avoiding any social situation where you might feel awkward?'

I didn't answer. In truth, I didn't want to think too much about the next two years. I supposed I'd just muddle through

300

as best I could. As a sixth-former, I'd have a good chance of being prioritised for one of the single rooms in Boarding, hopefully with an en suite. If I told Suzi and Kevin that I was a potential lesbian, this might also strengthen my case. I could claim that the experience of sharing with another girl might stop me from concentrating on my homework.

'You could have other friends if you wanted to,' Bethany said. 'I mean, if I thought it genuinely didn't bother you, then I'd say fine and leave it at that. But is that honestly the case?'

I shrugged, hoping this would be enough of a response. It was not. Bethany stopped walking and looked at me, creating a deliberate, uncomfortable silence. After ten seconds of this treatment, I caved in. I decided to tell her about the self-improvement regime I'd started back in October, the one that I'd largely abandoned due to the pregnancy and subsequent chain of events. Though in retrospect, I had my reservations about the whole endeavour; I wasn't convinced that it would have achieved any of the outcomes I had hoped for.

Bethany seemed to be of a similar opinion. 'Phoebe, you don't need to change yourself for people to like you. I'll keep on saying that until you believe it. You're kind, you're funny, you're interesting. You're the most honest and loyal person I know. And yes, you *are* really fucking weird in some ways, and you can be socially awkward, and some people will never get past that. But that's their problem, not yours. Trust me: there are tonnes of people out there who would love to have you as a friend.'

I felt deeply embarrassed by this speech, but I managed to suppress this reaction to some extent. I nodded. I found myself thinking about Hu. Things had not gone too well with him at first, when I'd viewed him as someone to *practise* talking to. It was only when I stopped trying so hard that we started having some enjoyable and interesting conversations. Now we spoke together in the common room semi-frequently – or we had done before I'd started exam leave. I still didn't know if I could classify him as a friend in the same sense that Bethany was a friend, but I could at least see that the potential was there.

'Will you at least consider going tomorrow?' Bethany asked. 'Just think of it as a social experiment, if it helps.'

'It probably would help,' I said.

Bethany smiled. An *actual* smile this time. 'I thought it would.'

When I got home that afternoon, I fulfilled my promise and spent an hour considering whether I'd attend the ceremonial Leavers' Evening. I made a list of pros and cons, starting with the cons, which were easier to think of because they were so numerous. They included: the large amount of unstructured time I'd have to navigate, the need to engage in small talk, 'mingling', formal photographs, loud music, dancing, and the need to dress up for the occasion. While the dress code (smart/formal) was 'suggested' rather than required, I understood that I would be judged negatively if I turned up in a hoodie and tracksuit bottoms. My best bet might be to reuse my abortion outfit.

When it came to listing the pros, I spent a long time staring at a blank column before eventually writing: *Bethany would like me to go; opportunity for personal growth.*

That was it. That was all I could come up with. So it was to my great surprise that I found myself scrunching up the sheet of paper and launching it across the room towards the bin. I texted Bethany to tell her I was going, and a few moments later, a smiley face came back, followed by another message:

I've got something for you – a gift. But no idea how I'm going to get it to you. Watch this space!

Here's the thing: I felt certain, as soon as I'd put the phone down, that I'd made the right decision. Stranger still, I wasn't even worried about it – or not to the extent I would have been at the beginning of the school year. I knew that I was capable of going to the Leavers' Evening alone, and perhaps even mingling a bit and exchanging some pleasantries. I might not enjoy it in the same way I'd enjoy being curled up in bed with a good book, but the notion of socialising for a couple of hours, with a mind to laying some simple foundations for the next two years, did not terrify me – and this was certainly progress. In a way, I could view it as the culmination of my self-improvement plan, but with the small mental adjustment suggested by Bethany: that I didn't have to change myself to be liked. The goal should not be to do a passable job of being someone else, but to do the best possible job of being me.

And yet, despite the clarity of these ideas, there was still this nagging sense of dissatisfaction lodged like a splinter at the back of my mind. When I thought about everything that had happened between me and Bethany since the autumn, I couldn't help but balk at the unfairness of the last few weeks. I'd spent so much time fearing the loss of my only friend, and taking every step to avert this outcome. Now our friendship felt deeper and more important than it ever had, but I was losing her anyway. It was the cruellest of ironies.

I was hitting the punch bag in the garden when her next message came through: *I've managed to persuade Mum to bring me over so I can leave your gift on the doorstep. Best I could do in the circumstances! X*

Getting out of my boxing gloves to read the message had

taken a while, and by the time I'd made it through the house and opened the front door, the gift bag was already there, waiting. There was a note attached, which I read as soon as I was back inside.

I got these for you ages ago, before everything went to hell. Please try your absolute best to have fun tomorrow – and send me pics! I know you'll look gorgeous. X

Inside the gift bag was a black dress with a textured pattern which, upon closer inspection, turned out to be an intricate tangle of black roses, their stems intertwining like the threads of a spider web. There was also a pair of black sandals – thankfully flat, but with a complicated ankle strap that I assumed was more decorative than practical.

I changed in my bedroom and stood for some time in front of the full-length mirror on my wardrobe door, a surprising lump in my throat. I remembered my birthday, when I'd been so unsure about the denim jacket Bethany had given me. I'd told Gee that it was the sort of thing Bethany would wear, but I wasn't sure it was really for me. This time I had no such qualms. This outfit wasn't like anything Bethany would have chosen for herself, and, needless to say, it was like nothing I'd ever owned. It looked like the sort of outfit Tarja from Nightwish might wear – dark and ornate and dramatic. It was perfect.

I took a picture in the mirror and sent it with a caption: *Thank you. I love it. X*

A moment later, I received back a smiley and a thumbs-up emoji, which I spent a long time looking at.

My own emotions were too complicated and contradictory to translate into pictures that would have made sense to anyone else. I felt happy and sad and grateful and bitter and angry. All of these, all at once.

I lay down on my bed with my eyes closed, and I started plotting.

I waited until 5.30 the following afternoon – an hour before the Leavers' Evening was due to start – and then headed down the lane in my black dress and strappy sandals. I passed the vicarage and joined the footpath that runs down the back of the house. Because it was June, the vegetation was quite profuse, but I managed to navigate the nettles and thistles without injury. The stone wall marking the perimeter of Bethany's garden was a bigger problem, especially in a dress. I waited for a couple of tourists to pass on their way down to the beach, then made the necessary adjustments to my costume to be able to clamber up, using the lower branches of the Collins's chestnut tree for additional support and concealment.

Having checked there was no one at the rear of the house, I sent a message to Bethany: *Look out your window – back of the garden!*

I saw her a moment later, in her bedroom window, and I popped my head out from behind the tree and waved. She did not wave back; I could see her texting.

Phoebe WTF?

I'd already worked out the best way to get her to come down. *I need someone to do my makeup. And by someone, I mean you. Any chance you could nip over the wall?*

Give me two minutes! Mum's in the front room so I should be OK. But if I get caught it's totally worth it! X

I gave her a quick thumbs up and then got back behind the tree.

She appeared shortly afterwards, wearing her shoulder bag. 'OK, let's make this snappy. How on earth did you manage to climb the wall in your dress? If you've ripped it, I'll kill you.'

'I basically had to hoick it up around my waist,' I told her. 'We should probably flee the scene before I get arrested for indecency.'

'Good plan,' Bethany said. 'I can't believe you're actually asking me to do your makeup. I thought it was going to be a once-only thing.'

I shrugged. 'I figured if I'm going to do this, I should do it properly. You know, fully commit.'

'Right!'

From her side, and wearing jeans and trainers, the wall was far less of an obstacle for Bethany. She found a foothold on the gnarled trunk of the chestnut tree and stepped up from there. Once she'd helped me back down to the footpath, we walked a short distance over the dunes, out of view from the house. I noted that we were in almost the exact same spot where I'd talked to Rachael Tibbet a month ago – the event that had led us, in a roundabout way, to this one.

I sat on the wind-flattened grass with the sun on my face and Bethany applied the cosmetics. Thankfully, it didn't take as long as last time, even though she said she was going a 'bit bolder' than before.

'I'm going to do your hair too,' she told me. 'Options are limited, obviously, but I'm thinking messy bun. A little bit grungy.'

'I've got no idea what that means.'

'You don't have to. Just stay still. It'll be worth it.'

The hair didn't take long, either – no more than five

minutes for it to be combed, twisted and tied, and another three spent loosening and pinning different strands to make it the correct level of messy.

'OK, don't freak out,' Bethany said as she took a compact mirror from her bag and held it up to my face.

I didn't freak out. I was prepared, this time, for the fact that I'd look quite different. Perhaps not quite *this* different, but the effect was far from displeasing. The girl in the mirror had dark, dramatic eyes, and hair that whirled around her crown like a piece of expressionist art. She looked confident, like she knew what she was doing, even if this wasn't one hundred per cent the case.

I took a deep breath and turned to Bethany. 'Thank you. I like it a lot, but I also have a small confession to make. The makeup's a pretext, at least in part. I don't want you to go home. I want you to come with me to the Leavers' Evening.'

Bethany gave a small shake of her head. 'I'd love to. But you'll be fine, honestly. You look gorgeous.'

'It's not about me,' I told her. 'I know I'll be fine. But I'll be finer if you're with me, and you'll be far, far finer if you come. You deserve the chance to say goodbye.'

'Seriously, Phoebe, I can't. You *know* I can't. I'm trying to fix things with my parents.'

'I don't think it's up to you to fix things. Not anymore. You've done everything you can.'

Bethany thought about this for a few moments, then shrugged. 'You might be right, but it doesn't really change anything, does it? They didn't say yes before, they're not going to now.'

'I'm not suggesting you ask,' I told her. 'I'm suggesting we just go. You've spent enough time being meek and compliant.

307

It hasn't worked and it doesn't suit you. It's time to take a stand.'

'Phoebe, I can't. Your dad's not going to agree to it, for a start, and it wouldn't be fair to ask him.'

'My dad's not taking us. I told him it would be easier for me to make my own way there. I've got a taxi booked for . . .' I checked the clock on my phone. 'Twenty minutes from now. So you've got a decision to make, and not that long to make it.'

Bethany looked at me in disbelief. 'Phoebe, you're nuts. My parents will flip out if I just disappear. I wouldn't be surprised if they phone the police to report me as a missing person!'

I shrugged. 'So send them a message from the taxi. Tell them that you love them but you're not a child anymore. You have the right to make your own decisions and live with the consequences.'

Bethany had her mouth open. I waited.

'I don't have anything to wear,' she said eventually. 'I can't go like this.'

Bethany was wearing a pale lilac vest top with her jeans. She looked perfectly acceptable. 'You can definitely go like that,' I told her. 'I've dressed up, you can dress down. Trust me, you'll find it liberating. Plus, if you say no again, I'm fully prepared to abduct you.'

Bethany put her fingers on her temples and shook her head for approximately ten seconds. 'OK. Fuck it,' she said. 'Fuck it. What do I actually have to lose?'

I didn't think. I threw my arms around her. The abduction back-up would not be necessary.

32

Rebellion

In the taxi, Bethany showed me the message she'd composed to her parents:

Mum, Dad, I've tried really hard to make things work over the last month. I thought if I stuck to your rules and was completely honest with you it would make a difference and you'd start to trust me again. I don't think this has happened and I'm starting to wonder if it ever will.

I've got to the point where I regret talking to you. I won't make that mistake again in the future. I'll keep anything important to myself and I won't risk asking for your support or understanding or acceptance. I don't know how that makes you feel but it makes me incredibly sad.

I'm on my way to the Leavers Evening with Phoebe. If I'm not going to see my friends again I'd like the chance to say goodbye. You can 'not punish' me when I get home.

I love you but I have to live my own life according to my own beliefs. x

'What do you think?' she asked.

'You need an apostrophe in *Leavers' Evening*,' I told her.

Bethany rolled her eyes. 'Other than that?'

'Other than that, it's perfect. It's what you need to say.'

Bethany didn't bother correcting the error. She hit send.

It took approximately thirty seconds for her phone to start ringing.

'I recommend you don't answer.'

Bethany ignored me. Obviously, I could only hear one side of the short conversation, which went like this:

'No, I'm not coming home . . . I understand that . . . If he's furious, he's furious. I don't see what difference it makes anymore . . . I don't think that's true. You've been punishing me since I told you . . . That's your decision. It's going to create a bit of a scene, but if you're comfortable having that conversation in public then I am too . . . No, it isn't a threat. If you're going to come and drag me home, there's not much I can do about that. But if anyone asks me why, then I'm going to tell them. I'm not going to lie about it . . . Because I'm not going to be made to feel ashamed anymore . . . No, it isn't. I just happen to agree with her . . .'

The conversation went on in this vein for another minute or so, with Bethany staying calm throughout. Then she shrugged and passed me the phone. 'My mum would like to speak to you.'

'Phoebe, this behaviour is extremely reckless!' Mrs Collins told me. Her voice was not calm. 'Can you please talk some sense into her?'

'I think she's made up her mind,' I said. 'And I support her decision. I think it's sensible.'

'It's going to make matters even worse!'

'We share the opinion that matters can't get any worse.'

'Was this your idea?'

'Yes. I thought she should come and explained why. She agreed with my argument.'

There was a significant pause before Mrs Collins spoke

again. 'Phoebe, in all honesty I don't care whose idea this was. You need to come back so we can talk calmly.'

'Bethany is extremely calm,' I pointed out.

'She's threatening to tell everyone what she did!'

'Yes, I deduced that from what she said. But I don't think it's a threat. It's only if people ask why she's leaving. It seems reasonable that she give them an honest explanation.'

'Reasonable! Phoebe, this is blackmail! She's going to do something she'll regret. She needs to think of the consequences.'

Mrs Collins was sounding increasingly frantic. It occurred to me that if Bethany *was* interested in blackmailing her parents, it would not be difficult; Mrs Collins, for one, was clearly distraught at the notion that Bethany's abortion might become public knowledge. However, it was not an optimum solution, even ignoring the morality of it. The goal was still reconciliation.

'Bethany's not blackmailing you,' I said. 'She just doesn't mind if people know anymore. I think that's admirable. It's important to stand up for your convictions.'

'Phoebe, be serious! What are people going to think?'

For the first time in the conversation, I felt myself getting annoyed. 'I don't know what they'll think, and I don't really care! It's irrelevant. What's important is how Bethany feels.'

'I see. And how will she feel when everyone's judging her? Gossiping about her?'

'Also irrelevant. She's not going to see any of them again after today. You've made sure of that.'

It was Mrs Collins's turn to speak, but she didn't. I could hear faint sniffing noises down the line; it was possible that she was crying. I looked at Bethany, who hadn't really reacted to the conversation so far. Her expression remained neutral.

I glanced in the rear-view mirror and saw the taxi driver's eyes reflected back at me, his gaze rather alarmed. I gestured with my fingers that he should keep his eyes on the road.

Mrs Collins was now sobbing unmistakably. It was unfortunate, but I decided this was not the time to backtrack. It was time to double down. 'Bethany is resilient,' I told her. 'She'll cope with whatever comes her way. But, to be honest, I think you're missing the bigger picture. It doesn't matter what anyone else says or thinks – not to Bethany. It matters what *you* think. That's what's hurting her.'

It took some time for Mrs Collins to stop crying. Bethany also looked upset now; she gestured for me to pass the phone back, which I did. They spoke for a further minute or so before Bethany hung up.

'She's going to talk to my dad,' Bethany said. 'After that . . . Well, I don't know what's going to happen after that. I guess we'll find out. She's pretty upset.'

'I think that's partly my fault. I wasn't very tactful.'

The corners of Bethany's mouth twitched in the smallest of smiles. 'If I'd been worried about that I wouldn't have given you the phone. I thought I could trust you *not* to be tactful.'

I nodded; I supposed not being tactful was one of my strengths, in the right circumstances. 'What now? Do you still want to go to the Leavers' Evening?'

'I still want to go. I guess there's a big chance my parents will turn up and try to drag me home, but that's out of my hands now. To be honest, I just want to enjoy myself for however long I've got. How does that sound to you?'

'It sounds good,' I said.

*

When we arrived at school, Bethany asked me if I minded taking a brief detour before we went in.

'How brief?' I asked. 'There's a chance we'll be late.'

'Fashionably late,' Bethany said.

'I don't think I've ever been fashionably anything.'

'Well, it's a good time to start. Come on, I need to clear my head first.'

I nodded. The conversation in the taxi had been intense, and, on reflection, I realised that I would also benefit from a bit of time to recalibrate. Being late was not the end of the world.

We walked around the edge of the Frowned-Upon Forest and across the empty sports fields, a warm wind blowing and the air smelling deeply of summer. Bethany seemed unusually pensive, with a faraway look in her eyes, but it took me a while to figure out what was probably going on. She may well have needed to clear her head, but the more I observed her, the more I suspected an additional motivation for our detour – her desire to have a last look around, knowing she wouldn't be back. I'm not usually sentimental, but as we walked through the familiar landscape of oak trees and neatly tended grass, I acknowledged to myself that this evening was the end of an era – the quiet closing of our shared childhood.

By the time we walked into the main hall, it was seventeen minutes after the designated start time. I don't know if this qualified as fashionable, but Mrs Holloway, who was handing out drinks on the door, didn't seem to mind. She smiled as she passed Bethany a flute of what I assumed was non-alcoholic champagne, then paused, mid-air, as she passed me mine. She had an extremely odd expression on her face.

'Oh my gosh! Phoebe? I didn't recognise you!'

It took me a moment to comprehend that she was referring to my altered hair, makeup and clothing; I'd been so preoccupied on the walk that I'd more or less forgotten about them.

'It's a social experiment,' I told her, taking the drink from her hand. 'Blame Bethany.'

Bethany laughed at this. After a moment, Mrs Holloway did, too.

Whoever was in charge of the decorations had done a good job, because the school hall didn't look much like the school hall. The curtains had been drawn and there were strings of golden lights hanging down the walls. There were tables draped in white tablecloths around the edge of a makeshift dancefloor, and to one side was a buffet with plates of snacks and neat rows of glasses waiting to be filled. I couldn't identify the pop music playing from the various speakers, but it was unobtrusively bland and only a little too loud.

A swift head count told me that most of our year had not decided to be fashionably late, and everyone had stuck to the recommended formal dress code. The boys were all wearing suits, though some had opted for kilts rather than trousers, and a few, including Will, had gone for tuxedos. Among the girls, only Bethany wasn't wearing a dress.

'Well, I feel out of place,' she said.

'Welcome to my world,' I told her. But when I glanced across, she was grinning; I don't think she cared very much how she looked right then. She was just happy to be there. Also, she was not the one attracting the majority of the stares.

I had changed my clothes and hair and was wearing some makeup, but you'd have thought I'd ridden into the hall on a unicycle, juggling fire. Of course, I was expecting some reaction, based on the previous experience of wearing a plait for the first time, along with Suzi's reaction on the morning of the abortion makeover and Mrs Holloway's reaction on the door. What I wasn't expecting was how I felt about it: in the best sense, I didn't really care. People were looking at me, judging me, and I didn't feel the usual sense of sinking into myself, of my skin tightening. I felt OK.

Jessica and Natasha came over.

'Phoebe, you look really different,' Jessica said. 'That dress is gorgeous.'

'Thank you. It's a social experiment,' I said.

Jessica laughed. Natasha laughed. I might have stolen the joke from Bethany, but it worked, and I got to recycle it several times. During the first part of the evening, people were continually approaching me to say more or less the same thing: that they hadn't recognised me, or that I looked so different, or some other variation on that theme. It was surprisingly enjoyable, and it solved the mingling problem to a large extent. It meant that I interacted with a lot of people, and the initial stage of the conversation pretty much wrote itself.

After half an hour or so, Will approached. I hadn't spoken a word to him for approximately five months; aside from the occasional glare in the corridors, the last interaction we'd had, of any kind, was when I handed him the abortion invoice at the end of January.

'Hello, ladies,' he said.

I looked at Bethany. Bethany started laughing. I assumed it was because of Will. Dressed as James Bond, attempting to be suave.

'Hello, William,' I said.

'You look . . . different,' he noted.

'He means you look fantastic,' Bethany clarified. 'Right, Will?'

'Of course, you look great.'

'I'm still weird,' I told him. 'Deeply weird. The rest is just window dressing.'

'Right . . .'

He didn't appear to know what else to say. Bethany was still looking extremely amused. 'I don't think your charms work on Phoebe,' she told him. 'She's completely immune. It's like some unfathomable superpower.'

'OK, very funny.' Will held up his hands in what I assumed was intended to be a placating manner. 'Look, I realise things have been very difficult between us for the last few months. I just wanted to apologise and try to make peace.'

I glanced at Bethany who rolled her eyes. 'Fine by me. I don't think it matters all that much anymore.'

'We accept your apology,' I confirmed, holding out my hand for him to shake. For some reason this caused Bethany to start laughing again, just as she was taking another sip from her drink. A small amount of liquid escaped her mouth.

Will narrowed his eyes. 'Are you drunk?'

'Just enjoying myself,' Bethany told him, between giggles.

I'm not certain Will believed her, but after a moment he shrugged and said: 'Whatever. I had something else to tell you. I'm leaving. My dad's got a new job. In Shanghai, starting September. I thought you might like to know.'

Obviously, this news made little difference to Bethany. 'Same here,' she said. 'We're also moving. Probably not anywhere exotic, though. Just away from here. I told my parents about the abortion.'

Will looked immediately panicked. 'Why? Why would you do that? I thought we had an agreement?'

'Relax! I didn't say anything about you. And I don't know why I said anything at all. It went about as well as you'd expect. I'm not actually supposed to be here at the moment. I'm not supposed to leave the house.' She gestured at her non-formalwear. 'Hence the outfit.'

Will nodded dumbly.

It was fortuitous timing because, at that moment, Bethany's phone buzzed. 'Oh. They're here,' she said. 'Waiting outside to talk to me.' She looked at Will. 'You can come and meet them, if you like?'

'I'm going to give it a miss,' Will said. And he turned and walked away, almost before the words were out of his mouth.

'Well, that was fun,' Bethany said. 'Closure, I guess.'

'Are they actually outside?' I asked.

'Yep. They actually are. Mum says they just want to talk, no big public showdown. But I guess we'll see.'

'Would you like me to come?'

Bethany looked at me a moment, then nodded. 'Did I ever tell you that you're a much better friend than Will?'

I shrugged. 'He sets an extremely low bar.'

Bethany smiled and took my hand, and together we walked out of the hall to see her parents.

They were waiting across the yard. Bethany's dad had his arm around Mrs Collins's shoulder, but it was a little too far to make out their expressions. At a squint, I thought they both looked grim, which was not a big surprise.

We only made it as far as the bottom step, outside of the portico, when Bethany stopped and turned to me. 'Would you mind just waiting for me here?' she asked. 'I think I need to do the rest on my own.'

'You're sure?'

She shrugged. 'I'm not sure. But it was my choice to be here, and I'm happy to face the consequences. My parents need to understand that.'

I sat on the bottom step and waited as Bethany crossed the yard to her parents, and for the next few minutes, I watched the scene unfold. Silently. Unexpectedly.

Mrs Collins had taken a step forwards and was exchanging words with Bethany, who was standing with her back to me, her posture stiff. Reverend Collins said something and Mrs Collins put her hands to her mouth, shaking slightly. I was almost certain she was crying, and took this as a bad sign. Various scenarios flashed through my head: a demand that Bethany come home, a refusal, threats and counter-threats, more anger and unhappiness. Then Mrs Collins took another step forward and opened her arms. She and Bethany spent a long time hugging. Shortly afterwards, her father hugged her too. He pulled back and told her something. I had no idea what; and I thought, then, that it didn't much matter. The words were just the surface. It was everything that lay beneath them that was important – the intentions, the attitudes, the feelings. When it comes down to it, reconciliation, like acceptance, is a simple thing – no more than the silent shifting of a perspective.

After a moment, Reverend Collins waved me over. It felt a little odd, as if I were stepping into a separate, private space, a scene from a film in which no extras were required, but I went over as requested. Bethany and her mum were hugging again and I could see now that they had both been crying. Yet I didn't need to see the smiles on their faces to know that these were happy tears.

I cleared my throat, a little awkwardly. 'Is everything resolved?'

Reverend Collins smiled at me. 'No, Phoebe. It's still a bit of a mess, I'm afraid. But we've decided we're just going to have to work through it together. It doesn't matter how difficult the circumstances are.'

The words were familiar, but it took me a second to figure out why. It was an echo of the conversation we'd had in the church two days ago – the conversation I'd thought had made no difference.

'You're going to stay, then?' I asked. 'On Holy Island?' I was almost certain, now, that this was the case, but old habits die hard, and I don't think I'll ever lose my distrust of subtext entirely.

'We're staying,' Reverend Collins confirmed.

Mrs Collins nodded, giving Bethany's shoulders a final squeeze before they separated. 'You look lovely, Phoebe,' she said. 'You should both go back inside. Enjoy the rest of your evening and we'll pick you up afterwards.'

'Thank you,' I said. 'That sounds like a nice plan.'

And as Bethany took my hand and we walked back towards the hall, I felt a bubble of happiness expanding within me, shooing all other emotions away.

Epilogue

Looking Forward

Dear Mum,

Summer was uneventful, in the best possible sense. I spent most of it writing. I spent some of it working in the shop. I spent some of it hanging out with Bethany, enjoying the simple fact of that.

My feelings for Bethany have become much clearer since the threat of her leaving came and went. She may have been my first crush, but now that the initial shock of that has passed, I'm happy to report that I have no lingering regrets about us remaining 'just' best friends. We're both agreed that this is one relationship that's perfect as it is. It requires no modifications.

As for Bethany and her parents, they are working through their issues one day at a time, and making significant progress. I went over for lunch at the beginning of August, and Reverend Collins performed a special non-religious grace, suggesting that we should all take thirty seconds to think about the things we're thankful for. It was a good idea. I've realised that there are innumerable things in my life that I'm thankful for, and I know that Bethany feels the same. I no longer have to ask her if she regrets telling her parents. She does not.

Despite everything else that was going on, we both did well in our exams. I attribute my success to my ability to compartmentalise – to focus obsessively on one thing at a time. Bethany attributes her success to being grounded for the duration of the exam period. It may have been a stressful time for her, but on a practical level, she didn't have much to do other than revise.

We started Sixth Form four weeks ago. Bethany is studying French, Spanish and Italian, to further her life goal of working with languages or something, probably somewhere sunny. I am studying English Literature, Psychology and Physics, to further my more immediate goal of raising a metaphorical middle finger to Mrs Shepherd, the travelling careers advisor. This is mostly a joke, of course. I still plan to be a writer because it's what I love and it's what I'm good at; that said, I'm no longer ruling out going to university, either. It's not necessary, but I can see why it might be good for me, in all sorts of ways. I'm going to visit Oxford and Cambridge and Durham and St Andrew's in the next year, and I'm going to get a better idea of what living in any of these places might be like; because I now realise, there's no reason I cannot.

In the meantime, school is providing plenty of stimulation and is, in all dimensions, far better than it was. The classes are smaller, which obviously suits me, and I now feel confident enough to raise my hand and talk in front of my peers. I was worried, at first, about not sharing any lessons with Bethany, but this, too, has had its positive side in that it has given me an extra push to make some new friends. There's a new girl called

Amara who sits next to me in Psychology, and so far, we seem to get on very well. She's from Nigeria and wants to study Medicine at university; we've arranged to visit the Anatomical Museum together during half term.

With a view to expanding my social circle even further, I have also set up my own after-school Enrichment activity, following a successful PowerPoint pitch to the English department. The Fantasy and Sci-Fi Book Club will have its inaugural meeting in the first week of November, and several students, including Hu, have already expressed an interest in joining. It has been scheduled for Thursdays, so it will not clash with Yoga, which I've now started doing on Wednesdays, or Chess Club, which I will continue to attend on Mondays. Having finished second in the league last year, Mr Finch has high hopes that we can 'go one better' this time round, and even though I'm not competitive, I must confess that I'm somewhat excited by the possibility. I have no plans to return to Jigsaw Club in the immediate future.

This brings us pretty much to the present.

It took me just under four months to get here, writing and rewriting an average of a thousand words per day over the summer. It wasn't my intention at first. I sat down to continue planning my fantasy novel (which I will get back to!), but found that I had an awful lot of clutter I needed to clear from my mind first. Writing it down seemed like the logical thing to do, and the project just sort of snowballed. It became a type of therapy.

Mrs Frost has been advising me again; I went to see her back in July to apologise for smashing her milk bottle, but it turned out she hadn't even realised I was the culprit. (She'd thought it was a wild animal.) Anyway, we've been on good terms ever since. I told her that I'd taken her earlier advice – namely, the last year, which had provided me with plenty of material. Once I'd outlined my proposed project for her (omitting the details about Bethany's abortion) she was generally supportive. She said in most cases, she'd question the wisdom of a sixteen-year-old writing a 'memoir', but in my case, she could just about see it working. At the very least, it would be good practice for me.

As to what comes next: I'm not sure.

I wrote this for you, Mum, because in the beginning, you were the only person I could imagine sharing it with. But I don't know if that's still the case. In the future, I might ask Daddy if he wants to read some of it, or Bethany, if she feels OK to do so. I don't know.

But one of the things I've learned in the past year is that you can't have a concrete plan for everything. Sometimes, you have to try different things to see what fits. Sometimes, life is messy, and you just have to work through it, one day at a time.

A little under a week from now I'll turn seventeen. I'm looking forward to it. Daddy says he'll start teaching me to drive over the quiet winter months, and I'm looking forward to that too.

I'm looking forward to at least two more years of education.

I'm looking forward to being myself, and not worrying too much about what that entails.

I'm looking forward to learning new things, experiencing new things.

I'm looking forward to reading new books and watching new films. I'm looking forward to hearing the new Nightwish album, which comes out next year. (I even considered listening to some *different* music, before deciding that I'm not quite there yet.)

Most of all, though, I'm looking forward to your next letter, the penultimate one. I'm looking forward to what you have to say.

Author's Note

Dear reader,

I wrote this book for my daughter, or a future version of my daughter. Let me explain.

When she was a baby, Amelia wasn't keen on being hugged. At eighteen months, pretty much all she wanted was to be read to, often for many hours at a time. She'd sit in my lap and stay perfectly still throughout, her eyes fixed on the page. Sometimes she'd repeat her favourite lines as we read them, and when we reached the end of the story, she'd immediately demand it 'gen' (and again and again; with some books she was insatiable).

By the time she was two, she could recite *Peter Rabbit* verbatim, and would do so several times a day. By two and a half, she could read fluently, having apparently taught herself. But she still wasn't fond of being hugged, and with most people, she wouldn't even tolerate being touched. If her grandmother tried to pick her up, she'd start screaming.

Amelia was diagnosed with autism at the age of four, which did not come as a surprise. But it did raise the question of how and when we – my wife and I –were going to talk to her about it. After some debate, we decided that we wanted her to know sooner rather than later. We wanted her to grow up understanding that she was not neurotypical, and this was just one thing among many that made her a special and unique human being.

So my wife wrote her a letter (I helped, but the words were hers, and are reproduced almost verbatim in chapter three). Our aim was to explain to Amelia, in as simple terms as possible, why she experienced the world a little differently to some other people; why she found some things hard and other things easy; why other children her age had to learn how to read, while she had to learn how to join in with social games (something she seemed interested in doing, as long as the rules of the game were set out and understood in advance!). The message, essentially, was that it's OK to be different – and often it's more than OK. That as much as our differences can present us with challenges, they can also, sometimes, be the source of our greatest strengths.

Amelia is ten now, but I know she'll be a teenager in the blink of an eye, and that will bring a whole host of new challenges. Being a teenager is tough for anyone, but it can be especially tough for autistic girls. It's the time when social dynamics change, when hormones kick in, when relationships with friends and parents become more complicated – when life, in general, becomes more complicated. In short, it's messy, and this book is about two girls, best friends since childhood, trying to navigate that mess. It's about love and friendship, self-acceptance and the acceptance of others. My original hope was that it might help my daughter to negotiate the weird, knotty and sometimes frightening transition from childhood to adulthood. My additional hope, of course, is that it's a compelling story that many readers – including you – will have enjoyed.

GE, *Sheffield, September 2022*

Acknowledgements

Huge thanks to Chloe Sackur for looking after Phoebe with such love, care and attention.

Many additional thanks to: Nicky Watkinson, Eloise Wilson, Charlie Sheppard, Jack Noel, Rob Farrimond, Sarah Kimmelman and Paul Black.

Final thanks, as always, to Stan for sticking with me through this long and arduous process, and to Alix, Amelia and Toby, for everything.